PRAISE FOR VICTORIA THOMPSON and *MURDER ON ASTOR PLACE*, THE FIRST IN THE GASLIGHT MYSTERY SERIES

"Victoria Thompson is off to a blazing start with Sarah Brandt and Frank Malloy in *Murder on Astor Place*. I do hope she's starting at the beginning of the alphabet. Don't miss her first tantalizing mystery."

—Catherine Coulter, author of *Double Take*

"A marvelous debut mystery with compelling characters, a fascinating setting, and a stunning resolution. It's the best mystery I've read in ages."

—Jill Churchill, author of *The Merchant of Menace*

"Fascinating . . . Sarah and Frank are appealing characters . . . Thompson vividly re-creates the gaslit world of old New York."

—*Publishers Weekly*

"Spellbinding. A bravura performance that will leave you impatient for the next installment."

—*Romantic Times*

"An exciting first in a series which will appeal to Anne Perry fans."

—*Mystery Scene*

Gaslight Mysteries by Victoria Thompson

MURDER ON ASTOR PLACE
MURDER ON ST. MARK'S PLACE
MURDER ON GRAMERCY PARK
MURDER ON WASHINGTON SQUARE
MURDER ON MULBERRY BEND
MURDER ON MARBLE ROW
MURDER ON LENOX HILL
MURDER IN LITTLE ITALY
MURDER IN CHINATOWN
MURDER ON BANK STREET

MURDER ON ST. MARK'S PLACE

Victoria Thompson

BERKLEY PRIME CRIME, NEW YORK

THE BERKLEY PUBLISHING GROUP
Published by the Penguin Group
Penguin Group (USA) Inc.
375 Hudson Street, New York, New York 10014, USA
Penguin Group (Canada), 90 Eglinton Avenue East, Suite 700, Toronto, Ontario M4P 2Y3, Canada
(a division of Pearson Penguin Canada Inc.)
Penguin Books Ltd., 80 Strand, London WC2R 0RL, England
Penguin Group Ireland, 25 St. Stephen's Green, Dublin 2, Ireland (a division of Penguin Books Ltd.)
Penguin Group (Australia), 250 Camberwell Road, Camberwell, Victoria 3124, Australia
(a division of Pearson Australia Group Pty. Ltd.)
Penguin Books India Pvt. Ltd., 11 Community Centre, Panchsheel Park, New Delhi—110 017, India
Penguin Group (NZ), Cnr. Airborne and Rosedale Roads, Albany, Auckland 1310, New Zealand
(a division of Pearson New Zealand Ltd.)
Penguin Books (South Africa) (Pty.) Ltd., 24 Sturdee Avenue, Rosebank, Johannesburg 2196,
South Africa

Penguin Books Ltd., Registered Offices: 80 Strand, London WC2R 0RL, England

MURDER ON ST. MARK'S PLACE

A Berkley Prime Crime Book / published by arrangement with the author

PRINTING HISTORY
Berkley Prime Crime edition / March 2000

ISBN: 978-0-425-17361-9

BERKLEY® PRIME CRIME
PRIME CRIME Books are published by The Berkley Publishing Group,
a division of Penguin Group (USA) Inc.,
375 Hudson Street, New York, New York 10014.
The name BERKLEY PRIME CRIME and the BERKLEY PRIME CRIME design
are trademarks belonging to Penguin Group (USA) Inc.

PRINTED IN THE UNITED STATES OF AMERICA

17 16 15 14 13 12

To Roselyn O'Brien and all the staff and volunteers of the March of Dimes, in appreciation for all you do to save babies.

I

SARAH HEARD THE WAILING WHEN SHE WAS STILL halfway down the street. She knew the sound only too well, the howl of a grief too great to bear, and she was certain she had arrived too late.

A midwife by trade, she had been summoned to deliver the third child of Agnes Otto, a strong, healthy young woman whom Sarah had seen only a few days earlier. Everything had seemed fine then, but if Sarah had learned nothing else from her years of midwifery, she knew that things sometimes went terribly wrong when a baby was making its way into the world, no matter how strong and healthy his mother might appear to be.

Certain of what she would find and praying she wasn't too late to save at least one of them, Sarah picked up her heavy skirts and tucked her medical bag under her arm. Dodging the puddles left from the freak rainstorm yesterday that had dropped over an inch of rain in a hour's time, she hurried down the sidewalk, past the neat row of tenement buildings here on St. Mark's Place, in the heart of Little Germany, until she reached the one where Agnes Otto lived. The front door stood open to catch what little air stirred in the early July heat, and Sarah was up the stoop and through it in an instant. Inside, the dark hallway was deserted, but the sound of weeping echoed down the stairwell. She followed it unerringly and found several women gathered on the landing above, just outside the door to the Ottos' flat. They were crying and wringing their hands and sobbing into their aprons. That was when Sarah began to suspect that whatever was wrong was not what she'd been expecting at all.

Then she saw the policeman.

He stood just inside the flat, the brass buttons of his uniform straining over his big belly, sweat streaming off his face in the oppressive heat, and his expression oddly panicked. His presence relieved her on one level. Nobody called the police because a baby or a mother died in childbirth. But the police didn't just show up for no reason, either. Something terrible had happened, even though it wasn't the thing Sarah had most feared.

"Oh, look, Mrs. Brandt has come," one of the neighbor women said, seeing Sarah. "Thank heaven you've come."

The policeman turned to look at her, and his sweaty face brightened. "The midwife's here now, missus," he said to someone inside, someone who was crying more loudly than any of the women in the hallway. "I'll just be on my way. Someone will let you know when you can claim the body."

The body? Good heavens, what was he talking about? Had something happened to Agnes's husband? No wonder everyone was hysterical.

"What's going on here?" Sarah demanded of the policeman, but he was in too much of a hurry to leave. He tipped his hat as he passed, but he did pass, as quickly as he could push his way through the group of women and squeeze by Sarah, and then he hustled his bulky frame down the dark stairwell and was gone.

"It is Mrs. Otto's sister, Gerda," one of the women obligingly explained, dabbing at her eyes with the corner of her apron. "Somebody has murdered her!"

The words brought back ugly memories that Sarah had worked very hard to store away forever. Her own husband had been murdered a little more than three years ago, and just last April, Sarah had helped solve the murder of another unfortunate young woman. Although she sometimes had to deal with death in the course of her work, that at least was natural. She'd hoped never again to encounter the kind that came unnaturally, from the violent hand of another.

Sarah didn't have to push her way into the Ottos' flat. The women parted to allow her to enter, apparently as grateful for her arrival as the policeman had been.

Agnes Otto sat at the table in her small kitchen with her head on her arms, sobbing as if her heart would break. Plainly, Sarah would get no straight answers from her.

She turned to the women still hovering in the doorway. "Is she in labor?"

"We do not know," one of them said. "But we were afraid, with the shock of it . . ."

Sarah nodded. Shock had a way of hurrying things along, and Agnes was due anytime now. Sarah set her medical bag on the table and started to unbutton the jacket that fashion dictated she wear out in public, in spite of the heat. From the front room of the flat, the one facing the street, Sarah could hear the cries of a young child. That would be Agnes's daughter, who was about two. Looking around, she found Agnes's son, a boy of about four. He was huddled in the corner, practically under the sink, and staring at his mother with wide, terrified eyes.

"Would one of you take care of the children, please?" Sarah asked as she rolled up her sleeves. "They shouldn't be here."

Two of the women hurried to do her bidding, removing the children from the flat and leaving her alone with Agnes.

"Do you want me to send for your husband?" Sarah asked, gently stroking the other woman's shoulders in a gesture of comfort.

Agnes didn't hesitate. She shook her head vehemently, then made an effort to raise her head. Her usually pale face was swollen and blotched with weeping. She brushed at her running nose with the cuff of her sleeve, and said, "He will not come. He would lose his day's wages."

Some men would count that a small cost to be able to comfort a pregnant wife, but Agnes knew her husband better than Sarah did. "How are you feeling? Are you having any pains?"

"Pains?" As if she'd forgotten for a moment that she was pregnant, Agnes sat up in the chair and wrapped her arms protectively around her distended belly. Then she looked at Sarah and seemed to recognize her for the first time. "*Nein*, I don't think so. Why have you come?" she asked in alarm.

"One of the neighbor boys came for me. I thought it must be your time."

"I did not send for you. I did not think of anything but—" Her voice broke as she remembered her sister, and she covered her face with her hands.

"I guess your neighbors thought you might need me." Sarah pulled out a chair and sat down beside Agnes. "Can you tell me what happened?"

For a long moment Sarah was afraid Agnes wouldn't be able to speak, but she continued to stroke her back and croon meaningless phrases of comfort until at last she was rewarded for her patience.

Slowly, Agnes lowered her hands, revealing eyes filled with so much pain, Sarah had to force herself not to look away. "It is Gerda. My little sister. You remember her?"

Sarah nodded. Gerda was a lively young girl of about sixteen, with blond hair and sparkling blue eyes who had come to America less than a year ago to live with her married sister. Her parents hoped she'd do as well as Agnes had, find a suitable husband and a good life here. She had a job in one of the sweatshops, where she would have earned enough to pay Agnes and her husband, Lars, for her keep, but not much more. Sarah vaguely recalled Agnes's concern for her.

"You were worried about her, weren't you?"

Agnes nodded, shuddering under a fresh onslaught of tears. "She would not listen. She would not stay home like a good girl. She was only sixteen . . ." Once again, the tears choked her, and Sarah had to wait, her own eyes welling with tears as she thought of a life so young being snuffed out. As much to distract herself as to help Agnes, she got up and fetched a glass of water from the pitcher and helped her patient drink it when she was calm again.

"Life is much different here than it is in Germany," Sarah suggested. "I expect Gerda had some trouble adjusting."

Agnes's expression grew instantly angry. "She had no trouble! She was like an American girl at once! As soon as she started working with those other girls—they are bad ones! They got Gerda in trouble, all the time, trouble. Staying out late at night so she would be too tired to get awake in the morning for work. Going to dancing, meeting strange men." Agnes shook her head in despair, and Sarah noticed she was rubbing her side without even realizing it. Sarah glanced at the pendant watch she wore pinned to her shirtwaist, making note of the time.

"Lars tried to tell her," Agnes explained, desperate to make Sarah understand that they had attempted to stop her. "He told her those men would not marry a girl who goes to dancing all the time and stays out half the night, but she would not listen. She would not listen to anyone. I know something bad will happen. I tell her that."

"And what *did* happen?" Sarah asked as gently as she could.

Agnes squeezed her eyes shut, as if she could close out the pain. "She did not come home last night. Lars, he goes out to look for her, but he cannot find her anywhere. No one can find her. I hardly sleep all night for fear. And then that police comes here. A police! To my house!" Her eyes pleaded with Sarah to understand her outrage, and Sarah had no trouble doing so. In Germany, the police would never have occasion to visit the home of a respectable family, and the same was true in America.

Then Agnes's blotched and swollen features crumbled under the weight of her grief again. "They find her today. In an alley. She was . . . Her face . . ." It was all she could do to choke out the words. "The police said someone beat her."

"She was beaten to death?" Sarah asked when Agnes hesitated, the words as painful to say as they were to hear. Only sixteen years old and beaten to death like an animal.

Agnes nodded stiffly, not trusting herself to speak. She took another sip of the water. "They could not tell . . . from her face . . . who she was."

Sarah couldn't stop herself from grasping at this last fragment of hope. "Then maybe it wasn't Gerda at all! How can you be sure if—"

"Her shoes," Agnes said, her voice barely a rasp.

"Her what?"

"Her shoes. She had new shoes. They were . . . *red*." She said the word as if it were vile. "*Red shoes,*" she repeated, silently asking if Sarah had ever heard of such a thing.

She had not. "How . . . unusual."

"She said she bought them herself. She said she saved the money by walking to work instead of taking the trolley. But she could not have saved so much money herself. Someone gave her those shoes. A man." Agnes's light blue eyes flared with fury. "We knew it, but we could not stop her. She would not listen, and now the police comes here to tell me my little sister is dead!"

She started to cry again, and once more Sarah saw her rubbing her side. A glance at her watch told her the contractions were only a few minutes apart. Agnes was in advanced labor.

"I think you should lie down for a while," Sarah said. "You have to think of yourself and the new baby. Come on, I'll help you."

Agnes looked around as if she had suddenly remembered something important. "My children? Where are my children?"

"Mrs. Shultz and Mrs. Neugebauer took them so you could get some rest. They'll be fine."

"My babies!" Agnes wailed as Sarah helped her to her feet, but the shifting of her weight resulted in a gush of fluid from beneath her skirt that succeeded in distracting her completely. Her water had broken. *"Mein Gott!"* she cried, and began to mutter hysterically in German as Sarah half led, half carried her into the bedroom.

TWO HOURS LATER Sarah was washing her hands at the kitchen sink when one of the neighbor women brought over a plate covered with a napkin.

"Mr. Otto will be hungry when he comes home," Mrs. Shultz explained, setting it down on the table. She was a short woman of ample girth who took great pride in the neatness of her appearance. "How is Mrs. Otto doing?"

"She's fine. She had another little girl."

"Already? I didn't hear a thing!"

"The labor went quickly." Sarah didn't mention that the baby had hardly cried. That worried her. That and the way Agnes had shown hardly any interest in the child. Sarah had made sure the baby nursed before Agnes fell into an exhausted sleep, but she was very much afraid Agnes's milk wouldn't come in if she didn't calm down soon. Unfortunately, Sarah couldn't think of any way to help her, short of bringing Agnes's sister back to life.

"Did she tell you what happened?" Mrs. Shultz asked. "To her sister, I mean."

"A little," Sarah admitted, wanting to hear the facts of the case from someone less emotional about them. "She said Gerda was killed."

"Someone beat her like a dog and left her to die in some filthy alley," Mrs. Shultz informed her righteously, folding her arms under her ample breasts. She was also of German descent, but had been in America long enough to have lost most of her accent.

"Do they know who did it?" Sarah asked, drying her hands on one of Agnes's immaculate towels.

"No, and they will never find out, either, if you ask me. That girl, she got just what she deserved. What did she expect? Going out every night, flaunting herself at those dance houses. No decent girls go to those places, I can tell you that."

"I'm sure she was only trying to have a good time," Sarah said, for some reason feeling obliged to defend the dead girl. Maybe because she was so young. Sarah could remember what it was like to be so young and wish for freedom and happiness.

"A good time!" Mrs. Shultz scoffed. "Girls don't need to have a good time. They should stay at home and help their mothers until they find a respectable man and get married. It's not natural for a girl to get work and go out alone with no chaperon to protect her. And this is what comes when she does. She ends up dead in an alley!"

Sarah glanced at the door into Agnes's bedroom, which she'd left open because of the heat. Fortunately, Agnes still seemed to be sleeping soundly, oblivious to the judgments of her neighbor. Still, she pushed the door closed, not wanting to cause Agnes any more pain than she'd already suffered.

"Young women *have* to work nowadays," Sarah reminded her. "Agnes and her husband couldn't afford to keep Gerda if she didn't pay her share of the expenses."

"*Ach,* she didn't have to run wild, though, did she? Going out every night, wearing those fancy clothes that she couldn't afford on her wages, not after she gave most of them to Mr. Otto for her board. And those shoes! I heard the policeman ask Agnes if her sister owned a pair of red shoes. That's how they knew it was her. Everybody in the neighborhood knew about those red shoes. And everybody knows what kind of a girl wears red shoes!"

"Yes, a girl who is now dead," Sarah reminded her grimly.

Mrs. Shultz huffed, plainly annoyed that Sarah wouldn't join her in condemning Gerda. "I must get back. My own husband will be home soon." Sarah wasn't sorry to see her go.

Sarah looked in on her patient again and found Agnes awake, her eyes brimming with tears. She'd overheard at least part of the conversation.

"That is what they will say about my Gerda now," Agnes moaned. "They will say she was a bad girl. They will say she deserved to be murdered, and no one will care that a poor German girl who worked in a shirt factory died in an alley. No one will bother to catch the man who did it, and no one will ever be punished."

Sarah knew this was true, so she had few words of comfort to offer. "At least Gerda has you to mourn her," she offered.

"She was not a bad girl," Agnes insisted, trying to make Sarah understand. "She only wanted to be free. That is what she says, all the time. She wants to be free, with no one telling her what to do. That is why she left Germany. She did not want our father telling her what to do and what man to marry. She wanted to make a new life for herself here in America where she could decide for herself what she did."

The same way Sarah had left her own father's house and married the man of her own choice instead of her father's. When Tom had died, again Sarah had decided to make her own way instead of moving back to her father's house. She'd wanted to be free, just like Gerda. She'd found a way to make her own living and her own life, just the way Gerda had tried to do. She'd simply been more successful at it than the dead girl had, because Gerda had met a man who had stolen her choices from her. *There but for the grace of God go I*, Sarah couldn't help thinking.

"The police, they will not care who killed my Gerda, will they?" Agnes asked.

Sarah could have lied to escape an awkward moment, to make Agnes feel better even though she knew the lie would do more harm than good. But because she did know, she told the truth. "The police might investigate if you could offer them a reward for finding Gerda's killer."

Agnes shook her head, tears running down her face. "We have no money for a reward."

Of course they didn't. And justice in New York City was only for the rich. Unless . . .

"I have a friend," Sarah heard herself saying. A small lie. She and Frank Malloy weren't exactly friends. "He's a police detective. I could ask him to help. He might be able to do something."

Agnes clasped Sarah's hand in both of hers. "Please!" she begged. "It is all we can do for Gerda now."

SOMEONE IN THE building was cooking cabbage for supper. Or maybe *everyone* was. With cabbage, it was hard to tell. The thin walls were also little barrier to the sounds of life within the flats she passed as she climbed the stairs to the second floor. A baby was crying in one, a mother screamed at her child in another. Pots clanged against each other as women prepared the evening meal, and the smells of cooking combined with the smells of rotting garbage from the streets to form a miasma of decay that seemed to hang over the entire city.

Sarah remembered the door. She remembered the last and only time she'd come here, just after she and Malloy had solved the murder of a young girl Sarah had known all her life. She'd left on good terms with Malloy that day, but certainly, he'd never expected to see her again. Just as she'd never expected to see him either. Not that she was going to see him now, of course. She'd been fairly certain he wouldn't be at home in the middle of the day. No, she just wanted to get word to him, and going to his home seemed much more sensible than going to police headquarters. The last time she'd sought him out at the Mulberry Street station, she'd found herself locked in an interrogation room!

Besides, she had another, very good reason for coming to his home: his son, Brian.

She raised her gloved hand and knocked more loudly than she'd intended to. From the other side of the door, she could hear the sound of grumbling, and then the door opened. The woman on the other side was small and sturdily built, her iron-gray hair pulled fiercely back into a bun. She looked ready for anything, but she was not ready to see Sarah Brandt. Her wrinkled face grew slack with surprise for an instant before it hardened into anger.

"He ain't here, and he ain't expected," Mrs. Malloy said, turning up her nose. Or maybe she was just looking up. Sarah was much taller.

Sarah feigned surprise. "Brian isn't here? Where is he, then?"

Now Mrs. Malloy was surprised again. And confused. "Brian? What would you be wanting with the boy?"

"I brought him a present," Sarah informed her with a smile as genuine as she could make it, knowing full well that Frank Malloy's mother would rather push her down the stairs than allow her inside their apartment. "Oh, here he comes!" Indeed, Brian was crawling over to where his grandmother was trying to block the door with her black-clad body.

His beautiful face was alive with happiness at having a visitor. Surely, he didn't remember Sarah. He'd seen her only once, for a few minutes, and that had been over two months ago. And he was feebleminded, as his grandmother had explained to Sarah with perverse satisfaction on her first visit, in addition to being crippled by a clubfoot. But Brian's life would be very uneventful, and the arrival of anyone at all would be a cause for joy.

Mrs. Malloy instinctively turned to see what Brian was doing, and Sarah took shameless advantage of her momentary distraction to slip past her guard and into the flat.

"Hello, Brian," Sarah said, leaning over to greet him. She ignored Mrs. Malloy's gasp of outrage. "Look what I've brought for you." She reached into her satchel and pulled out a small wooden horse and rider. The horse had been fitted with a miniature leather saddle and bridle, and the rider was done up in someone's idea of what a western cowboy would wear. It was designed to delight any little boy, and Brian was no exception.

"He don't need no toys from the likes of you," Mrs. Malloy tried, but Brian was already snatching the horse from Sarah's hand, his luminous green eyes huge with wonder. He sat back on his haunches and began to examine his prize.

"It won't make no difference," Mrs. Malloy told her fiercely. "You can bring the boy a cartload of toys, and it won't make no difference to Frances. He don't have no use for any woman but Brian's mam, God rest her soul, so don't go thinking you'll win him through the boy."

Sarah was hard-pressed not to laugh out loud at the ridiculous notion that she had designs on Frank Malloy. "I'm not looking for a husband, Mrs. Malloy," she said instead, even though the old woman plainly didn't believe her. "But I do need the services of a police detective once again, so I thought I'd stop by and leave word for him. Would you mind telling him I need to speak with him?"

"I'll do no such thing! I'm not some servant you can order around and—"

She stopped speaking for the same reason Sarah stopped listening to her. They were both distracted by the realization that Brian had, within seconds, figured out how to remove the toy rider from his saddle, unbuckle the saddle and remove it, and then put everything back together again.

"Aren't you clever, Brian," Sarah told him, expecting him to beam his glorious smile at her. Instead he didn't even look up. He had already started working on removing the horse's delicate bridle.

Perhaps he was simply engrossed in his project, but Sarah didn't think so.

"That's a horse, Brian. You probably see them in the street when you look out the window," she tried.

"That's right, Bri, don't pay her no mind," Mrs. Malloy said, and the boy paid her no mind either. "He won't talk to you," she told Sarah with just a trace of satisfaction. "If he won't talk to me in three years, he ain't going to talk to you just because you brought him a present."

Sarah didn't acknowledge her. She was too busy studying the boy. His tiny hands were nimble as he worked the intricacies of the horse's tack. He'd needed no more than a moment of study to figure out how to remove and replace it. And yet his grandmother claimed he'd never uttered a word.

"Has he always been mute?" Sarah asked as the tiny seed of an idea sprouted in her mind.

"Mute? What's that, a fancy name for simple?" Mrs. Malloy demanded.

"No, it means someone who doesn't speak. Did he cry when he was a baby?"

"Hardly at all," she bragged. "He was the best baby on earth. Never gave his old Nana a second of trouble, did you, Bohyo?"

Brian didn't deign to reply. He was moving the horse along the floor, as if the cowboy were going for a ride across the wooden planks. He turned away as the horse rode over toward the sofa. He seemed oblivious to the conversation going on around him. Or maybe not oblivious at all.

"Hah!" Sarah shouted as loudly as she dared.

Mrs. Malloy squeaked in shock, her hand going instantly to her heart. "Whatever is the matter with you?" she cried, outraged at Sarah's bizarre behavior. "You scared me out of ten years' growth!"

Indeed, the woman had fairly jumped when Sarah shouted, but the boy hadn't moved a muscle. He hadn't so much as hesitated in his determination to take his cowboy on the ride of his life all around the parlor. He hadn't even noticed.

Which made Sarah think that she knew the real reason why Brian never spoke, and it had nothing at all to do with him being feebleminded.

"He seems very clever with his hands. Did you see how quickly he figured out how to work the saddle?" she asked.

"He's always been good at figuring things out," Mrs. Malloy said defensively, as if Sarah had somehow insulted him by hinting his brain might not be as damaged as she had been led to believe.

She glanced at Mrs. Malloy, then back at the boy. Dare she voice her suspicion? No, not to the old woman. She wouldn't be interested in Sarah's theories about her grandson, not from a woman she had decided was out to usurp her position in Frank Malloy's life. Malloy might not be interested either, but at least he would listen. And if Sarah was wrong, as well she might be . . .

"Next time I come, I'll bring you some cookies, Brian," she tried. The boy was riding his horse up the side of the sofa and didn't respond.

"Next time!" Mrs. Malloy huffed. "What makes you think you'd be welcome?"

Sarah smiled sweetly. "Not a thing," she admitted. "But I would appreciate it if you would tell Mr. Malloy that I stopped by. If you do, I won't have to come back again."

There, that might be just the motive the old woman needed. But probably she wouldn't have been able to resist venting her spleen on Malloy over Sarah's brazenness in calling on a man without so much as an invitation. Whatever her reason, Mrs. Malloy was sure to complain to her son about Sarah, which would, in turn, bring him right to her door. Satisfied that she had accomplished her mission in coming, she took her leave. Brian hardly noticed.

SARAH WAS GLAD she'd bought an extra chop and a loaf of bread at the Gansevoort Market a few blocks away when she saw the man sitting on her doorstep. He didn't look particularly pleased to be there, but Sarah had expected that. She was pretty sure she could coax him out of his bad mood if she cooked for him, though. It had worked once before.

"Mrs. Brandt!"

The familiar voice distracted Sarah from Malloy's glowering expression, and she turned to see her neighbor peering at her through her partially opened window. Nothing happened in the neighborhood that Mrs. Elsworth didn't see and note, and someone as large and formidable as Detective Sergeant Frank Malloy was certainly noteworthy.

"I knew someone would be coming today. I had bubbles in my teacup this morning," she reported.

"Bubbles?" Sarah echoed in amusement.

"Yes, a sure sign that visitors are coming. Or at least one visitor, in this case. I didn't think you'd mind if he waited, or I would have told him to be on his way. It's that police detective, isn't it? He hasn't been around in a while."

The question Mrs. Elsworth was too well bred to ask was fairly screaming for an answer, but Sarah felt compelled to discourage her nosiness since she hadn't been able to do a thing to quell her superstitions. "No, he hasn't been around in a while," Sarah confirmed, "and it's perfectly fine that he waited for me. I need to speak with him. But maybe you just had some soapsuds in your cup. Did you ever think of that?"

Not waiting for a reply, Sarah strolled on down the sidewalk to where Malloy now stood beside her front stoop, glowering furiously.

"Good evening, Mr. Malloy," she said. "It was so good of you to come."

He looked as if he'd like to throttle her, but she was fairly certain he wouldn't, at least not with Mrs. Elsworth watching.

"What did you think you were doing this afternoon?" he

asked, his voice rough but pitched low, so he couldn't be overheard.

"I was visiting your son, and a delightful boy he is, too." She'd passed him and gone on up the steps, leaving him no choice but to follow unless he wanted to shout at her.

"My mother almost had a stroke, she was that upset," he told her as she unlocked her front door.

Sarah could believe it. "She thinks I've set my cap for you, Malloy," she informed him wickedly, pushing the door open.

"*What?*" he asked, but he was talking to himself because she'd gone into the house. Left with no other choice, he followed her inside.

"Your mother thinks I'm looking for a husband," Sarah explained, closing the door behind him, "and she obviously believes you're a good catch, so naturally, she wasn't very happy to see me, but you can assure her I am no threat to your independence."

Malloy planted his hands on his hips and made every attempt to intimidate her. She had to admit, he almost succeeded. Malloy could be horribly intimidating when he set his mind to it. "That's not what she was going on about," he informed her. "She said you upset the boy."

"Brian?" she asked, genuinely shocked. She should have guessed Mrs. Malloy would lie to make her look bad to her son. "He wasn't upset. In fact, he was very happy when I left. Did he show you the horse I gave him?"

"He didn't show me anything. He was sitting in a corner, banging his head on the wall when I got home, and the old woman was screaming like a banshee."

"Oh, my." Sarah frowned, trying to figure this out. Brian had been blissfully happy when she left, and would have remained so as long as he had his new toy to play with. Was it possible? Could the old woman have been cruel enough to take the toy away to upset the boy for his father's sake? Of course she could, if she believed she was protecting her family from a she-devil, which she obviously did. "Well, then, you'd probably enjoy having your supper in some peace and quiet. Lucky for you I got some extra meat."

"Mrs. Brandt!" he called after her as she made her way into the kitchen.

Sarah turned back just before disappearing through the doorway. "Aren't you the least bit curious about why I went to the trouble to get you over here?"

Frank swore under his breath as he watched her go. What on earth had possessed him to come here tonight? He should have remembered what an infuriating piece of baggage Sarah Brandt could be. Oh, she was smart and a damn fine-looking woman, but Frank had never considered intelligence a particularly attractive trait in a female, and beauty is as beauty does, as his mother would have said. He couldn't have cared less why she wanted to see him, and he felt obliged to tell her so. Besides, she'd left him standing in her office with its strange instruments and equipment, and the mere sight of those things made his flesh crawl.

He found her stoking the fire in her stove. "Mrs. Brandt—"

"It's too hot in here. Why don't you go sit on the back porch and wait. I have a little table set up out there to catch the breeze, and I poured you some beer." She nodded toward a tall glass of amber liquid sitting on her table. "My neighbor makes it," she explained with one of her sly grins when Frank registered surprise.

Maybe he was being too hasty. He'd tell her whatever it was he intended to tell her *after* he'd had the beer. And maybe he'd let her feed him, too. She wasn't a bad cook, if he remembered correctly. And then . . . Well, then he'd make sure she understood she was never to show her face in his mother's presence again.

By the time she set his plate in front of him, he'd mellowed somewhat. Maybe it was the beer or maybe it was the peacefulness of his surroundings. Her back porch overlooked the tiny patch of ground that passed for a yard in the city. Sarah Brandt had filled that patch of ground with flowers of every description. Their beauty and fragrance disguised the stench and bleakness that stretched in every direction outside the boundaries of her fence.

She'd fried up a pork chop and some potatoes and onions. Bakery bread completed the meal, and Frank realized he was starving. She sat down opposite him at the small wicker table she'd placed on the porch, still smiling the way she did when she thought she knew something he didn't.

"Somebody's been murdered," he guessed, trying to wipe that grin off her face. He found it far too disturbing.

To his relief, she frowned. "The sister of one of my patients, a girl named Gerda Reinhard. She was only sixteen. Her family doesn't have any money, and her sister is afraid her murder will never be solved."

"She's probably right," Frank said before allowing himself to taste the meat. It was juicy and tender, not fried to shoe leather the way his mother would have done.

That really made her frown. "I thought maybe you could help."

He gave her a look that usually turned hardened criminals into quivering, terrified jelly, but she didn't bat an eye.

"I promised her sister that I'd find out what I could, at least," she said. "Can you at least tell me if there are any suspects? If the police think they know who did it or something?"

Frank took another bite of the meat and told himself he was only asking for trouble. There was nothing he could do for this girl's family, and it was cruel of Sarah Brandt to let them think otherwise. Still, he heard himself say, "What happened to her?"

"They found her in an alley. Someone had beaten her and—"

"Oh, the red shoes," he said knowingly.

"What?"

"She was wearing red shoes, wasn't she?"

"Yes. How did you know?" She seemed pleased that he'd guessed so quickly.

"Everybody at Mulberry Street was talking about it," he said, referring to the offices of police headquarters on Mulberry Street. "And you're wasting your time. They'll never find out who killed her without offering a reward . . . and not for the police," he added when she would have interrupted him. It was common knowledge that the New York City police only investigated crimes for which they would receive a reward. "You'd need a reward to get a witness to come forward. They'll never find her killer unless somebody saw him do it. There's just too many possible suspects."

"What do you mean?"

"I mean this is no society girl this time," he said, reminding her of the murder the two of them had solved last spring. "Gerda Reinhard was pretty free with her favors, if you know what I mean. Out every night, different men each time, she was just asking for trouble. Got what she deserved, if you ask me."

"Nobody asked you!" she cried, outraged. "Are you saying that a girl who tries to have a little fun deserves to have the life beaten out of her?"

How could he have forgotten how unreasonable she could be? He swallowed down the last bite of his chop, which no longer tasted quite so delicious. "I'm saying that when a girl takes up with strange men the way this one did, night after night, she's bound to find a bad one sooner or later."

"And you think this bad one should be allowed to go out and kill another unsuspecting young woman because this girl's family is too poor to pay a reward to catch him?"

Frank's dinner was turning into a molten ball in his stomach. "I'm saying that it's not very likely he'll be caught."

"Isn't it worth a try, though? Things are changing in the police force. You're bound to get noticed if you solved a case like this."

"Noticed by who? Your friend Teddy Roosevelt? Haven't you been reading the newspapers?"

"I certainly have! His testimony is going to get that corrupt Commissioner Parker removed from office, and then he'll finally be able to accomplish the reforms he wants. That will mean excellent officers—and detectives—will be promoted."

He shook his head. "Not likely. Parker is a Platt man," he said, naming the Democratic party boss who ran the city by pulling the strings of elected politicians. "The governor would have to approve his removal, and that won't ever happen, no matter what the mayor decides. So if you think I'll waste my time trying to impress the likes of Roosevelt—the man who offended every man who likes a Sunday afternoon beer in this town—then you're out of your mind."

She sighed in disgust and stabbed at her meat with her fork without making any attempt to eat it. Another man might have thought she'd given up, but Frank knew Sarah Brandt better than that. She never gave up. He braced himself for her next angle of attack, but even still, she caught him on his blind side.

"I also wanted to talk to you about Brian."

"There's nothing to talk about," Frank informed her. "My mother takes care of him, and she knows what's best for him. Seeing you upsets him, so I'm going to have to insist that—"

"Your mother told me he's feebleminded," she said baldly, without the slightest regard for the pain this would cause him.

And it did cause him pain, the kind of agony someone like Sarah Brandt with her privileged background could never understand. "You must have noticed that yourself," he said, his teeth gritted in an attempt to control himself.

"I don't think he is," she said, laying down her fork and crossing her arms over her well-padded bosom. "I don't think there's anything wrong with his mind at all."

Now Frank was really sorry he hadn't throttled her earlier. He could have spared himself this, at least. "My son's mind is none of your concern," he tried, but she was having none of it.

"I told you I gave him a horse when I visited him today. It was a fancy carved thing I picked up from a street peddler. It had a real leather saddle and bridle, and Brian had them off that horse in seconds. Your mother said he's very clever at figuring things out, even though he's only three years old."

Frank had to grip the edge of the table to hold himself in check. "Maybe she also told you he doesn't talk. Doesn't make a sound, and he can't understand a damn thing you say to him." He was fairly shouting now, but even that didn't seem to bother her. She just stared back at him, cool as you please.

"Of course he doesn't understand what you say to him. That's because he's deaf."

2

"*D*EAF?" HE SAID THE WORD AS IF HE'D NEVER heard it before. Plainly, he'd never heard it in connection with his son.

"When I met Brian the first time, I only saw him for a few minutes, and your mother told me he was feeble-minded, so I didn't think anything about his behavior. But something bothered me. He was so silent. I've seen lots of children with damaged brains, and they were all as loud and boisterous as other children. But not Brian. I think that's one reason why I went to your home instead of leaving word for you at the station. I wanted to see Brian again and figure out why he was so silent."

He was still trying to get his understanding around this. "And now you think he's *deaf*?" he asked incredulously. He obviously also thought she was insane.

"Let me tell you some things that I suspect are true about Brian. He's a very sound sleeper. Loud noises don't wake him up. In fact, no noise of any kind wakes him up. And when you call him, he ignores you. Unless perhaps he's looking at you, and then he comes. He has signs that he uses for things, and even though he doesn't talk, he uses the signs to make his needs known to your mother. Am I right?"

He was frowning. Of course, he was *usually* frowning when he was with her, but this frown was different. He wasn't trying to frighten her this time. He was thinking, and not liking the things he was thinking about.

"I'm right, aren't I?" she prodded, knowing he must be testing her theory against what he knew of Brian's behavior. "Your mother even told me he's clever about taking things apart. That proves there's nothing wrong with his mind. In fact, he's probably very bright."

If she'd thought to comfort him, she failed. "Do you think this is news I want to hear?" he asked her in amazement. "Do you think I want my son to be deaf? He's already a cripple!"

"But don't you see, if he's deaf, he can be educated. He can even learn a trade and—"

"He's still a cripple," he reminded her, his face dark with the anger he still felt over this fact.

"I've been thinking about that, too, and I know this surgeon who—"

"Do you think I didn't take him to a doctor when he was born?" He was beyond angry now. She'd wounded his pride. "I took him before he was a week old. I would've paid any amount of money to have him made right again, but they said nothing could be done."

"Who told you that?" she asked, outraged.

"The *doctor,*" he reminded her impatiently.

"Which one?"

"How should I know? That was three years ago!"

Sarah somehow managed not to sigh in dismay. "Malloy, let me ask you something. Are all the detectives on the New York City police force as good at their jobs as you are?"

Once again, she'd stung his pride. "No!"

"Of course they aren't. Some of them are just as good

as you are and some are not quite as good and some are completely worthless."

"What does that have to do with—?"

"Doctors are the same way. Some are very good at what they do and some are not quite as good, and some are completely worthless."

"He was a *doctor*!" Malloy insisted.

"Malloy, where do you think the expression 'quack doctor' came from? Some doctors don't know any more about medicine than you do! Well, perhaps a bit more, but not much. It's entirely possible that the doctor who saw Brian didn't know much about clubfoot, and that this surgeon I know might be able to help Brian walk. I can't make any promises, but I can at least arrange for you to—"

"Mrs. Brandt, I don't need for you to arrange anything for me," he told her, gritting his teeth again. "And I don't need your help. I can take care of my son myself."

Sarah caught herself just short of issuing another lecture. Malloy wouldn't appreciate it, and she might very well alienate him completely. Besides, he was right. He *could* take care of his son himself. "Of course you can," she agreed reasonably. "All I'm suggesting is that you go home and test my theory. See if Brian can hear. And if he can't, well, there are schools for the deaf in the city. I'm sure they would be happy to help you learn how to communicate with him."

He pushed his plate away. He couldn't push it very far because the table was so small, but the gesture told her he was finished with her and this conversation. Too bad she wasn't finished with him.

"Think about it, Malloy," she tried. "If Brian is only deaf, he won't need someone to take care of him for the rest of his life. He can earn his own living, and he might even marry and have a family of his own and—"

"No woman would marry a deaf cripple."

"Don't be so sure." She could see she'd given him

enough to think about without planning Brian's future, so she let it drop.

"I've got to go," he said, rising from his chair.

"Of course you do," she agreed, standing also.

"Thanks for the . . ." He waved toward his plate, and Sarah nodded in acknowledgment.

He looked ready to bolt, but before he did, she had one last request. He didn't realize it yet, but she had done him a good turn with Brian, and he would soon feel the need to repay her.

"Malloy, if it wouldn't be too much trouble, could you at least find out if there are any suspects in Gerda Reinhard's death? It would mean a lot to her sister."

He was still shaking his head in wonder as he disappeared through her garden gate.

SARAH SAT DOWN at the back of the United German Lutheran Church on Sixth Street. The crowd at Gerda Reinhard's funeral looked pitifully small in the cavernous interior. Gerda's sister Agnes was still in bed, on Sarah's orders, and the rest of her family was still in Germany and probably didn't even yet know of her death. A few of Agnes's friends and neighbors had come, and a small group of young women who must have known Gerda were sitting on the other side of the church. At the very last moment, just before the minister took his place in the pulpit, a young man Sarah recognized as Lars Otto, Agnes's husband, came in. He wore an ill-fitting black suit, probably borrowed for the occasion, and his sandy-brown hair had been slicked down with an abundance of hair tonic. He walked stiffly down the aisle, his lanky frame all knees and elbows, carrying his hat clutched tightly in both hands. He seated himself with obvious reluctance at the front of the church, took out a handkerchief, and mopped the sweat from his face. The weather had cooled considerably today, but Mr. Otto was under a lot of strain.

Sarah could sympathize with him. Burying his sister-in-law would be an ordeal under the best of circumstances. Gerda, however, had not simply died an untimely death. She had been murdered under scandalous circumstances. The shame and embarrassment the family must feel would be considerable. Added to their grief, the burden must be great indeed.

Lars hung his head, not even glancing at the closed casket that sat only a few feet away from him. The minister took his place and began reciting the appropriate Scriptures, the ones that offered hope to the bereaved. Sarah wondered how much hope they would offer in this case. Most people believed Gerda had only gotten what she deserved. Could a girl as sinful as Gerda was rumored to be really be expected to walk the streets of gold?

As she mulled over these questions, Sarah glanced at the group of young women who had known Gerda in life, girls who must be much like her. They stared straight ahead, apparently hanging on the minister's words, their young faces stricken beneath the layers of heavily applied makeup. Their cheap finery looked out of place in the solemn surroundings, like peacocks in a chicken coop. Gaudy and tasteless peacocks, too.

Sarah wished for organ music to drown the oppressive silence, but the Ottos wouldn't waste money on an organist for this occasion. From Lars Otto's expression, he would not have wasted money on any of this, except that common decency demanded at least the minimum of ceremony, even for a girl as undeserving as Gerda. A girl so thoughtless as to get herself murdered.

The service was not a moment longer than necessary. The minister seemed aware that he should waste no time in committing this girl to the ground, and before Sarah knew it, he was pronouncing the benediction. She waited a moment, expecting some pallbearers to come forward to carry the casket out, but no one did. Instead, Lars Otto made his way out of the pew and started down the aisle. There was to be no graveside service, which would have required a hearse and more expense. Gerda's remains would be carried to the cemetery in the gravedigger's wagon and deposited in lonely solitude with no one to mourn her.

As Lars passed, Sarah hurried to follow him, wishing at least to find out how Agnes was doing.

"Mr. Otto," she called, stopping him as he started down the front steps outside. He turned to face her.

Lars Otto was a tall man, thin and lanky, with big hands and feet, and a face too sharp and angular to be called handsome. Sarah noticed his knuckles were skinned when he adjusted his hat, testimony to how difficult his job must be. She thought she remembered he was a butcher by trade. He frowned when he saw Sarah, not recognizing her.

"I'm Mrs. Brandt, the midwife. I'm very sorry about Gerda. How is Mrs. Otto doing?"

"How do you think? Can't even hold her head up now, with all her friends whispering behind their hands. I work hard to give her a good life, and her sister does this to ruin everything."

Sarah blinked. She had forgotten the bitter anger cases like this engendered. She resisted the temptation to point out that Gerda hadn't gotten herself murdered on purpose. "I'm sure no one will hold this against you and your family. Not your true friends, at least," she added at his grunt of disdain.

Unimpressed, he turned away, anxious no doubt to get back to his family.

"Please tell you wife I'll come by to see her this afternoon," she called after him. He gave her no acknowledgment. Well, if he was always this rude, he was probably right to worry, since he probably had no true friends to stick by him.

"Oh, look, he's already gone!" a voice behind her cried in dismay.

"Go after him, then," another suggested sarcastically.

"Oh, and chase him down the street, I guess," the first voice replied, equally sarcastic.

Sarah turned to see the three young women she had noticed earlier emerging from the massive doorway of the church. In the merciless sunlight, their clothes looked even more garish. Plaids and feathers and too much jewelry, painted lips and painted cheeks. Sarah couldn't believe the girls thought the paint looked better than their natural skin, which was young and smooth and should have still had the flush of health beneath the startling brightness of the rouge.

Behind them, the other mourners came out, casting disapproving looks as they made their way around them. Sarah nodded to those she knew as she made her way back to where the girls stood, arguing about something.

"Are you friends of Gerda's?" she asked, trying a friendly smile.

They looked up, startled, then grew instantly wary. "Yes, ma'am," one of them said after a moment. Did they look guilty? Sarah could hardly credit it, but she had to admit they did. Perhaps her instincts had been surer than she'd imagined. She'd thought only to approach them and find out a little about Gerda, but could they know something about her death, too?

"I'm a friend of Mrs. Otto, her sister," Sarah said, stretching the truth just a bit. "I knew Gerda a little, but not very well. She seemed like a nice girl. I'm sure you're going to miss her."

They nodded uncertainly, making the feathers on their ridiculous hats shiver. They were studying Sarah, as if trying to decide what to make of her. Then the plump one prodded the one in the red plaid jacket with her elbow and said, "Ask her. Maybe she knows."

The girl in the plaid jacket shot her friend an angry glare, but she turned to Sarah and said, "Excuse me for asking, miss, but do you know . . . I mean . . ." She hesitated, glancing at her friend for help, but none was forthcoming. The two stared at each other for along moment, silently communicating things at which Sarah could only guess.

"She wants to know did they bury her in the shoes," the third girl finally said. She was small and fragile looking, her golden hair glittering in the sunlight beneath the frothy confection of a hat she was wearing. Her lips were very red, and the blush on her cheeks was unevenly applied, larger on one side than the other, making her look like a child who had gotten into her mother's things. But then Sarah looked into her eyes, and there she saw a steely determination quite at odds with her apparent fragility.

"The shoes?" Sarah echoed stupidly.

"The red shoes," the plump girl clarified. "They was brand-new. Seems a shame to put them in the ground with her, don't it? Bertha here was wondering—"

"*Me!*" the girl in the plaid jacket cried in outrage. "You was the one said it first!"

"I was only agreeing with you!" the plump girl insisted.

"Bertha and Hetty both want the shoes," the blond girl explained patiently, her disapproval obvious.

"To remember her by," Hetty added hastily, lest Sarah think them ghouls.

Which of course she did, although she decided not to betray her true sentiments. "I can understand that. You were good friends, then?" she guessed.

"We all were," Hetty said, determined to make Sarah believe her. "Since the day she come to work at Faircloths."

"She couldn't hardly talk a word of English," Bertha added, "but we didn't care about that. She learned quick, she did. Wanted to be an American, like us. That's what she always said."

"You were very kind to befriend her," Sarah said, and allowed the girls a moment to absorb the compliment before adding, "Since there isn't going to be a wake, perhaps you'd allow me to buy you ladies a cup of coffee. There's a shop just around the corner."

"It's a little warm for coffee," Hetty said. "How about some lemonade?"

Sarah was more than happy to supply them with champagne if it meant she'd be able to learn more about the dead girl, so she readily greed. By the time they found the shop, Sarah had learned that the girls were named Hetty Hall, Bertha Hoffman, and the blond girl was Lisle Lasher. They were fascinated to learn Sarah was a midwife, although they couldn't understand why she'd taken up a trade instead of remarrying. Plainly, they believed—as did most of the population—that a woman needed a man to look after her.

Sarah treated them to cake as well as lemonade, knowing full well their meager salaries would hardly stretch to such an extravagance and figuring they'd be more talkative if they were fed. They sat in the café, glad to be out of the sun, and Sarah tried to imagine what questions Malloy would ask these girls if he were here.

"Does anyone have any idea who might have killed Gerda?" she tried, starting with the most important matters.

"I think it was a robbery," Hetty said between mouthfuls of cake.

"Are you crazy?" Bertha demanded. "What would a robber want with Gerda? She didn't have anything worth stealing except them shoes, and they was left right on her feet!"

"Which is why he killed her," Hetty reasoned. "He got mad when she didn't have any money, and he killed her."

Sarah glanced at Lisle while Bertha and Hetty continued to bicker over the theory of the robber. She sipped her lemonade delicately, listening but unmoved by their arguments. She was remarkably self-possessed for a girl of her class, her intelligence obvious. Dressed properly, she would have looked at home in Mrs. Astor's parlor. When she met Sarah's gaze, she smiled slightly, as if to acknowledge Sarah's good opinion of her.

"And what do you think, Lisle?" Sarah asked, interrupting Bertha and Hetty's squabbling.

Both of the other girls fell silent, waiting for Lisle's opinion. She was the leader of the group, her delicate appearance notwithstanding.

"I don't think it was no robber," she said. "A robber wouldn't of bothered with Gerda, and if he did, he'd never take the time to beat her up. He might smack her a bit, but they said she was beat to death. That takes time, and a robber wouldn't take the chance of getting caught."

Sarah hadn't been mistaken about her intelligence. "I was thinking that it must have been someone who knew her. Someone who was very angry with her, so angry he didn't even think about getting caught."

But Lisle didn't agree. Her red lips turned downward in a frown. "You might think that except . . ." She glanced at the other girls who shifted uneasily.

"What is it?" Sarah asked. "Do you know something I don't?"

The girls exchanged wary glances, silently debating whether to share their knowledge with her. Finally, Lisle said, "Gerda ain't the first girl ended up that way."

Of course not. Women were beaten to death every day in the city, usually by their husbands or lovers or fathers. Men who took out their frustrations with life by beating those closest to them, those weaker and defenseless. Women who would conceal this violence by telling stories about walking into a door or falling down stairs to explain the bruises. Women so afraid of not being able to support themselves without a man that they would tolerate any abuse in exchange for a roof over their heads.

"I know," Sarah agreed. "Lots of women end up like Gerda did. That's why you should be careful about the men you become involved with—"

"No, you don't understand," Lisle explained, her voice patient and confident with her certainty. "Gerda ain't the first girl to get murdered just that way."

"The same way exactly," Bertha added, her brown eyes wide with fright.

"They go out to a dance and never come home," Hetty added, her full lips quivering a bit.

"Somebody beats them and leaves them in an alley, just like a dead cat," Lisle said bitterly.

"You mean . . . other girls have died the same way?" Sarah asked, unable to grasp this completely.

"That's what we just said," Hetty pointed out, a little insulted. "Somebody's looking for girls to kill. At least that's what everybody at Faircloths is saying. The other girls, they was at dances, too, and they leaves their friends to walk home, but they never got there."

"How many other girls?" Sarah asked, a strange sense of foreboding quivering inside of her.

"Three others," Lisle said.

"That we know about," Hetty added.

"Might be more, not from the neighborhood, that we didn't hear about," Bertha said.

Their fear was a palpable thing, and Sarah could feel a shiver of it herself. Was it possible that one man was responsible for all these deaths? Sarah understood crimes of passion, where the killer knew his victim and murdered for one of the usual reasons—jealousy, hatred, lust, or greed. But if someone was selecting victims at random and killing them for no apparent reason, then how would anyone ever catch him? She recalled a similar set of murders in London a decade ago and the difficulties the police had encountered in trying to solve them.

Solving a crime when the circle of suspects was small and the motives were discernible was difficult enough, as Sarah knew from her experience last spring, helping Malloy discover the killer of another young woman. Finding a killer whose only connection with the victims was meeting them at a dance seemed impossible! They'd certainly never found Jack the Ripper.

But maybe it wouldn't be as difficult as she thought. If the connection was the dances, perhaps someone with a trained eye could spot the killer. Sarah's eye wasn't exactly trained, but she did have some experience identifying a killer. "Where did Gerda go dancing the night she died?"

The girls looked at each other, as if they were trying to remember. Surely, that shouldn't be so difficult. Sarah could remember everyplace she'd ever gone dancing in her life.

"Was that the night we was at New Irving Hall?" Hetty asked the others.

Bertha shook her head. "No, it wasn't that big. Someplace small, I think. I remember we was thinking there wasn't enough room to dance there."

"It was Harmony Hall," Lisle said. "Gerda said she wasn't having any fun, but she'd met a swell who was going to blow a lot of money on her, so she left with him."

"Did any of you see who he was?"

They shook their heads.

"It didn't seem important then." Bertha sighed. "We didn't know . . . what was going to happen."

"Maybe . . ." Sarah hesitated, wondering if she dared do what she was thinking. "Could you take me there with you the next time there's a dance?"

"There's a dance every night," Hetty said, surprised she wouldn't know that.

"Every night?" Sarah could hardly credit it.

"Well, maybe not there, but somewhere," Lisle corrected. "I think there's one at the Harmony tomorrow, though. The Barn Stormers are having it," she added, naming a local social club.

"On a weeknight?" Sarah asked in surprise.

"I told you, there's dancing every night," Hetty reminded her.

"Were you planning to go?" Sarah asked, then immediately realized how cold she sounded. "I mean, if you wouldn't feel . . ." She let her voice trail off, knowing she was making it worse.

Bertha and Hetty looked away, uncertain. Plainly, they were leaving the decision up to Lisle.

"Why would you want to go?" Lisle asked her suspiciously.

"I . . . I told you I knew Gerda slightly. Last spring, another girl I knew was killed. The police weren't able to solve the case, so I helped, and we were able to find the killer. I don't think the police will be very interested in solving Gerda's murder, either, and I don't want her killer to go free."

"You solved a murder?" Hetty asked, fascinated and seeing Sarah in a whole new light.

"A police detective helped me," Sarah admitted, wondering what Malloy would have to say to that. He'd probably say that *she* had helped *him,* which was more correct but less likely to impress these girls.

"You said the police didn't want to solve it," Lisle reminded her shrewdly.

"They didn't. In fact, this detective was ordered to stop the investigation. That's why he needed my help. I've already asked my friend to look into Gerda's case, but he didn't think much would be done."

The girls nodded sagely. "They didn't care about them other girls that was killed," Hetty said. "Why should they care about Gerda? She wasn't even an American."

A very good point, and Sarah knew she didn't have to say so. The girls, young as they were, probably knew more about the realities of life than she did.

"Will you take me to the dance?" Sarah asked.

"You won't find out nothing," Lisle warned her.

"You might be surprised," Sarah said, feeling the familiar surge of emotion. Not excitement, surely not that, but something closer to power and purpose. A feeling she hadn't experienced since the other time she'd worked so hard to find a young woman's killer.

"You're way too old for these dances," Hetty pointed out unkindly. "They'll think you're somebody's mother."

Sarah ignored the flash of annoyance she felt. After all,

she *was* nearly twice their age, so she shouldn't feel insulted.

"You'd have to fix yourself up some, too," Lisle said. "You need some flash if you want to get noticed."

"I don't want to get noticed," Sarah assured her. Just the opposite, in fact. "I only want to look around and see who comes to these dances."

"You think he'll be there? The killer, I mean," Bertha asked uneasily.

"He must go to these dances. How else would he find his victims?" Sarah pointed out. "And I hope you girls are being careful."

"We're always careful." Bertha sniffed. "We go in pairs. If a girl has a friend with her, they can help each other out, in case a fellow gets too friendly."

Sarah decided not to point out that having a friend hadn't saved Gerda. "Then you'll need a fourth person along, won't you? So you each have a companion. Why not take me?"

Lisle was considering. She didn't know whether to trust Sarah or not, but she must also know that Sarah was the only person who had displayed the slightest interest in finding Gerda's killer—and the killer of several other young girls, too, if what they had told her was true. If nothing else, at least Sarah would be able to prevent these girls from making the same mistake Gerda did in going out with someone she didn't know.

"We'll take you, then," Lisle said at last, "but you've got to get some flash whether you want it or not. It won't do for you to be so plain. You'd draw attention to yourself for that, won't you?"

Sarah thought perhaps she was right. "And what, exactly, must I do to get some flash?" she asked with a smile.

FRANK MALLOY FOUND the man he wanted slumped over his desk in the detectives' office. The large, untidy room was crammed with desks which were usually deserted because their owners were out on cases. Bill Broughan could be counted upon to spend as much time as possible at his desk, however. He avoided work whenever he could.

"Broughan!" Frank shouted right beside the sleeping man's ear.

Broughan jerked awake, blinking furiously until he brought Frank's face into focus. "Malloy, I'd kill you for that, but if I move that sudden, my head'll explode."

"Bad night?" Frank asked without much sympathy. He'd had a bad night himself. He could thank Sarah Brandt for that.

Broughan clamped both hands on his head, as if he really were trying to keep it all in one piece. "My nephew Andrew had a baby boy yesterday. We was celebrating till the wee hours."

"Congratulations to the proud father," Frank said with more courtesy than sincerity. He didn't know Bill's nephew. "Look, Bill, somebody asked me about a case, the one where the girl was wearing red shoes."

Bill squinted, as if the act of trying to remember caused him pain. Broughan was a portly man, his round face flushed from too many years of "celebrating." His thinning brown hair was mussed, as if he hadn't combed it this morning. He probably hadn't. There was a yellow stain on his lapel. "Oh, yeah, the red shoes," he recalled after a moment. "German girl. Hadn't been here long, from what I heard. Damnedest thing. I never heard of nobody wearing red shoes. Not even a German. You ask me, she got 'em whoring. Who else would have red shoes?"

Frank agreed, but he didn't want to say so. He'd get more information if he argued with Bill. "A friend of mine knows the family. Says they're respectable."

"Maybe they are, but that never stopped a girl from whoring if she needed money."

Frank couldn't argue with that, no matter how much he thought it might help him get information. He sighed. "This friend of mine, she wants to know if you've got any idea who killed this girl."

"She?" Broughan asked, his bloodshot eyes brightening with interest.

"She who?" Frank asked, feigning innocence.

"You said your friend who wants to know is a *she.*" His face squinched up in the effort of thought. "This *friend* wouldn't be that blonde who come to the station for you that time, would it? The one the sergeant locked in an interrogation room?"

Frank was never going to live that down, but maybe he could get it to work in his favor this time. Even if this might be even harder to live down. "Yeah, well, you know how women can be when they get started on something."

"Frank, you devil, you." Broughan rubbed his hands in glee. "You never said a word. How long has this been going on?"

Frank gave him a disdainful glare. "I'd tell you if I thought it was any of your business."

Bill frowned. "This must be serious. You thinking about getting hitched again? She know about your kid?"

"Look," Frank said, growing impatient and more than a little annoyed, "right now I just want to make her happy by telling her you're going to arrest somebody for killing this girl." That much was true. If he could make her happy by solving this case, he wouldn't have to see Sarah Brandt again.

Bill rubbed his temples with both hands, closing his eyes against the pounding that must be going on inside his head. "Wish I could help you, son, but nobody'll ever find out who killed that girl."

"Why not?" Frank figured he already knew, but if there was the slightest hope, he wanted to grasp it.

"I told you. She was a whore. Or the next thing to it," he added when Frank was going to protest. "Out every night dancing with her friends. You know what goes on at them dance halls. Lots of strange men, some stranger than others. She went out to Coney Island, too, from what I hear. Always taking up with a new fellow. Somebody give her a hat, right before she died. And them shoes, too. Maybe not the same fellow. Nobody's real sure about that. But at least two men give her presents in the last week or so. Which means maybe one of them found out about the other and beat her for cheating on him, or maybe some other fellow found out about one or both of them and beat her for the same reason. Or maybe she just met somebody new and asked him for a present, and he got insulted. Who knows? And more important, who cares?"

"Her family cares."

Broughan didn't look impressed. "These people got any money? They offering a reward or anything?"

Frank considered lying. Maybe Mrs. Brandt would offer a reward. Did she care that much? He couldn't be sure, and if she didn't, he certainly had no intention of paying a reward himself to find the killer of a girl he'd never even set eyes on just to please Sarah Brandt. "I don't think so."

"Then they might as well forget about her. Put her in the ground and wash their hands. Ain't nobody ever gonna know who killed her, and that's a fact."

Broughan reached into his coat pocket and pulled out a cheap metal flask. The hand that pulled the cork from the top trembled slightly, and he needed both hands to guide it to his lips. He took a long pull, emptying it.

Frank managed not to wince. His father had been a drinker, and it had killed him young. To this day, he couldn't abide hard liquor.

"Was she raped?" Frank asked without knowing why. It just seemed important to have all the facts, and that one might be relevant.

Broughan shrugged one shoulder as he dropped the empty flask back into his pocket. "The doc said she'd been doing it with somebody recent, but he couldn't say that she was raped. Her clothes was all in place when they found her, and she wasn't . . ." He hesitated, searching for the right word. "Damaged" was what he settled for. "No cuts or bruises down there. Had enough of 'em everyplace else, though. Whoever killed her made a good job of it. I'd guess he wanted a piece, and she said no, though it might've been the first time she did. Poor bastard was the only one she wouldn't spread 'em for, I guess, and look what it got her."

"Yeah," Frank said, discouraged. This wasn't going to help. Sarah Brandt wouldn't be satisfied, not by a long shot. She'd want to dig, although where else she would dig, he had no idea.

Well, if she was that interested, maybe she could find out something Bill hadn't. In fact, she could most certainly find out a whole lot of things Bill hadn't, since Bill wasn't particularly interested in solving this case. In fact, unless her family or someone came up with a reward of some kind, Bill was completely finished with it already. Girls turned up dead every day in the city. Some starved, some killed themselves, and some were killed by others. The world didn't seem to care or even to notice, so why should the police exert themselves? Frank certainly wouldn't, not under normal circumstances.

But these weren't normal circumstances. Because he'd gone home from Mrs. Brandt's house last night and stood beside his sleeping son's bed and shouted until the neighbors complained. And just like she'd predicted, the boy hadn't even flinched. Sleeping like an angel, he'd lain there peaceful and quiet and undisturbed while his mother ranted at him, demanding to know had he lost his mind.

"The boy is deaf," he'd told her, silencing her instantly.

She'd looked at him in stunned surprise that turned quickly to terror as she realized the meaning of his words. Or tried to. In truth, neither of them knew what this really meant. It changed everything. The only question now was how.

3

SARAH COULDN'T BELIEVE SHE WAS DOING THIS. She'd gone shopping with Lisle Lasher after Gerda's funeral, and Lisle had convinced her to buy a hat that could only be called ridiculous. She'd done her hair in a fancy pouf, then pinned the outrageous hat with its huge silk roses and oversized brim onto the top of it. She'd even painted her lips, which was as far as she would go, even though Lisle advised some rouge, too.

She wouldn't look too out of place in a shirtwaist and skirt. Lots of working girls wore them to the dances, Lisle had told her, but she should have some beads to dress it up. Sarah was now the proud owner of a strand of gaudy glass ones. She would make Lisle a gift of them when the evening was over.

Harmony Hall was a large empty room over a saloon on Fourteenth Street. The sound from the band—it couldn't be called music—was audible down the street. Sarah decided it must be unbearable inside the hall. The girls had met her a few blocks away, and as they strolled down the street toward it, Sarah began to sense their nervousness.

"If you'd rather not do this, I'll understand," Sarah said

guiltily. How could she have been so insensitive? They must be terrified of going to the last place Gerda had been before she was murdered.

"Oh, don't worry, missus," Hetty said, patting her hair to make sure it was securely in place. "We want to help."

"Sure we do," Bertha said, glancing at Lisle.

Lisle looked like a China doll whose paint had been inexpertly applied. Her blue eyes shone in the fading sunlight, and her hair looked like spun gold beneath the brim of her elaborate hat. The paint on her lips and cheeks, probably applied to make her look older and more sophisticated, actually made her look more fragile and vulnerable. Only when one looked deep into her eyes did one see the inner hardness.

That hardness flashed like steel when she looked at Sarah. "We want to find out who killed Gerda, Mrs. Brandt. If you think this'll help, we'll do it."

Plainly, she didn't think it would, but Sarah knew better. She knew she would find the killer if she just put herself in the right place.

The entrance to the hall was an outside stairway on the side of the saloon. Half a dozen men in loud, checked suits hovered near its entrance, inspecting everyone who passed, as if their approval were necessary for admittance. They were a little the worse for time spent inside the saloon.

"Hetty!" one of them called, a smarmy-looking fellow with slicked-down hair beneath his straw boater. "Who's that with you? Did you bring your ma to chaperone?"

The others found this hilariously funny and laughed uproariously. Sarah felt her cheeks heating, but she was certain it was from anger.

"At least I know who my ma is!" Hetty replied without missing a beat, tipping up her chin haughtily.

The other men found this even more hilarious, as drunks will. Sarah quickened her step to keep up with the other girls who were scurrying up the stairs to escape the drunks below. At the top of the steps, a burly young man sat at a rickety table collecting the fifteen-cent admission fee. Sarah treated the girls, knowing they had to count their pennies and skip lunches to afford such outings.

The hall was much hotter than the street outside, and the stench of human sweat was strong. Mixed with the smell of stale beer, cigarette smoke, and the other unpleasant odors of the city, it was nearly overwhelming, but Sarah fought off a wave of dizziness and reminded herself that she could get used to anything. She'd delivered babies in enough hovels to know that after a few minutes she wouldn't even notice the smell anymore. The heat was another matter. She'd just have to ignore it.

The band had been playing a rousing rendition of "After the Ball," but as soon as they arrived, the music stopped with unnatural abruptness, leaving Sarah's ears ringing in the sudden stillness. The silence lasted only a moment, however, since the hundred or so people in the room instantly took advantage of the opportunity to converse without screaming over the din of the musicians.

"Let's find a table," Bertha said, taking Sarah's arm and propelling her across the dance floor to where a few empty tables stood. They claimed one crammed in between two groups of drunken young men who might have been related to the men they'd encountered downstairs, so closely did they resemble each other. Or maybe it was just that all their suits were uniformly ugly and garish and their manner equally obnoxious. They hooted at the girls, making suggestive remarks which the girls studiously ignored.

"Don't pay no attention, Mrs. Brandt," Lisle advised her. "They like you better if you ignore them."

Sarah didn't want them to like her at all, so she wondered if she should openly flirt with them to discourage their attention. That strategy seemed foolish, even if Sarah had the courage to carry it out, so she just sat down with the rest of the girls and concentrated on looking for a killer.

In no more than a few seconds, Sarah realized that Lisle had been only too right in predicting this trip was a waste of time. Easily half the people in the room were men, and all of them seemed to be dressed in tasteless plaid or checked suits. Most of them appeared to be already drunk, and the rest were on their way to it. They were all leering or jeering or both, vying for the attention of a female, *any* female, it seemed. To Sarah, they *all* looked exactly like the kind of man who would beat a woman to death. How could she possibly differentiate between them?

Sarah was shocked to see so many of the young women lighting up cigarettes as soon as the dance was over. Or rather, their male companions were lighting the cigarettes for them. Sarah had never seen a respectable woman smoking. She'd never seen a respectable woman drink more than a sip of anything alcoholic, either, but now the couples who had been dancing were making their way over to the bar on the far wall where several harried bartenders were serving drinks. The girls were doing much more than sipping.

"We'll have to wait till the next time," Hetty explained to her, nodding toward the bar.

"The next time for what?" Sarah asked.

Bertha rolled her eyes, but Hetty gave her a dirty look that put Bertha in her place. "The band plays for a few minutes, then everybody goes to buy a drink. Or the fellows buy drinks, that is. For the girls they dance with."

The dancers must need a drink to keep from expiring in this heat, which would provide some excuse for the girls to imbibe, Sarah thought, and realized she was thirsty herself from the walk over. "I'll treat you to drinks," she offered, but the girls gaped at her in horror.

"A girl don't buy her own drinks, missus," Bertha said, as if explaining one of the more profound truths of life.

"You do, and what'll the fellows think? They'll think you don't need them, that's what, and you'll be sitting on the bench all night!"

Sarah managed not to smile. Sitting on the bench all night was exactly what she intended to do, but she wouldn't spoil their chance to have a good time. By the time the band began to play again, men had begun to buzz around, like flies attracted by the sweet scent of honey. To Sarah, the men looked like people she would cross the street to avoid, but Bertha, Hetty, and Lisle seemed more than pleased with their attention. When the band struck up the first discordant notes to "A Hot Time in the Old Town Tonight" all three of them got up to dance, leaving Sarah to observe.

Hours later Sarah was still observing. She'd bought herself some beer, ignoring the pitying looks she received from the bartender and the other women standing around, and she'd rebuffed the few men who were too drunk to notice her advanced age. Indeed, she was too old by a generation for this event. She was probably the only woman in the place older than twenty, and most were nearer fifteen.

The men tended to be older, probably because a man needed ready cash to impress the girls, and a young boy wouldn't be able to afford it. In fact, some of the men seemed *much* older. And when Sarah looked more closely, she realized the older ones were very well dressed, too. Even though their suits were just as tasteless as the others, the quality was much better and the fit one only a tailor could accomplish. Once the sun went down and the shadows grew deep in the hall, Sarah began to understand what men of means might be doing in a working-class dance hall, too. When she had, she was ashamed of her naïveté.

The dancing was merely a ruse to get people into the hall to drink. The band would play one number and then take a break for about ten minutes while everyone went to the bar for a libation. Much more time was spent drinking than dancing, and as the girls became drunk, the men began to take advantage. Or maybe the girls simply began allowing them to.

The most obvious result of this loss of inhibition was the way the style of dancing grew wilder. Several couples were engaged in the kind of dance Sarah overheard someone call "spieling." The girl would stand stiff as a poker, her left arm out straight, and the man would sidle up to her, positioning himself so that his chin was on her shoulder, regardless of the difference in their heights. She'd put her chin on his shoulder, too, and they'd start pivoting or spinning around in the tightest possible circle, their bodies locked together, in a frenzy of sexual excitement. As if inflamed by the sight of this, other couples stole away to the dark recesses of the hall to engage in the kind of kissing and groping Sarah had never seen in public.

She'd lost sight of Hetty and Bertha, and she feared they had succumbed to the temptations offered by their partners. Lisle was still on the dance floor, but she was offering only token resistance to the man who was using his hands in ways never taught at the dance academy Sarah had attended as a child. Lisle's gaze met hers across the room, and Sarah suddenly realized the girl was checking to see if Sarah was watching her. She had the uncomfortable feeling that if she wasn't here, Lisle wouldn't even be offering token resistance.

This whole evening had been a waste of her time, and an unpleasant waste, too. Seeing the things she'd seen here, she was overwhelmed with dismay and pity at the desperation that would drive young girls to a place like this and compel them to submit to indignities and worse in exchange for the dubious pleasures of male attention.

She should leave. Her presence was an embarrassment to her companions, and she certainly wasn't going to find Gerda's killer here. What had ever made her think it would be that easy? She'd have to be careful that Malloy never found out about this foolishness, or she'd never hear the end of it.

As Sarah debated the propriety—and the wisdom—of simply leaving without telling her companions, the last, crashing notes of "Ta-Ra-Ra Boom-De-Ay" rang out, and Lisle came straight back over to the table for the first time in over an hour. Her partner was at her heels, half-angry and half-pleading, trying to convince her to go to the bar with him for a drink.

"I don't have to put up with your sass, Billy," Lisle told him, the color in her cheeks real this time. She'd sweated off her rouge long ago. "I'm leaving."

"Since when did you get so particular?" Billy demanded. "I know how you got that hat. George don't give them away for free!"

"Shut your mouth!" Lisle snapped, refusing even to look at him. She'd reached the table, and she said to Sarah, "Do you mind if we leave now?"

Sarah was on her feet in an instant, only too happy for an excuse to escape this bedlam. "Should we find Bertha and Hetty?" she asked, gathering her things.

"They know their way home," Lisle said, heading toward the door. Sarah had to hurry to catch up to her, but she was no match for Billy, who was still pleading his case.

"Don't be this way, Lisle. I told you, I get paid on Friday. I'll get you something nicer than a hat! How about some jewelry?"

Lisle pretended not to hear him, but when she looked back to see if Sarah was coming, her face was scarlet in the smoky light of the hall. "I don't want nothing from you, Billy. Find yourself another girl."

Billy said something obscene that made Sarah gasp, and she realized her heart was pounding. This is exactly the scenario she'd imagined had led to Gerda's death. A young man furious at being spurned follows her and waits for an opportunity to . . .

But Billy wasn't following anymore. He'd turned on his heel and returned to the hall, most likely seeking easier pickings. Indeed, the hall was full of young women who would be more than willing to accept his attentions. Why should he subject himself to further rejection when within minutes he could most likely be enjoying success with someone else?

Lisle didn't stop to wait for Sarah when she reached the

street. She plunged through the group of drunks still lingering at the foot of the stairs and was halfway down the block when Sarah caught up with her.

"Wait, Lisle, there's no need to run!" Sarah cried, finally stopping her. Lisle's slender body fairly radiated fury as she stood on the sidewalk, waiting. Tapping her foot impatiently, she wouldn't look at Sarah, either.

Sarah couldn't resist looking over her shoulder to see if anyone was following them, but no one seemed to care that they were leaving the dance. "Come on, I'll walk you home," Sarah said, taking Lisle's arm gently.

Lisle signed, the anger draining out of her and leaving her looking very young and extremely vulnerable. Sarah had to resist an urge to hug her.

"That Billy," she said, her disgust sounding sad.

They started walking, and Sarah waited awhile, letting Lisle calm down a bit. Finally, she said, "You were right about that being a waste of time. I don't know what made me think we'd find Gerda's killer that way."

Lisle glanced over, her expression wary. "You didn't look like you was having much fun."

"I didn't go to have fun," Sarah reminded her. "You didn't have much fun there at the end. Don't you like Billy?"

"He was being . . . fresh," she admitted.

Sarah didn't point out that every man in the room was being fresh with someone or that Sarah had concluded taking or allow such liberties was the entire purpose of coming to these dances. They walked another block down Fourteenth Street before Sarah said, "Who's George?"

Lisle's head snapped up, her expression frightened now. "Nobody. He's just . . . He's a fellow I know."

"Did he give you a hat?"

Her mouth tightened. "Don't pay no attention to what Billy says. He don't know what he's talking about."

Sarah waited a few seconds before saying, "Someone gave Gerda a hat right before she died. Was it George?"

"Could've been anybody," Lisle said defensively.

"But if it *was* George, maybe the police should talk to him. Find out where he was the night Gerda died. Who is this George?"

At first she thought Lisle wouldn't answer. Then Sarah realized she was weighing her words very carefully. "He . . . he's a salesman. Sells ladies things."

"And he gives girls presents?"

Lisle seemed to flinch. "He's real generous," she allowed, although the admission seemed to pain her.

"You mean he's generous to girls who are generous to him," Sarah corrected.

"It ain't what you think!" Lisle insisted.

"How do you know what I think?" Sarah asked.

"We ain't whores!" Lisle said. "We don't take no money!"

"Lisle, I didn't—" Sarah tried, but Lisle ignored her.

"It ain't whoring if you don't take money!"

"Lisle, I'm not going to judge you," Sarah assured her. "I'm just trying to find out who could have killed Gerda before he kills someone else, and the more I know about her, the easier that will be."

Lisle didn't say anything for another block. They were getting close to St. Mark's Place. Sarah didn't have much time left before Lisle would be home. She gambled. "Lisle, you know this is a dangerous way to live. You could become pregnant. You could get a disease."

"You think I don't know that? But how else can we get nice things? Do you know how much I earn at Faircloths? Six dollars a week, that's how much! And my family'd take it all if I'd let them! As it is, they only let me keep a dollar or two for myself. I've got to make do on that, and I have to skip lunch or walk instead of taking the trolley so I can afford to go to a dance."

Sarah was calculating in her head. The last suit she'd bought for herself cost seven dollars and fifty cents. How many lunches and trolley rides would girls like Lisle and

Gerda have to skip and how long would they have to save before they could afford a new outfit? Even a few dollars for a hat or a shirtwaist would require great sacrifice.

Now Sarah understood another truth about the dance she'd just attended. The men were obviously there for sexual favors, and Sarah had assumed the girls gave them for attention. She'd never dreamed there was more at stake.

Both Gerda and Lisle had probably exchanged sex for a hat from the man named George. "What kind of a man is he? This George, I mean."

Lisle shrugged one shoulder. "He's all right, I guess. Likes to have fun. Never minds dropping a few dollars to show a girl a good time."

"Does he have a temper?"

Lisle looked at her with disdain. "All men got a temper if a woman says no. Don't you know nothing at all?"

Sarah decided not to mention that her husband, Tom, had been at least one exception to that rule. Lisle probably wouldn't believe her anyway.

"But do you think this George would be violent? Is he the kind of man who—?"

"Who would've killed Gerda?" Lisle asked grimly. "I don't have no idea. Who knows what a man'll do if a woman pushes him far enough?"

"Would Gerda have pushed him?"

"Gerda liked to make them mad," Lisle admitted after a moment. "She liked to make them beg her. Lot of men, they don't like that."

"Wouldn't that be dangerous?" Sarah asked, instantly realizing how foolish the question was. Of course it was dangerous. Gerda was dead. "I mean, is that what you do? Is that why Billy was angry?"

Lisle didn't like talking about this. "I ain't like Gerda. I don't like a fuss. I . . . I just like pretty things."

They had reached St. Mark's Place, and they turned toward Tompkins Park. The streets weren't as deserted as they should have been this time of night. Many people were sleeping on the fire escapes and stoops because of the heat. Others were leaning out of windows or sitting wherever they could find a spot, trying to catch whatever breeze might be stirring.

Lisle lived down a few blocks, in one of the tenements. Sarah remembered how little she knew about the girl.

"Do you live with your family, Lisle?"

"My mother and stepfather."

"You don't like him very much," Sarah guessed from the tone of her voice.

"I hate him," Lisle said with surprisingly little rancor. It was just another fact of her life.

"I don't suppose he approves of you going to dances."

"He don't have nothing to say about it. I told him if he made any trouble, I'd leave. I've got some friends I could stay with. Then he wouldn't get my money anymore. He didn't say anything after that."

"Could you really do that? Live on your own, I mean?"

Lisle made a disgusted sound. "Not likely. Not on six dollars a week, even with three of us to a room. He don't know it, though, so he leaves me alone."

The bleakness of Lisle's existence weighed on Sarah, especially when she thought of Gerda and the other dead girls. Their lives had been equally as bleak and hopeless. "What are your plans, Lisle? What are you going to do with your life?"

Lisle looked up in surprise, as if no one had ever asked her such a question before. "I don't know," she said after a moment. "I'll get me a steady fellow, I guess, and we'll get married."

Then the babies would come, too many, too quickly, and fragile Lisle would be old before her time. Maybe she wouldn't even survive. Life was hard for girls like this, and they had few options. Survival was all they could hope for. Happiness wasn't even something they dreamed about.

Sarah knew she couldn't change Lisle's destiny, but she felt compelled to warn her anyway. "Be careful, Lisle.

There are good men out there. Don't settle for less."

Lisle gave her an unfathomable look, and Sarah didn't know how much she'd appreciated the advice. Probably not at all, but at least Sarah had tried.

Lisle's step slowed, indicating they had reached her building. Some children were sleeping on a blanket on the sidewalk out front, and an old woman crouched on the stoop, staring vacantly out into the darkness. Lisle looked up, apparently checking her family's apartment windows.

"Looks like it's safe to go in. No lights. They must be asleep." Her smile was wan in the glow of the gaslight.

"Thank you for taking me with you tonight," Sarah said. "I hope I didn't ruin your evening."

"There's always tomorrow," she said philosophically.

"Gerda thought that, too," Sarah reminded her gently. "Don't take any foolish chances."

Lisle smiled slightly and shook her head, as if unable believe Sarah was real. "Good night, Mrs. Brandt."

Sarah waited until she had disappeared into the building. She glanced at the old woman, but she hadn't moved, and Sarah realized she was asleep. Sitting straight up but fast asleep. Probably she was guarding the children.

Leaving them to their rest, Sarah made her way back down St. Mark's and back toward her own home in Greenwich Village.

SARAH DIDN'T KNOW exactly what she could say to Agnes Otto. The new mother was still in bed, just as Sarah had recommended, and Sarah suspected she was suffering just as much from grief as she was from the exertions of childbirth. Her eyes were red-rimmed, as if she'd been crying, when Sarah arrived the next day.

"Mrs. Brandt, do you know anything about my Gerda? Did the police tell you anything?" she asked eagerly.

"I spoke with my friend, but he hasn't told me anything yet. The police are probably still investigating," she added, knowing it was most likely a lie, but not wanting to hurt

Agnes any more than was necessary. "How are you feeling?"

Agnes's head rolled on the pillow, and she closed her eyes against fresh tears. "I cry all the time. I cannot stop," she said.

The baby was sleeping beside her on the bed, swaddled in spite of the heat, and Sarah carefully unwrapped her. The baby's arms and legs were still spindly, and when she pinched the baby's skin, it didn't spring back the way it should have.

"How often do you feed the baby?" she asked.

Agnes waved her hand vaguely. "When she cries."

"She's not thriving. She should have put on more weight than this, and she's dehydrated . . . not getting enough to eat," Sarah explained when she saw the alarm in Agnes's eyes. "She might just be a good baby who doesn't wake up often enough. You'll have to feed her even when she doesn't cry. Every two or three hours. Listen for the clock to chime and feed her." The Ottos wouldn't have a clock of their own, but the city was full of public clocks by which people regulated their lives. "Wake her up if you have to."

She could see Agnes's despair. Sarah was making demands of her, and she didn't think she could cope. "Maybe one of your neighbors would help you remember," Sarah suggested.

"They already do enough," Agnes said. "They take care of my children and bring us supper every night. I cannot ask more."

Maybe she couldn't, but Sarah wasn't afraid to, not if it might save this baby's life.

Sarah finished checking Agnes and the baby, and as she stepped away from the bed, she nearly tripped over a small wooden box sitting on the floor.

"Oh, that is Gerda's things," Agnes said, new tears welling in her eyes. "All that is left of her."

The lid had come loose, and Sarah used that as an excuse

to kneel down and peek inside. A thought occurred to her. "Did Gerda keep a diary?"

That was how she and Malloy had finally solved the first murder they'd investigated together. The victim's own words written in her diary had led them to the killer.

"A what?" Agnes didn't recognize the word.

"A . . . a journal?" Sarah tried. "A book she wrote things in, private things?"

Agnes found the very idea ridiculous. "*Nein.* Why would she do such a thing?"

Of course she wouldn't, Sarah thought. That would have made finding her killer so much easier. Assuming she'd even known her killer before that night, that is.

Sarah pretended to repack the items in the box more carefully while she was really examining them for any clues. She found little of interest, however. Only a few strings of glass beads, a handkerchief with ragged lace, and there, in the very bottom, a photograph. Sarah opened the cardboard frame, expecting to see a picture of the dead girl. Instead she found what appeared to be a picture of people in a boat, and they all appeared to be screaming.

Puzzled, she looked up at Agnes for an explanation.

"It is Gerda. There in the front row," she said, pointing.

Sarah looked again and recognized Gerda Reinhard. She was sitting with a young man in a bowler hat. He had his arm around her, and they were obviously only pretending to be frightened. "Where was it taken?"

"At that place, what do they call it? It is on an island . . ."

"Coney Island?" Sarah asked, looking at the photograph again.

"*Ja,* Gerda said they have this boat ride. The boat goes down a . . . a hill and makes a big splash."

"And they take a photograph of it?" Sarah knew that couldn't be true. Photography required that the subjects sit very still. Taking a picture of an amusement-park ride would be impossible.

"Yes," Agnes said, "but not when it is going." She

searched for the proper words to explain. "They have a special boat. That one," she added, pointing to the picture. "You sit in it, and they make a photograph. The people in the boat are just pretending to be riding down the hill."

"Oh, I see, so they have a souvenir of their adventure," Sarah said, looking more closely at the picture. "Do you know the man sitting with Gerda?"

"No, we do not, and that made Lars very angry. He say Gerda should not be making photographs with men he does not know."

Sarah only wished Gerda had only been posing for photographs with such men. That was the least of her transgressions.

"At least you have her picture," Sarah pointed out. "To remember her by."

"But such a picture," Agnes lamented, closing her eyes again.

Sarah discreetly finished examining the contents of the box, carefully replaced the lid, and set it back where she had found it. Maybe she could ask Lisle and the other girls if they knew the man in the photograph, although the chance that he was Gerda's killer was probably remote.

"That was the day when she got the red shoes," Agnes murmured, her eyes still closed so that Sarah wasn't sure if she'd been addressing her or not.

"Gerda got the red shoes when she went to Coney Island?" Sarah asked.

Agnes nodded, her face a mask of pain. "Just before she . . ."

"Agnes, would you mind if I borrowed this photograph for a few days? I'd like to see if I can find out who this man with Gerda is."

Agnes's eyes flew open, and her pain instantly turned to horror. "Do you think he is the one?"

"That's something we can let the police find out," she demurred.

Malloy would be proud of her restraint. She'd have to make sure he heard about it very soon.

4

MALLOY CALLED ON HER IN THE MIDDLE OF THE afternoon. He figured this would be the best time. She wouldn't try to feed him, so he wouldn't have to stay very long. He just needed to repay the debt he owed by telling her what he knew about the German girl's death, and then he'd be free of her for good.

It was a good plan. Why did he have such a sickening feeling it wouldn't be quite that simple?

The moment she opened the door to him, he knew he should have let her know he was coming. Because of the heat, she was wearing hardly any clothes at all. Well, she did have a dress on, but her arms were bare, and the dress was so light, it left little of her figure to the imagination. He wondered she considered it decent. He certainly didn't.

"Malloy," she said, the way she always did, and smiled. The way a cat smiles when it's been in the cream. "Come in. I was visiting with my neighbor, Mrs. Elsworth, but I'm sure she'll excuse us. Like your mother, she thinks there's something more between us than a mutual interest in a murder case, and she'll be only too happy to leave us alone."

Plainly, she found this amusing. Malloy did not.

She left him no choice but to follow her out to her backyard. The old woman from next door was sitting there, fanning herself with the most elaborate fan Frank had ever seen. Her wrinkled face lit with happiness when she saw him.

"Detective Sergeant Malloy, Mrs. Brandt didn't tell me you were expected. I'll take myself off so you two can discuss . . . uh . . . whatever it is you need to discuss," she said with a sly grin.

"That's kind of you, ma'am," Frank said, wishing he didn't feel embarrassed. He had nothing to feel embarrassed about. This meeting was strictly business.

The old woman rolled her eyes as she gathered her things to leave. "I guess I should've expected Mr. Malloy. I broke a needle today, you know. And yesterday I saw three crows together."

Mrs. Brandt smiled patiently. "Does that mean a visitor is coming?" she asked.

"Oh, no," Mrs. Elsworth said smugly. "Both those things mean a wedding. I'll be off now. You two enjoy your afternoon."

As soon as the old woman had disappeared through the gate connecting the two yards, Mrs. Brandt said, "Don't look so terrified. Her omens hardly ever come true."

"I'm not—" he began, then caught himself. He wasn't going to get into a conversation about *that*. He cleared his throat. "I talked to the detective who's investigating the girl's death," he said instead, figuring that would distract her.

It did. "Sit down and tell me everything," she said eagerly. "I've found out some things, too." She took the other chair and began to pour some lemonade from a pitcher. "Take your jacket off. You must be sweltering."

Frank briefly considered doing so. He *was* sweltering, but he didn't want to start getting comfortable with Sarah Brandt. He wasn't going to know her that much longer. Besides, his shirt was probably badly wrinkled.

He did sit down, though, and he did drink the lemonade she offered him. Then he took out his handkerchief and mopped his brow and for just a moment allowed himself to enjoy the cool shade of her yard and the sweet scent of her flowers. But only for a moment.

"Bill Broughan is investigating the case," he began.

She nodded. "I remember him. I tried to get him to tell me where you lived, but he wouldn't do it. He said it would be worth his life, if I recall correctly."

"He's the one," Frank confirmed.

"Is he any good? As a detective, I mean?"

"When he's sober."

"Which isn't very often, I'd guess."

She was right about that. No need to tell her, either. "He said the girl was out dancing every night. Went with a lot of men. Didn't have a steady fellow, so there's no telling who she was with that night."

"Even her friends don't know, the ones who were with her at Harmony Hall," she confirmed.

He looked at her in surprise. "Harmony Hall?"

"It's a dance hall on Fourteenth Street, over a saloon. That's where she went dancing the night she died."

"If you knew all this, why do you need me?" He was feeling annoyed, although he knew that was irrational.

"Because I didn't know it when I saw you last. I met Gerda's friends at her funeral, and they told me all this. I feel sure the police have uncovered a lot more about her, though. What else did you find out?"

"Nothing," Malloy admitted reluctantly. "You might as well forget finding who killed her. Nobody is going to bother to investigate."

"They're giving up already?" she asked, outraged.

"I told you, there's no way to find out who killed her. There's just too many possibilities."

"What if I could help you narrow it down to a few?" she asked slyly.

Frank didn't like that expression one bit. "How?"

"Someone gave Gerda a hat shortly before she died. His name is George, he spends a lot of time at dances, and he sells ladies' furnishing. Someone else gave her red shoes, someone who was with her at Coney Island, and I have a photograph of him. Wait right here. I'll get it."

Frank felt like he'd been poleaxed. The woman was a caution. How on God's earth did she get a photograph of the killer?

Before he had time even to form a theory, she was back. She handed him a cheap cardboard cover, the kind photographers used. He opened it to the strangest picture he'd ever seen. "Is this some kind of a boat?"

"It's a ride at Sea Lion Park."

"Sea Lion *what*?"

"Sea Lion Park. It's an amusement park at Coney Island. Surely, you must have heard about it."

Frank grunted noncommittally.

"I think this is a picture of the Shoot-the-Chutes ride, from what Gerda's sister described. I read about it in the paper when the park opened. They have these boats that travel in water-filled chutes, and they pull them up to the top of a steep incline and let them slide all the way to the bottom. They make quite a splash when they hit the pool below."

Frank looked at the photograph again, trying to picture what she was describing. "And this is the boat?"

"From what I understand, this is a duplicate of the boat. A photographer poses people as if they're on the ride. See how they're pretending to be frightened? Then they buy the photograph as a souvenir."

"And you think this fellow with her bought her the shoes?"

"It's certainly possible. According to her sister, she got them at Coney Island that day."

Frank looked at the photograph more closely. "Well, even if this fellow did buy her the shoes, that doesn't prove he killed her, does it?"

She frowned. "I hadn't thought of that."

Frank gave her a look that told her that was why she wasn't a professional detective, and she didn't like it one bit. "If she'd been killed the day she got the shoes, you might have something here. *If*," he added, "you could even identify this fellow from the photograph. It's not a very clear picture of his face. The shadow of his hat brim is covering half of it."

She took the photograph out of his hands and looked at it again, very closely. "I'm sure if you knew this fellow, you'd recognize him."

"But I don't know him," Frank pointed out. "Do you?"

"Gerda's friends will." She sounded awfully certain, which made Frank think she wasn't certain at all.

"If they do, are you just going to go find him and ask him if he killed this girl?"

His sarcasm was wasted on her. "I think it would be a better idea to find out if the other girls who were murdered knew him, too."

"What other girls?"

"I don't know their names, but three other girls from that neighborhood have been murdered the same way Gerda was."

"Beaten, you mean?" Frank was getting an uneasy feeling.

"Yes, and their murders are unsolved, too. I think there's a good chance the same man killed all of them. I'm sure if you questioned their friends, you could find out which men all the girls knew in common and—"

Frank wasn't listening anymore. He was remembering a case he'd investigated last winter. The girl was from the same German neighborhood near Tompkins Park, and she'd been beaten until her face was practically smashed in. They'd identified her from her clothes and a birthmark on her back. No one had cared much about her death, except her family of course, but they were working folks with no money to spare. She'd been one of those girls who went out dancing all the time, and Frank had soon realized that finding the one man who'd killed her would be nearly impossible. He'd gotten busy with other things, and now he couldn't even remember the girl's name.

Why had no one told him there were others?

"When were these girls killed?"

"I don't know. I guess I should have found out, but I thought you'd know all about it."

"I'm not the only detective sergeant on the New York City police force," he reminded her more sharply than she deserved. "There's no reason for me to know about cases I don't work on."

She didn't take offense. She was too amazed. "Then there's no way for anyone to realize these four girls' deaths might be connected somehow?"

"You don't know that they are," he pointed out.

This time she gave him a condescending look. "Are you asking me to believe that four different men beat four different young women from the same neighborhood to death in exactly the same way during the past few months?"

"It could've happened," he said, but he didn't sound convincing, even to himself.

She smiled sweetly. "If you're that naive, I guess I'll have to make sure you don't play any games of chance when we go to Coney Island tomorrow, then."

"What?" Frank was certain he'd misunderstood her.

"I think we should go to Coney Island, don't you?" she asked. "We can look around and ask questions and get an idea of what happens out there. Maybe we can figure out how Gerda met this fellow. We might even find someone who recognizes him from the photograph. We should at least be able to find out where she got the shoes. Someone might remember who bought them for her."

"This isn't my case," he reminded her, although his conscience was pricking him. The nameless girl who had died last winter had been his case. If he'd solved that one, this Gerda might still be alive.

"It's *my* case," she said, "and you'd be helping me. As a friend," she added, taking a sip of her lemonade.

When he didn't reply, she said, "Did I tell you I left a message for Dr. Broadstreet? He's the surgeon I told you about, the one I thought might be able to help Brian."

The lemonade that had been so refreshing a moment ago now felt like acid in his stomach. He hated being in debt to anyone, and Sarah Brandt was dragging him deeper and deeper into her debt every time he saw her.

"Mrs. Brandt, your talents are wasted. You should have been a criminal."

"A criminal!" she asked in surprise, although she seemed more pleased than insulted. "Whatever do you mean?"

"I mean you're awful good at blackmail and making people do what you want them to."

"It's just my female powers of persuasion, Malloy. Since women don't have any real power in the worldly sense, we have to compensate by using the powers we do have."

Frank didn't think he agreed with that. Women might not be able to vote or own property or go into business, but they certainly managed to do whatever else they wanted. "Find out the names of the other girls who were killed," he said. "I'll see if there's any connection between them."

She sat back in her chair, looking smug. "I'll have that information for you on Sunday when we go to Coney Island."

FRANK COULDN'T BELIEVE he was going to Coney Island. He'd never been to the beach in his life, and he had no desire to go now. At least he wouldn't be expected to bathe in the ocean. He'd done some research on Coney Island and learned that the main attraction nowadays was the amusements and rides that had been built near the beach. You didn't have to go in the water unless you wanted to, and Frank had no intention of putting on one of those ridiculous bathing outfits and jumping in the ocean. If God had intended for men to go in the water, they'd have fins.

Coney Island had always been a place where people from the city went to escape the summer heat, but the place had eventually been overrun by gamblers, roughnecks, confidence men, pickpockets, and prostitutes, so that decent folks had stopped going. Fires in '93 and '95 had destroyed the worst sections of West Brighton, however, and then a fellow calling himself Captain Paul Boyton built an enclosed park where people of modest means could pay an admission price of ten cents and enjoy themselves all day without being bothered by the riffraff that used to prowl the streets of the island.

From what he'd learned, the park was like a carnival, only larger and far more elaborate. The games of chance and the freak shows were there, but this Captain Boyton had added rides designed to thrill and frighten people. Frank saw plenty of things in his everyday life that thrilled and frightened him. He didn't need to pay ten cents to have the life scared out of him in a phony boat.

Which explained his foul mood when he met Sarah Brandt early Sunday morning at the trolley. He'd been pleasantly surprised to learn he didn't have to take a boat ride just to get to Coney Island. Last he'd heard, the ferry was the easiest method of transportation. But progress had come when he wasn't looking, and now a nickel trolley ride would take anyone out to Captain Boyton's park.

"Oh, Malloy, you look like you're going to your own funeral," Mrs. Brandt said when he found her. "This is supposed to be fun!" She certainly looked ready for fun in her flowered summer dress and broad-brimmed hat.

Malloy cast a jaundiced eye around at the crowd of people waiting for the trolley. There were middle-class families decked out in their Sunday best, children scrubbed and brushed and braided and fidgeting with excitement already. There were young women, girls really, decked out in the kind of finery that pennies could buy. Frippery, his mother would have called it. They looked cheap and gaudy and very, very young. Hovering around them were young men in their checked suits and straw hats, preening for attention from the girls who were studiously ignoring them.

"It's fascinating, isn't it?" Mrs. Brandt asked.

"What?"

"Watching the way they act. The girls are so desperate for attention, but the men are equally desperate. You'd think that would make it easier, since they both want the same thing, but it somehow makes it more difficult."

Frank had no idea what she was talking about, but he did think it was interesting the way the men were sniffing around the girls. He could imagine what his mother would say about those girls, too. They didn't look like decent females, yet he knew they weren't prostitutes either. They fell in some mysterious gray area between.

In Frank's experience, young girls went nowhere unescorted by a chaperon. He himself had never been alone with his own wife until their wedding night. Kathleen's parents and brothers had seen to that, and he'd understood completely. He'd respected Kathleen as much as he'd loved her and wouldn't have dreamed of taking advantage of her innocence. Had she flaunted herself the way these girls were doing, he would have been shocked. These girls lived in a different world than the one he'd known, however. The rules were different there, and Frank didn't understand them.

And he understood Sarah Brandt even less.

"What do you hope to accomplish with this . . . this . . ." He gestured vaguely at all the people gathered for the trolley to Coney Island on what was promising to be the first truly nice Sunday of the season.

"Excursion?" she offered, smiling. "I don't know. It's awfully hot and uncomfortable in the city. You should thank me for making you go to the country for some sea air."

Frank was saved from answering by the arrival of the trolley. He and Mrs. Brandt waited until last to board, watching how the other people conducted themselves. The girls got on first, then the families, and then the young men, who jockeyed for position near the girls they had picked out. There was much jostling and arguing, and Frank was glad he and Mrs. Brandt got separated in the crowd. It saved him from making conversation with her on the ride out, even if he did have to stand up the whole way because of the crowd.

After what seemed an interminable time later—but which was less than an hour—they arrived at the station at West Brighton Beach. During the ride, Frank had learned that criminals weren't the only people who used outrageous slang and that flirting had changed a lot since he was a young man.

Mrs. Brandt was waiting for him when he got off the trolley. She still looked as fresh as she had when they'd left the city, although Frank felt damp and rumpled.

"What do you think?" she asked, surveying the view.

Frank didn't know what to think. The place looked like something out of a storybook. A band played nearby, apparently to welcome the new arrivals, and in the distance he could see the dark expanse of the ocean, ominous and never-ending. On the other side he saw what must be the amusement park Mrs. Brandt had told him about. Surrounded by a fence to keep out nonpaying customers, it seemed to stretch for acres and probably did. Odd-looking structures rose above the fence, hinting at the wonders inside.

"Look," she said. "The girls have already paired off with those fellows. That's so they'll pay their admission fee to the park."

The girls who had so studiously avoided the men at the station and had offered only token interest during the ride out were now accepting offered arms and allowing themselves to be escorted through the front gates. As the men fished in their pockets for the fee, the girls giggled and batted their eyes and acted coy.

"How long will they stay with the fellows once they're inside?" Frank wondered aloud.

"I'm sure they have their idea of what's appropriate. Maybe if they like the fellow, they let him spend money on them all day long."

"Whoever called them Charity Girls was wrong. They're outright thieves."

"Don't judge them too harshly," she said as she started walking toward the entrance gate to the park. "It's the only way they can have a good time."

"By making men spend their hard earned money on them?" Frank hurried to catch up.

She gave him a disapproving glance. "Those girls only earn about six or seven dollars a week. After they give their families money for their room and board, they usually have only a dollar or two left for themselves. Out of that they've got to buy their lunches, ride the trolley, and keep themselves clothed. With a budget like that, the five cents for the trolley ride out here is about all they can manage."

"They why don't they just stay home?" Frank asked reasonably.

"It's a new world, Malloy. Women don't just stay home anymore."

Of course she'd say that, a woman who had a trade and made her own living, just like a man. Kathleen had just stayed home, and if she was still alive, she'd be home still, taking care of their son.

At the gate, an obnoxious young man took Frank's money so fast he didn't even feel it leave his fingers, and the fellow never even missed a word in his ongoing spiel. "Step right up, ladies and gents, see the Seven Wonders of the World, see Little Egypt dance the dance of the seven veils, see the two-headed calf and the bearded lady, sights you'll never see again. Come one, come all, only ten cents for a day in Paradise. Step right up!"

As if these people needed encouragement. They'd already ridden an hour on the trolley to get there. They were hardly likely to decide to turn right around and go back, now, were they?

"You didn't have to treat me, Malloy," Mrs. Brandt said. "I wouldn't want you to get the wrong impression of my motives."

She was laughing at him, but Frank could get in the last word. "Just don't expect me to buy you a hat, Mrs. Brandt."

That sobered her instantly.

They stepped through the gates and into another world. The noise was overwhelming. People talking and screaming in terror on the rides, barkers trying to lure the unsuspecting in to see the freak shows or play the games of chance, the clank of machinery, the shots from the shooting gallery, the din of the calliope, and the brass of an oompah band somewhere.

"People come here to get away from the noise of the city?" Frank shouted into her ear.

She merely shrugged.

They strolled along the avenues running through the park, looking at the various attractions and studying the people. Everywhere they saw groups of young men and women, obviously enjoying themselves, or at least pretending to. There was food and drink and entertainment everywhere, and nickel postcards, with photographs of the beach and bathing beauties in skimpy costumes that showed practically all of their legs, were available to send back to friends and family who hadn't made the trip.

"This way for the Streets of Cairo!" a barker shouted as they passed a booth where several buxom girls dressed in shimmering veils and little else were gyrating suggestively. "One hundred and fifty Oriental beauties! The warmest spectacle on earth! See her dance the Hootchy-Kootchy! Anywhere else but in the ocean breezes of Coney Island she would be consumed by her own fire! Don't rush! Don't crowd! Plenty of seats for all!"

"I'll wait if you want to go inside and see the show," Mrs. Brandt offered with a sly grin.

"Oh, it's perfectly respectable," a man standing behind them said. "Don't have to worry about taking the missus inside."

Frank looked at him in amazement. In Frank's experience, total strangers didn't offer their opinions on such matters. In fact, total strangers didn't speak to one another at all except perhaps to say excuse me.

He was a short, round man in a suit that had been bought when he weighed twenty pounds less. With him was a woman of equal girth, and both of them were smiling at Frank and his companion as if they were old friends.

"Sam's right," the woman offered. "You won't be offended at all. The only thing I couldn't figure out was how those girls could be so limber!"

Frank knew Mrs. Brandt must be offended at being addressed so familiarly by people she didn't know, so he took her arm and steered her away. "He must be drunk," he said by way of explanation when they were out of earshot.

She nodded, still looking as puzzled as Frank felt.

In the crowd, they came face-to-face with another couple, a tall lanky young man with a scraggly mustache and a girl with buckteeth who was holding a stuffed bear. "Hey, old man, you should try your hand over there. Ring the bell and win a prize for your wife. Big fellow like you shouldn't have any trouble at all!"

Frank nodded as politely as he could and guided Mrs. Brandt around them. They passed an attraction at which a man was using a large hammer to strike the base of a tall tower in an attempt to drive a ball up and ring the bell on the top. The sign called it the HI-STRIKER MACHINE.

"People here are certainly friendly," Mrs. Brandt observed.

"Or rude," Frank offered.

Frank lived in two very different worlds in his life, and the rules for each of those worlds were strictly prescribed. Prostitutes spoke to strangers and strangers spoke to them—and did a lot more besides—without the formality of an introduction, but a respectable man didn't so much as tip his hat at a respectable female unless they were acquainted.

Here, however, those rules seemed to have been forgotten. Since no one could possibly mistake Mrs. Brandt for a prostitute, there could be no other explanation. As Frank looked around, he quickly realized that everywhere strangers were meeting and conversing like old friends, then going on their way, never to meet again.

"I can see why young people like this place so much," Mrs. Brandt observed. "No one seems to observe any of the rules of propriety. Strangers become friends in a moment, and there's no chaperon looking over your shoulder to disapprove."

"Why would you want to take up with a stranger?"

"To have some fun. The young men here are different and interesting, and they have money to spend. The girls' lives would be horribly dull without a diversion like this."

Frank was still of the opinion that the girls would be far better off with dull lives than with exciting deaths, but he didn't bother to mention that to Mrs. Brandt. She probably agreed anyway.

"Oh, look, the carousel. Let's ride it!" she said.

Frank would have protested, but she looked so excited, he didn't have the heart to refuse her. Feeling like a consummate fool, he helped her up onto the platform and lifted her onto one of the gaily painted horses. She was a well-made woman, soft and round in all the right places, and Frank found himself oddly breathless after he'd settled her on her horse. Probably from the exertion, he told himself. She wasn't exactly skinny.

"Oh, Malloy, at least *try* to have fun, won't you?" she chided him.

He climbed up onto the horse beside her before anyone else could claim it and tried not to look unhappy. It was the best he could do.

The music was too loud, and Frank wasn't fond of going around and around in a circle, but at least Mrs. Brandt didn't encourage him to exert himself to catch the brass ring. That honor went to a young man in a derby hat whose accomplishment earned him the adoration of his female companion, a girl with a grating laugh who found everything hilarious.

When the ride stopped, Mrs. Brandt slid down from her horse herself without waiting for help, which suited Frank just fine. He had already decided he shouldn't touch her again. He'd been alone for far too long, and he obviously couldn't be trusted.

"Did riding the carousel help you figure out who killed Gerda Reinhard?" he couldn't resist asking as they walked away.

"I didn't expect to find the killer today," she told him, not the least bit repentant. "But we need to understand what Gerda's life was like those last days. That will help us figure out who might have killed her. Once we can narrow down the list of suspects, we'll have a better chance of finding the killer."

That was so reasonable, he almost said so. Fortunately, good sense prevailed. He couldn't start complimenting Sarah Brandt. She was already way too confident as it was. Instead he said, "What do you mean by 'we'? Has your friend Teddy appointed you to the police force?"

She didn't like being reminded that Police Commissioner Theodore Roosevelt was a family friend. Or maybe she just didn't like being reminded that women couldn't be police officers. "No," she admitted, "but maybe I could ask him to order Detective Sergeant Broughan to continue the investigation into Gerda's death."

"That's not likely to help. *All* of Broughan's attention would practically guarantee the killer is never found. You're better off letting him ignore it and working on it yourself."

She widened her eyes at him in surprise, and he had to admit he'd surprised himself. What was he thinking to advise her to solve the case herself? On the other hand, she was going to try to do it anyway. He felt an obligation at least to prepare her, however.

"Look, Mrs. Brandt, solving a murder isn't always as easy as it was with the VanDamm girl," he said, referring to the case they'd worked on together last spring.

Now she just looked shocked. "You think solving that case was *easy*?"

"It got solved, didn't it? A lot of them don't. Oh, sometimes we know who the killer is five minutes after we find the body. Those are the easy ones. The killer's standing over the body with a bloody knife still in his hand, all eager to tell you how he didn't mean to do it. But the ones like this girl—"

"And the other girls," she interjected.

"And the other girls," he allowed grudgingly, "the killer's been real careful to cover his tracks. Maybe he never even met the girls before that night. These girls go with strangers all the time, and even if they did know the man before, he's only one of dozens they knew. The girls are no better than they should be, and if we arrested all the men who take advantage of girls like that and might be the killer, we'd have half the men in the city locked up."

She didn't look impressed. In fact, she'd set her chin at an angle he didn't like at all. "I told you, Malloy, we can find out which men all the dead girls knew in common. That's got to narrow down the suspects considerably."

"If they even knew the men's right names—or any name, for that matter."

"The girls weren't prostitutes, Malloy. They wouldn't go with a complete stranger, no matter what you think. They have to pretend there's a little romance involved and that the gifts are tokens of esteem, not payment for services rendered. They knew their killer, and he'd been wooing them for a while before they agreed to go with him that last time. I don't think for a moment that it will be easy to find him, but I think it's possible. Your friend Broughan might believe it's too much trouble, but I'm willing to give some effort to the cause."

"And you're willing to bribe me into helping you," he said, thinking of her interest in Brian. "I guess that makes me no better than the Charity Girls."

"It's not like that, Malloy," she said, stopping in the middle of the midway and forcing people to go around them. "Helping your son is something I'd do whether you helped me in return or not."

Frank didn't want to believe her, since *he* certainly wouldn't be helping *her* unless he felt he owed her something. He was afraid she was telling the truth, however, so he didn't press her. Better to leave some doubt in his mind so he could keep a little self-respect.

He touched her arm to indicate they should start walking again. People were becoming annoyed at the way they were blocking the way. "It doesn't look to me like these girls are very particular who they go with, but if you're right about them wanting to know the man a little first, then maybe there is a chance we can figure out who the killer is," he admitted reluctantly.

She smiled at that, recognizing a victory. At least she was gracious enough not to gloat.

Frank refused her entreaties to ride the Flip-Flap Railway, which looked like a very dangerous proposition indeed. A car went sliding down a steep incline, building up speed, until it was going fast enough to propel it around a vertical loop. No matter how many times they watched it go around and saw no one fall out, Frank wouldn't be convinced it was safe.

They watched the performing sea lions who had been the original attraction of the park and saw the newest addition to the park, an alligator just arrived from Florida. They ate Vienna sausages on rolls, called Red Hots, at one of the sidewalk cafés under a striped umbrella and were allowed to buy beer in spite of the Sunday closing laws Theodore

Roosevelt was now vigorously enforcing, because they were eating, too.

Sarah couldn't help noticing, however, that at many tables the only food was a dried-up-looking sandwich that no one touched.

"That's to obey the letter of the law," Malloy explained when she pointed it out to him. "So long as they serve some kind of food, they can also serve liquor. The law doesn't say what kind of food it has to be or that anybody has to actually eat it." The same sandwich was apparently served over and over again all day.

After their meal, they allowed themselves to be lured into one of the freak shows to see a bearded lady and a man who could make his eyes bulge nearly out of their sockets. Frank had seen more frightening things on Fifth Avenue.

"Are you a good shot, Malloy?" Mrs. Brandt asked when they passed a shooting gallery. Young men were using the rifles to shoot at moving targets in hopes of winning their companions one of the cheap trinkets on display. "Have you passed the police-department shooting test?"

She was referring to the regulation that her friend Commissioner Teddy had made last December, after a police shooting mishap, that every man on the force must be trained to use a .32-caliber, double-action Colt revolver. It was the first type of formal training ever required of a police officer, and resentment ran high. Tammany Hall had complained because the men were required to buy their own guns, accusing the department of charging them ten dollars for a gun worth only four. Roosevelt countered that the gun actually cost fifteen dollars, and suddenly the controversy had ended.

"I knew how to shoot before your friend made it a rule," Malloy assured her.

"Prove it, then," she challenged, gesturing toward the shooting booth. "Win me a prize."

"Do you need a set of glass beads that bad?" he teased.

"Are you afraid you won't win?" she teased back.

He couldn't allow her to think he was, especially when he wasn't. He stepped up to the counter, plunked down his nickel, and picked up a rifle. He kept shooting for a while, until a small crowd had gathered and the barker was trying to draw an even larger one.

"Step right up, folks, see how easy it is! This gentleman's already won himself whatever he wants from our vast array of prizes. Just point the rifle and shoot, that's how easy it is! Take home a treasure for your sweetheart! Step right up!"

When Frank figured he'd proven his point, he laid the rifle down and turned to Mrs. Brandt with a satisfied smile. She was smiling back, well aware of why he had continued to shoot long after he'd won her the glass beads. "What would you like?" he asked, indicating the "vast array of prizes."

"That fire wagon, I think," she said, pointing to the toy at the bottom of the display. It was obviously worth only a few cents and totally unsuitable for a lady. "For Brian," she added at his surprised look.

Of course. She knew his weakness. He wouldn't be able to refuse her anything now that she did.

With the toy bulging in his pocket, they continued down the midway until they heard the shouts and screams and thundering splash that told them they'd finally reached the place where Gerda Reinhard may have met her killer.

"It's the Shoot-the-Chutes," she said unnecessarily. Frank had already recognized the boats from the photograph.

They watched as one of the boats crested the top of the final incline and went shooting down the water-filled trough into the lagoon below. The angle of descent caused the boat to strike the surface of the water with a bone-jarring crash that sent water splashing in all directions. The passengers screamed with either terror or delight, Frank wasn't certain which, but from the way they were laughing as they climbed out of the boat, they seemed none the worse for their experience.

"That's the place where they take the photographs," she said, drawing his attention to a replica of the boats used on the ride. This one was propped up on a wooden stand, and the photographer was assembling a group of people in it for a photograph.

Frank looked back as another boat went crashing down the chute. "I hope you don't think you have to ride that thing to find out who the killer is," he said, but when he looked at Mrs. Brandt, ready for her smart reply, she wasn't even paying attention. Instead she was staring intently at the people posing in the boat.

"What is it?" he asked, looking, too, but seeing nothing noteworthy.

"That man in the third row. I think I know him."

5

"WHICH ONE?"

Sarah looked again. The man was turned away now, speaking to his companion, a young girl who couldn't seem to stop giggling. Sarah couldn't be certain, but he looked like one of the Schyler boys. Then he turned to pose for the photographer who had commanded them all to look suitably frightened for the picture, and she was sure.

"Dirk Schyler," she told Malloy. "His family and mine have known each other forever."

"Knickerbockers," Malloy said with disapproval, referring to the nickname for the wealthy old Dutch families who had been the original settlers of New York City.

"Don't say it like it's an insult, Malloy," she chided him. "Some people are proud of being a Knickerbocker family."

He knew she wasn't, of course, so he just gave her one of his looks, which she ignored.

They watched as the people in the boat posed, trying to look frightened, and the photographer snapped the picture.

"What do you suppose the son of a Knickerbocker family is doing at Coney Island with a shop girl?" Malloy mused aloud.

Sarah had been wondering the same thing. Dirk was helping the girl out of the boat now, and they could see the cheapness of her outfit and the tawdriness of her accessories. She didn't appear to be more than sixteen, either. Dirk himself was dressed the part of a Coney Island swain in a plaid suit and a straw boater, which was amazing in itself. Someone of Dirk's station in life would never be seen in such a costume, or so Sarah would have thought.

All this actually made Sarah doubt her own judgment for a moment, but she waited until the couple was within earshot, and she called, "Dirk!"

Sure enough, his head jerked around in surprise. When he saw Sarah staring back at him, he didn't seem to recognize her at first. His surprise slid into confusion and then, just for a moment, alarm, as recognition dawned. She hadn't seen him in years, but they had been children together, sharing the agonies of dancing classes and tea parties. He knew her now and for just that second had been horrified to know she had seen him here, like this.

She understood it all in the second before his expression twisted itself into the semblance of delighted surprise, the kind he would have genuinely felt to have encountered her while dining at Delmonico's in the city, for example. He leaned down and spoke to his companion, who shot a look in Sarah's direction, plainly ready to object to his leaving her, even for an instant. But then she saw Sarah and recognized that someone of Sarah's advanced years could not be a threat to her, and besides, Sarah already had Malloy for an escort. Reluctantly, she released the arm to which she had been clinging possessively and allowed him to make his way over to Sarah and Malloy.

"Sarah, is that you?" he asked, his features now schooled into the proper combination of amazement and pleasure.

"It certainly is. How have you been, Dirk?" she asked, taking the hand he offered.

He clasped hers in both of his, holding it fast while they exchanged pleasantries about the health of their respective families. Sarah thought she was going to have to pull it free by force until she realized she could simply introduce him to her companion instead.

"Are you enjoying the sights?" Dirk was asking politely, plainly expecting her to deny it. His eyes were dancing with the assumption of a shared contempt for the amusements found here.

"Very much," Sarah said truthfully. "I was just trying to convince Mr. Malloy to take me on the Shoot-the-Chutes."

"Malloy?" Dirk said with some amazement, as if the name were some foreign language he didn't quite recognize. His tone told her he was shocked at the idea of her consorting with an Irishman, but at least he released her hand at last to shake hands with Malloy.

"Frank Malloy, Dirk Schyler," Sarah said, offering Dirk no more information about Malloy, even though his curiosity was obvious.

"Do you come here a lot, Schyler?" Malloy asked him with all the subtlety of a police interrogator.

Dirk was taken aback by his bluntness, but he couldn't quite bring himself to refuse to answer. That would have been beyond rude, and Dirk had been bred to obey the rules of etiquette as if they held the force of law. "I . . . now and again," was all he would admit. "I find it . . . amusing."

Malloy glanced meaningfully at the girl, who was waiting with increasing impatience for his return. "Yes, she looks . . . amusing."

Sarah wanted to smack him. Certainly, Dirk's ill-disguised contempt for Malloy was annoying, but insulting him back wouldn't get them anywhere.

The girl saw them looking at her, and she called, "Will you come on?" to Dirk, who replied with a placating wave, indicating he'd join her in a moment.

"We were just wondering if this ride is dangerous," Sarah asked, drawing his attention back to her. "I couldn't get Mr. Malloy to take me on the Flip-Flap Railway. He was afraid we'd fall out." She smiled sweetly, knowing Malloy would probably like to choke her for saying such a thing.

"Oh, there's no need to worry, old man," Dirk assured him generously, plainly delighted to gain an advantage over Malloy. "Everything here is perfectly safe. The Flip-Flap relies on centrifugal force to keep people in their seats. Works just like gravity, don't you know?"

Malloy didn't know any such thing, but he wasn't going to show weakness in front of Dirk. "That's what I heard," he lied.

"And the boat ride here"—Dirk gestured toward the Shoot-the-Chutes—"is quite a thrill, but not dangerous at all. And you'll like the beginning of the ride even better than the ending. It's a very different kind of thrill, especially with a companion like our lovely Sarah."

Malloy didn't like the suggestive tone of Dirk's voice. Sarah could tell by the way his neck got red. But for once in his life he held his tongue, thank heaven.

"I'm afraid you might have the wrong idea, Dirk," she hastened to explain. "Mr. Malloy and I are here on Coney Island for business."

"Business?" He looked at Malloy again, as if trying to imagine what kind of business he might be in. "Police business, by any chance?"

Sarah was surprised he'd guessed so quickly, but Malloy wasn't. The two men understood each other perfectly.

"Not all Irishmen are coppers," Malloy reminded him.

"And not all coppers are Irishmen anymore, are they?" Dirk countered. "I heard my old friend Teddy has even hired some Jews to police our fair city. But no one would mistake you for one of them, Officer Malloy."

"Detective Sergeant Malloy," Malloy corrected him.

Dirk's eyebrows rose, and Sarah thought he might have paled a bit, but perhaps she only imagined it. In any case, they were all distracted by the sudden appearance of the young lady Dirk had left standing nearby while he conversed with them.

"You promised me some ice cream!" she reminded him,

shooting Sarah a look meant to freeze her blood. The girl was even younger than Sarah had thought, but her eyes were old with experience, just as Lisle's were.

"So I did, my dear," he said, tucking her hand into the crook of his arm and patting it soothingly. "I'm afraid I must excuse myself now. Sarah, it was so nice to see you. Malloy, enjoy the ride."

His smirk was knowing as he steered the girl away. Sarah turned on Malloy.

"That was a fine job," she said as soon as Dirk was out of earshot.

"What are you talking about?"

"I'm talking about all that male posturing," Sarah said furiously. "The two of you were like schoolboys, puffing out your chests and trying to see who could be King of the Mountain."

"You're crazy!"

"No, I'm angry!" she corrected him. "If you hadn't insisted on taking offense, I might have gotten some information out of him."

"Information about what?" he scoffed.

"About Coney Island and what goes on here. It's obvious he comes here often."

"Yes, and you know why he comes here, don't you?"

"Of course. To meet shop girls."

"He does more than meet them," Malloy said, his expression hardening.

"I'm sure he does. He buys them treats and takes them on the rides, and they reward him with their favors. It's the kind of exchange that goes on all over the city every day."

"And maybe he even buys them things, like hats. Or red shoes."

That silenced Sarah, but only for a moment. "Dirk isn't a killer."

"Why not? Because you know him?"

Sarah remembered she had known the killer of Alicia

VanDamm, too, and it had been someone she had never suspected.

"All right, Malloy, you win. Dirk could be the killer just as easily as every other man here."

"Maybe even more easily than some. He doesn't have to come all the way out here for female companionship. And why would he dress like a dry-goods salesman and prowl around a place where he'll probably never see anyone who knows him?"

"Because the female companionship of girls of his own class would be heavily chaperoned. A liaison with one of them would be impossible. He's probably dressed the way he is so none of the girls will suspect he's wealthy and try to blackmail him. And he certainly doesn't want any of his friends to know how he satisfies his baser urges. Keeping a mistress would be perfectly acceptable in their eyes, but apparently, Dirk doesn't want to go to the trouble."

"Or the expense, maybe."

Sarah shook her head. "He could keep a woman if that's what he wanted. I'm sure his father would provide for him if he knew the alternative was to have him consorting with the trash he'd consider these girls to be."

"Maybe this is his way of rebelling. Maybe he hopes you'll go back and tell everyone you saw him here. Maybe he wants to embarrass his family."

Sarah didn't know what Dirk's motives were, and she really didn't care, but she did know she could learn a lot from him. But not when Malloy was around. She'd have to seek him out when she got back to the city.

"Well, Malloy, since you cost me a chance to find out something from Dirk, you have to take me on the Shoot-the-Chutes."

"What?"

"You heard me. Or are you going to make me go alone?"

"What would you want to go on that thing for?" He stared at the contraption in horror as yet another boat came splashing down into the artificial lagoon.

"I want to find out everything I can about Gerda Reinhard's last days, and on the last Sunday of her life, she rode on that ride. Now, are you coming or do I have to find another escort?"

He opened his mouth, ready with another argument, but Sarah beat him to it.

"You're not afraid, are you?" she challenged.

Of course he was, but he'd die before he admitted it. Sarah knew that, and she managed not to grin with triumph when he grabbed her elbow and determinedly steered her toward the line of people waiting to board the boats.

He was muttering something under his breath, and Sarah chose not to hear. It was easier than getting into an argument. She could sympathize with his fear of mechanical contraptions. She wasn't overly fond of them herself, but she was terribly curious to learn what Dirk had meant about the thrills on the first part of the ride.

They waited the better part of half an hour before they were handed into a boat. Malloy nearly upset the thing when he climbed in beside her, but the water was so shallow that truly upsetting was actually impossible.

"Easy there, sir," the young boy assisting them cautioned, helping Malloy sit down on the seat beside her. They were crowded in with their knees pressing against the people on the seat in front of them and the knees of those behind them pressing against their backs.

Malloy shot her a reproachful look, but she simply smiled serenely.

When everyone was seated, the boat started with a jerk, and Sarah realized it was being propelled by some sort of motorized pulley device. They glided down the chute, and the next thing they knew, their boat was swallowed up by a tunnel.

"So this is what he meant!" Sarah whispered to Malloy as the darkness enveloped them.

In the sudden silence of the tunnel, where they were shielded from the raucous noises of the rest of the park, they could hear the sounds of rustling clothing and provocative giggling and even the smack of lips as the other couples in the boat took advantage of the momentary privacy for some hasty petting.

"If that's all you wanted to know, I could've told you," Malloy said, the disgust evident in his voice. "We didn't have to get on this cursed thing."

"At least try to enjoy yourself, Malloy," she chided.

Just then the couple in front of them nearly toppled into their laps, and by the time they were all untangled, amid much giggling and cursing, the boat was emerging into the daylight again.

The couples discreetly stopped kissing, but they kept their arms around each other as the boat began to travel upward at an increasingly steep angle.

"Oh, my," Sarah said as the ground fell away and the boat seemed to be going almost straight up into the air.

"I tried to warn you," Malloy reminded her as she instinctively clutched at his arm for support, but by then she was too distracted to take offense.

What had she been thinking? This was insane! She could be killed! She most certainly *would* be killed! This flimsy boat would never withstand the impact she knew it would take when it went plummeting down the chute to splash into the water below. Malloy was right, but she would never have the opportunity to tell him so because suddenly the whole world was tipping over, and they were going down and down and down, faster and faster, until a scream was literally ripped from her throat, and she thought her very heart must be torn out with it. And just when she thought she couldn't bear it another second, the boat hit the water with an impact that sent them slamming into their seats. The spray of water showered them, and then it was over, and they were gliding safely, surely to the shore, where men with grappling hooks were waiting to pull the boat in so they could disembark.

Only then did Sarah realize that in her terror she had

thrown her arms around Malloy and that she was still clinging to him desperately.

"Oh!" she cried, mortified, and released him at once, except she couldn't exactly release him because he was clinging to her, too, in equal desperation.

But his reaction was only an instant later than hers, and they sprang guiltily apart, or at least as far apart as they could get in the crowded boat. For a moment their gazes locked and they shared their mutual embarrassment, but a moment was all they could stand. They looked away, up or down or anywhere but at each other.

Good heavens, what had come over her? Sarah wasn't clingy or helpless or at all the kind of woman to clutch at a man for *anything*. Or at least she wasn't in the normal course of her life. The normal course of her life had not, until now, involved a terrifying plummet down a water-filled chute to what felt like certain and imminent death, however. That, apparently, changed her into a quivering mass of feminine weakness.

And it had turned Malloy into a quivering mass of male weakness, too, it seemed. He was the first one out of the boat when the attendant had secured it to the wooden wharf, and he let the attendant help her out, too. Which suited Sarah fine. She didn't feel quite ready to have Malloy's hands on her again.

She immediately changed her mind, however, when she discovered that her knees were trembling as she made her way toward the exit. She could have used a steady arm to support her, but one look at Malloy's expression told her not even to consider it.

"That was certainly an experience, wasn't it?" she managed, hoping her voice didn't sound as breathless as she was afraid it did.

Malloy didn't bother to respond.

Luckily, there was a vacant bench nearby, and Sarah and Malloy both plopped down on it. For a few moments they just sat there, staring at the people walking by. Sarah was waiting for her heart rate to return to normal, and she supposed Malloy was doing the same.

Finally, he said, "I hope you know who the killer is now, because I don't think I can survive any more of this investigation."

Sarah looked at him in amazement, but then she saw the glint of amusement in his dark eyes and realized he was teasing her. Malloy was *teasing* her! She knew it wasn't funny, but she had an irresistible urge to laugh, and before she could stop herself she *was* laughing, and then Malloy was laughing, too. Or chuckling at least. And shaking his head and chuckling some more. She had never seen him laugh. It was so amazing, she laughed even harder, until she had to wipe the tears from her eyes and take some deep breaths to compose herself.

"Oh, Malloy, I'm sorry I put you through that," she said when she could speak again. "I had no idea it would be so frightening. Everybody looked like they were having such a good time!"

"You thought they were screaming because it was so much fun?" he asked skeptically.

He had a point, but she didn't give it to him. "And I'm sorry I behaved so . . . so foolishly. Clinging to you the way I did," she added with chagrin when his look grew puzzled.

He nodded in understanding, then turned his head away, seemingly studying the passing throng for several moments. "I didn't mind," he said quite casually.

This time Sarah was dumbfounded. "Malloy, are you flirting with me?" she demanded, not at all displeased.

When he turned back to her, his expression was bland. "I thought you were flirting with me."

Had she been? She thought back to her behavior throughout the day and realized she hadn't been acting at all like herself, at least not the way she usually acted with Malloy. And he hadn't been acting at all like himself, either, if the truth were told. They'd both been almost playful and slightly adventurous and much more informal than they had ever been in each other's company.

"It's this place, isn't it?" she realized. "Here a person can break all the rules of propriety and not suffer any consequences!"

Malloy frowned, but she was too busy thinking aloud to notice.

"In the city, strangers don't speak to each other, but here they offer advice as if they were dear friends. In the city, a man wouldn't dare even tip his hat to a woman he didn't know, but here he can introduce himself to a girl he's never seen before, treat her to rides and buy her food and even kiss her in the darkness of the tunnels."

Malloy was still frowning, but not in disapproval. He was thinking, too. "You're right. People don't act like themselves here," he said. "No one knows them, so they don't have to worry about what anyone else will think of them."

"Which is why young people come here, so they can meet new people and have fun and their families won't know what they're doing. A girl can be forward and flirt and do things she wouldn't dream of doing in her neighborhood where anyone might see her and ruin her reputation. Even going to the dance halls, a girl has to be a little careful because word might get back to her family, but not about what happens on Coney Island."

"And men like your friend Dirk come out here to prey on those girls," Malloy reminded her.

"Men of *all* kinds prey on them," Sarah corrected him. She looked at the crowd passing down the midway before them, hundreds of people of every size and shape and age and status in life. Any one of them might have met Gerda Reinhard and treated her and tempted her and lured her to a dark corner and beaten the life out of her. "It's hopeless, isn't it?" she asked in despair.

"Finding the killer, you mean?"

She nodded glumly.

He sighed and watched the crowd with unseeing eyes

while he considered. "If it was just one girl, then yes, it *would* be impossible."

"But it wasn't just one girl, was it?" How could she have forgotten? "There were three others! I found out their names from Gerda's friends. I was going to tell you today, but in all the excitement, I forgot!"

He didn't look at her. "They were Eva Bower, Luisa Isenberg, and Fredrika Lutz."

"That's right!" Sarah's surprise quickly became anger. "You knew all along! You were just playing with me!"

"Don't be a fool. I would've told you if I did."

She supposed this was true, although she really had no way of knowing for sure. "Well, then, if you didn't know their names before, how do you know them now?"

"I know Eva's name because I worked on her case. She was the first one, as near as I can figure, which is why nobody thought it was anything out of the ordinary. Just another girl who took up with the wrong man and got beaten to death for her mistake."

"You didn't investigate?" Sarah was outraged.

Malloy just gave her one of his long-suffering looks. "She was just like this Gerda. She'd known dozens of men, and the ones we could find all had alibis. Nobody saw it, nobody knew anything, nobody cared."

"But what about the others! Why didn't you start questioning their friends to find out what men they all knew in common?"

"I didn't know about the others until you told me the other day, remember?"

"But you know their names now!"

"Only because you told me other girls had been killed. I started asking around, and that's when I found out about the other two cases. Two different detectives had them, and they didn't know about any of the others, either."

"How could this happen? Don't policemen talk to each other?" Sarah was incredulous.

Malloy rubbed the bridge of his nose, as if he were getting a headache. "We talk to each other about important cases."

"And the deaths of four girls isn't important?" Sarah cried, but she didn't need Malloy's pitying look to remind her that no, these deaths *weren't* very important in the grand scheme of things. No one outside their families cared about them, and none of their families had the money or connections necessary to ensure a thorough investigation. Even *with* all the resources money could buy at their disposal, the police were unlikely to solve any single one of these murders, simply because the pool of suspects was so very large.

But now Sarah saw a way to surmount all these difficulties. "The deaths of *four* girls *is* important if we can prove they were all killed by the same man, especially since he's likely to kill again."

"We don't know the murders were committed by one man," Malloy pointed out reasonably.

This time Sarah was the one giving the pitying look. "Oh, Malloy, I thought we already settled that. All the girls had been to a dance hall, and they were all killed the same way in the same neighborhood. How many men do you think are skulking around the city beating young women to death?"

"More than you'd like to imagine, I'm sure," Malloy said. "And even if one man did kill all these girls, we don't have any reason to think he'll kill again."

"How can you say that? He's gotten away with it four times! He must think he's invincible by now. If anything, he'll start to kill more often!"

"What makes you such an expert on the criminal mind, Mrs. Brandt?" he asked sourly.

Sarah couldn't resist. "All the training I've received from a very wise police detective."

Malloy's expression was priceless, but Sarah didn't gloat. She merely smiled serenely.

Malloy finally found his tongue. "Do you feel up to

walking back to the trolley station now? I've had enough of this place."

"So have I," Sarah agreed. "On the way back to the city, we can discuss how we're going to proceed with our investigation."

SARAH WAS ACTUALLY quite surprised that Malloy had agreed to allow her to help investigate the murders. She'd only been teasing him when she suggested they work out a system, but he had been willing—if not eager—for her to assist him. Apparently, the investigation into the murders of all the other girls had been abandoned just as Malloy had abandoned his, and for the same reasons. Sarah suspected that Malloy felt a bit guilty for not trying harder to solve the case that had been his originally, even though they both agreed the task had been hopeless with only one victim. Now, of course, they had a way of narrowing down the list of suspects.

Sarah had planned to begin with Gerda's sister first thing the next day, but an early morning call delayed her. By the time she'd brought a healthy baby boy safely into the world, it was late in the afternoon. Men were returning to their homes carrying their now empty lunch pails, and the smells of thousands of suppers being prepared filled the hot, summer air as thunderclouds gathered overhead. At least a storm might break the oppressive heat.

Sarah hated to intrude on the Otto family at this time of day, and she certainly didn't want to encounter Lars Otto again, but she also didn't want to lose any more time in her quest to find Gerda's killer. Maybe she could catch Agnes before her husband came home from work.

She climbed the dark stairs to the Ottos' flat, the heat from dozens of cooking stoves turning the stairwell into a giant oven. The two older Otto children were playing on the landing, the boy entertaining the girl as best he could, probably trying to keep her out of their mother's way.

Young as he was, he could understand that his mother didn't need any distractions just now.

Sarah could see Agnes sitting in her kitchen through the door that stood open to catch whatever air might be stirring, superheated though it might be. Agnes was listlessly rolling out dough for biscuits. On the floor beside the table sat a cradle which she was rocking with one of her slippered feet. Inside the cradle lay the new baby, clad only in a ragged diaper. She looked no healthier than she had the last time Sarah saw her, and she was mewling pitifully. Agnes appeared oblivious to the child's complaints.

"Good afternoon, Mrs. Otto," Sarah called, startling her.

When Agnes turned to face her, Sarah was startled in turn by how haggard she looked. Like a dishrag that had been thoroughly wrung out. Sweat had dampened the hair around her face, her lips had little color, and her eyes were red-rimmed and dark-circled. Sarah instantly diagnosed anemia and no relief from the postnatal depression. Agnes's condition was alarming, but the baby was in even more danger.

"Mrs. Brandt?" Agnes said after a moment, as if she needed that time to properly identify her visitor. "Why are you here? Is it Mrs. Gertz's time?"

Sarah smiled. "Not that I know of. I was just in the neighborhood and thought I'd stop by and see how you're doing. The little one seems unhappy."

Agnes glanced down at the cradle she still rocked automatically, as if the action of her foot was independent of the rest of her body. Only then did she appear to become aware of the child's misery.

"She is so good, I hardly remember she is there," the new mother said, picking the baby up out of the cradle with little tenderness.

Sarah thought it more likely she hardly *noticed,* but she said nothing, waiting for Agnes to offer the child her breast. Instead, she tried bouncing the baby, as if that would soothe her cries.

Sarah's fear was a tight ball in her stomach, but she tried not to show it. In her fragile state, Agnes probably wouldn't be able to tolerate any perceived criticism of her mothering. Making her feel attacked would only harden her against the child. "She might be hungry," Sarah suggested mildly.

The baby was rooting frantically, digging her face fruitlessly into the bodice of her mother's dress, looking for milk. "I do not have time now. I have to finish supper," Agnes said, laying the babe back in the cradle. "Lars will be angry if his supper is not ready when he comes home."

The child's little face was pinched and red, but she appeared too weak to cry any harder than the small, pitiful sounds she was making. Sarah knew what was happening. The baby wasn't getting enough attention or sustenance, and she would die. Not today or tomorrow, but eventually. She wouldn't grow, wouldn't fatten, would shrivel and grow sickly and die. Sarah had seen it happen often enough. Too many unwanted babies seemed to recognize their fate and choose oblivion to further suffering. Some might say they were better off dead than alive in a world that didn't want them, but not Sarah. Sarah hated death. Too many tiny lives had ended from injury and disease already. In the city, one in every three infants died from any number of reasons. Sarah never surrendered those in her care easily, and she wasn't going to stand by helplessly and allow this one to go for no good reason at all.

"I can keep an eye on the other children and finish making those biscuits while you take the baby into the front room and nurse her. I'm prescribing some rest and relaxation for you." She smiled with what she hoped looked like kindness, and prayed Agnes wouldn't sense her desperation.

But Agnes was far too withdrawn into her own anguish even to notice Sarah's expression, much less to divine her intentions. For a long moment she simply stared at the half-flattened dough ball sitting on the table in front of her, as if she were trying to remember what she had been doing with it.

"Lars will be angry," she repeated. "He wants his supper waiting when he comes home."

"He won't like listening to a crying baby, either," Sarah said. "I can roll out biscuits as well as you."

That might be a lie, but Sarah felt no guilt in telling it. Instead she waited patiently while Agnes considered the possible ramifications and the baby continued to whimper. Finally, Agnes pulled herself to her feet. Her faded house-dress hung on her, and Sarah was amazed at how quickly she had lost the extra weight from her pregnancy. In fact, she was *too* thin, as if she were starving herself as well as the child.

Sarah was so concerned about Agnes's weight loss that she almost didn't notice the way she clutched at her side when she rose, as if she felt a pain there.

"Are you all right?" Sarah asked, automatically reaching to help her.

Agnes recoiled, cringing as if in fear of a blow, but then seemed to catch herself. She straightened, pride overcoming her obvious discomfort. "I am fine."

"Your side hurts," Sarah said, mentally running through a list of possible complications from the pregnancy. She couldn't think of anything offhand that would cause pain up high on Agnes's side, though. "I'd be happy to examine you and see if—"

"It is nothing," Agnes insisted. "Just a bruise. I . . . I fall out of bed. *Ja*, I fall out of the bed. In the night. It was foolish. Like a little child. I have the bad dreams still. About Gerda."

Sarah nodded. She sometimes had dreams about her dead sister, too, even though Maggie had been gone for more than a decade. Maggie, who had died bringing a child into the world. Maggie who had taught Sarah to hate death with a vengeance and fight it at every turn.

"Go on now and lie down. Feed the baby and get a little

rest. I'll get the biscuits in the oven for you."

Agnes's expression was heartbreakingly pitiful as she struggled with emotions Sarah couldn't begin to understand. Finally, she said, "I cannot pay you."

"I don't charge people for doing them a favor," Sarah replied gently. "Please get some rest. If you get sick after having a baby that I delivered, it will hurt my reputation," she added with a small smile.

Agnes didn't appreciate Sarah's attempt at humor, but she allowed Sarah to pick the baby up and place her in her arms.

"I forgot to ask what you'd named her," Sarah said.

Agnes glanced down at the child, as if she needed to remind herself. "Marta," she said after a moment. "After Lars's mother. I wanted to call her Gerda, but—" Her voice broke, and Sarah was afraid she would collapse if she didn't get into bed soon.

With professional efficiency, Sarah guided her patient to her unmade bed and tucked her into it, making sure the baby was suckling properly before leaving them. She checked on the other two children, who were still playing so quietly Sarah found it disturbing. They stared at her with large, wary eyes when she told them their mother was resting, but they didn't make a sound. She remembered Malloy's silent son and wondered for a moment . . . But then she recalled hearing them speak on earlier visits and realized that they were most likely simply cowed by things they couldn't understand.

Sarah made short work of the biscuits. She was afraid she'd added too much flour to the dough, but she hated when it stuck to the rolling pin. She hated everything about dough, in fact. It was either sticky and messy or powdery and messy. She cut the biscuits with the top of a drinking glass, found a sheet of tin to bake them on, and stuck them in the oven. By then her clothes were damp and her face running with sweat. All that work, and she still hadn't so much as asked Agnes a single question about her sister.

She was just cleaning up the last of the flour from the kitchen table when she heard footsteps on the stairs and cries of, "Papa! Papa!" Lars Otto must be home, and he'd be annoyed because his supper wasn't ready. He'd probably be even more annoyed to find Sarah there. She steeled herself to face him.

Lars Otto called something in German, something that sounded a bit angry to Sarah, as he stepped through the doorway, his small daughter perched on one hip while his son proudly carried his father's lunch pail in with both hands. His work clothes were dirty, probably stained with dried blood from the animals he butchered, but he'd made some attempt to clean himself up before coming home. He stopped short when he saw Sarah and frowned.

"Something is wrong with Agnes?" he asked, apparently more angry than concerned. Or maybe he was just one of those men who hid his finer feelings behind anger. Sarah hoped that was true.

"She's very tired, and she still hasn't recovered from the birth. I'm worried about her and the baby. Marta isn't thriving and—"

"Why should you worry about the baby? That is not your job."

"I'm a trained nurse, Mr. Otto. I treat sick babies as well as their mothers."

"Is Marta sick?" Plainly, he believed she was not.

"She will be soon if her mother doesn't recover her strength. She's not getting enough to eat. You could try giving her canned milk, but babies rarely do well on that. I'd suggest—"

"Agnes will feed this baby just like she fed the others," he interrupted her, outraged. "We have no money to waste on milk from a store!"

"I don't want that, either. Mother's milk is best, in any case, but Agnes—"

"Did Agnes send for you?" he demanded, setting his

daughter down. The little girl was starting to cry, upset at seeing adults argue.

"No," Sarah admitted. "I just stopped by to see how she was doing."

"I will not pay you for this visit," he informed her haughtily. "We did not send for you, and nothing is wrong here."

"Something is very wrong, Mr. Otto. Your wife is mourning her sister, and she isn't able to properly take care of the baby."

"Lars?" Agnes's voice was hardly more than a whisper, and when Sarah turned to see her standing in the bedroom doorway, she was shocked at the look of naked terror on her face. "Your supper is almost ready."

Only then did Sarah remember the biscuits, and when she looked, she saw a suspicious curl of smoke coming from the oven door. Quickly, she grabbed a towel and pulled the door open. The biscuits were just starting to burn, and Sarah was able to pull them out before any serious damage was done. Still, she could see that Lars wasn't pleased. In fact, his face was scarlet.

"Now you are cooking in my house?" he asked her.

"I was just helping Agnes so she could get some rest. She needs some time to mourn her sister and—"

"No one will mourn that woman here! She does not deserve any of our tears." He glared at Agnes as if daring her to contradict him. She ducked her head like a whipped dog and scurried to put the now sleeping baby back in her cradle. Without looking up, she hurried to the stove and began dishing up something from the pot that had been simmering there.

"You will go now," Lars told Sarah. "And do not come back here. We do not need a midwife any longer."

Sarah decided not to mention the other reason for her visit, which was to see if Agnes had any useful information about Gerda's male companions. Under the circumstances, she didn't think he would be too pleased to know she was helping investigate Gerda's death.

Not wanting to linger any more than Mr. Otto wanted her to stay, Sarah gathered her things. "If you need me, just let me know," she told Agnes, but the woman gave no indication she even heard. She was too busy setting her husband's meal on the table.

Sarah saw herself out, gratefully escaping into the busy street, where the air was marginally fresher, at least. She could feel her cheeks burning with indignation at the way Lars Otto had treated her. He could be excused for being angry at the scandal his sister-in-law had brought down on them, but he should be more understanding of his wife's grief. He should at least feel concern for the health of his wife and his baby daughter, if nothing else. But Sarah knew that many men cared little for such things.

Agnes Otto was afraid of displeasing her husband, and she might well have good reason to be. Sarah would do nothing further to annoy him. At least that he would know about. And he certainly wouldn't know if she questioned Gerda's friends.

6

"MRS. BRANDT, ARE YOU OFF TO DELIVER A baby?" a voice called as Sarah descended her front stoop the next evening.

"Not this evening," Sarah replied to her next-door neighbor Mrs. Elsworth, who never seemed to miss a single event that happened in their neighborhood. Mrs. Elsworth spent an inordinate amount of time sweeping her front steps just so she'd have a good vantage point. That's what she was doing just now, but at least she had an excuse. The showers that had fallen throughout the day had left leaves and small twigs in their wake. "I'm going to meet some friends."

"Not that nice detective sergeant?" she asked hopefully.

"No, I'm afraid not," Sarah said, unable to hide her smile. She wondered what Malloy would say to being characterized as "nice."

"Are you expecting visitors, then? I found a button today while I was cleaning upstairs, which means I'm going to make a new friend. I wonder if you've got any babies due soon. If someone comes while you're out, I'll certainly take a message for you."

"No babies due that I know of, but certainly take a message if anyone comes. I won't be late, I'm sure."

"Oh, that won't matter to me. I hardly sleep anymore as it is. The slightest noise wakes me, and then I'm awake for the rest of the night. Getting old is such a bother."

"But far preferable to the alternative, don't you think?" Sarah replied with a smile.

Mrs. Elsworth smiled back. "I expect you're right about that."

Sarah left her still sweeping as she watched for other activity which might excite her interest.

A few minutes later Sarah was outside Faircloths when the girls came out at the end of their shift. She tried to imagine Gerda working in this place, sitting over a sewing machine for long hours, making men's shirts, then coming out at the end of the day, tired but rejuvenated at the prospect of going dancing that evening and meeting a young man who might marry her and change her life.

Of course, changing her life might not necessarily have been a change for the better. She would most likely have traded her good times for life in a tenement apartment with too many children and too little money. Unfortunately, Gerda's only alternatives would have been prostitution and an early death or spinsterhood, living on the charity and goodwill of relatives. When Sarah thought of Lars Otto's potential for showing goodwill, she knew why women chose spinsterhood only when they had no other choice.

At first Sarah was afraid she might miss Gerda's friends in the crowd of girls pouring out of the building, but then she saw Bertha's outrageous hat with the red bird on top, and she called out to attract her attention. Bertha was surprised, and as Sarah had expected, she directed the attention of the other two girls, who were with her, to Sarah. They made their way over to where she stood beside the building.

"Mrs. Brandt, what're you doing here?" Lisle asked "Did you find out something?"

"Did you find the killer?" Bertha asked, saying what Lisle wouldn't.

"Not yet, which is why I need your help. Is there someplace we can go to talk? I'll treat you to supper," she added when the girls looked doubtful.

She knew that the girls frequently skipped lunch to have money for their frolics, and they eagerly accepted the invitation. They found a German beer garden nearby, where they feasted on bratwurst and sauerkraut and chunks of freshly baked bread.

"What do you want from us?" Lisle asked when they were settled at their table, heaping plates in front of them.

"I need to know the names of all the men that Gerda had been seeing right before she died," Sarah explained. "My friend Detective Malloy is going to question the friends of all the other murdered girls, too. We're going to try to narrow down the list of suspects to men that all the girls knew. Try to think of men who paid Gerda particular attention those last days."

The girls thought and argued. "He did so dance with her!" "No, he didn't!" It was a frustrating process, and Sarah was afraid it might be equally fruitless since evenings at the dance halls seemed to run together in their minds.

Still, she jotted down every name the girls mentioned in relation to Gerda, no matter how casual the contact. Sarah thought perhaps the killer wouldn't want to have been seen with the victim very much before the crime. Perhaps he'd kept their contact mostly private. The thought was discouraging. That would mean he was clever enough to hide his identity from everyone.

"And there was George, don't forget," Bertha reminded them. "He bought her that fancy hat."

Hetty nodded grimly. "George liked her a lot. He got mad one night when she danced with somebody else."

"What night was that?" Sarah asked, her interest quickened. "Was it near the time she died? Was it before or after he gave her the hat?"

"After, I think," Bertha said, glancing at Lisle, who was

frowning. Plainly, she didn't like the turn the conversation had taken.

Sarah waited for her verdict. "Yes, it was after," Lisle reluctantly recalled. "She was wearing the hat that night, I think. That's what started the fuss. George thought she should only dance with him, but she was tired of him."

"That's right," Hetty remembered. "She'd found somebody she liked better. He had more money to spend, too. He'd treated her to dinner at a real nice place, she said."

The other girls nodded.

"And George was jealous," Sarah guessed.

"I guess you could call it that," Bertha allowed as the girls exchanged a look.

"What do you mean?"

"It's not like George was in love with her or anything," Lisle explained. She sounded almost as if she were defending him. "He just . . . he wanted to . . ."

"She'd let him do it," Hetty said baldly when Lisle couldn't find the proper words. "He wanted to do it some more, but Gerda was finished with him once she got the hat."

"Was Gerda fickle?" Sarah asked.

The girls gave her a blank stare, not understanding.

"Did she often change her mind about which man she liked best?" Sarah tried.

"She never liked any of them," Bertha said. "Not really."

Lisle nodded her agreement. "She never cared for anybody much. She just went with anyone who could show her some fun."

"She liked a man who'd treat her," Hetty added. "The more he'd spend on her, the better she liked him."

"And she'd found someone more generous than George, so naturally, he was angry," Sarah said. "Do you know George's last name or where he lives?"

"He wouldn't kill anyone," Lisle said too quickly, and Sarah remembered that Lisle had also taken a gift from him. That meant she'd had a relationship with him, too. Did

Lisle have tender feelings for him? If so, she'd better tread softly.

"I didn't say I thought he was the killer," Sarah said. "But maybe he would remember who the other man was or know his name. We need to question everyone who might know anything at all. It's the only way we'll find Gerda's killer before he kills someone else."

This sobered them instantly. After a moment Lisle said, "I never heard George's last name."

"I think he said Smith, but that's probably a lie," Hetty said. "Sometimes they don't tell you their real names."

Sarah could believe that. She wrote "George Smith" with a question mark. "What else do you know about him?"

"He sells ladies notions to the stores in town. Siegel-Cooper, Ehrichs, Simpson-Crawford, Adams & Co., and O'Neils," Hetty said, naming all the big department stores on Sixth Avenue. "At least he claimed he did," she added.

"He had nice things in his sample case, that's certain," Lisle said. Sarah thought she sounded wistful.

"Have you seen him lately?" Sarah asked.

The girls tried to remember. "I don't think so," Bertha finally decided. The others agreed.

"He ain't been around since Gerda . . ." Lisle didn't have to finish the thought.

"Please let me know if you see him in any of the dance halls, won't you?" Sarah asked. "And it wouldn't hurt to ask around and find out if anyone knows more about him."

They looked grim now. Plainly, they didn't relish the role of detective the way Sarah did.

"Do you know any of the other girls who were killed?" she asked. "Well enough to know who their male companions might have been?"

They considered.

"I used to see Luisa at the dances sometimes," Hetty allowed.

The others weren't sure. Obviously, they weren't too interested in which other females attended the dances.

"Do you know any of their families?" Sarah asked. "Maybe you could introduce me."

"Why would you want to meet them?" Lisle asked.

"To find out what men they knew in common."

The girls looked at her pityingly. "Their families ain't likely to know such a thing," Lisle said. "You'd best ask their friends. Like us, that's who'd know."

They were right, of course.

"Do you know any of their friends, then?" she asked with a smile.

TWO MORE DAYS passed before Malloy came in response to the note she'd sent him. She was sitting in her backyard, savoring the cooler evening breeze and feeling awful because she'd lost a baby that afternoon. The cord had been wrapped around his throat, and he'd suffocated before ever seeing the world. Sarah knew there was nothing she could have done, no way she could have known or prevented it from happening, but she still hated failure. The mother had been inconsolable. She'd lost another one before this, too, a baby born before its time and too small to live. She had placed all her hopes on this one since she'd managed to carry it to term. The babe had been perfectly formed, too. All his fingers and toes and a face like an angel. But dead. Sarah had tried every trick she knew to revive him, but to no avail.

When she heard someone knocking on her door, she rose wearily, praying it wasn't someone summoning her to another birth. She didn't think she could face another possible tragedy today. Which made her actually happy to see Malloy on her front stoop.

He looked as formidable as ever in his wrinkled suit and bowler hat. His shirt needed a fresh collar. She thought of her father, always impeccably dressed. Felix Decker considered himself a force in the city, a man to be reckoned with because he had money and power. Sarah imagined he wouldn't last five minutes if Malloy decided to give him the third degree. The thought cheered her a little.

"Malloy, come in, and you'd better have some information. You kept me waiting long enough."

"It's always a pleasure to see you, too, Mrs. Brandt," he replied, and she thought she caught a twinkle in his eye as he passed her.

"I hope you let Mrs. Elsworth see you coming in here," she said, closing the door behind him. "She's a great admirer of yours."

"I doubt anybody comes in here without that old bat seeing them," Malloy said sourly, removing his hat. His dark hair was mussed, and he made an attempt to smooth it with his fingers, making it worse.

"Let's sit outside where it's cooler," she suggested. "I didn't have a chance to get any lemons today, so all I've got to offer is water or coffee."

"Water," Malloy said, probably thinking as she did that it was too hot for coffee, even though a freak storm the day before had dropped the temperature sixteen degrees in just a short while.

When they were seated at the table on her back porch, he reached into his coat and pulled out a small notebook. Sarah already had her notes in front of her.

"These girls knew a lot of men," he said.

"All we have to do is figure out which ones they *all* knew," Sarah reminded him.

"Except they might not have known the man's real name. Or maybe their friends didn't know they'd met the fellow or—"

"Stop being so discouraging, Malloy! Just show me the names you've gotten."

"I wouldn't think I'd need to show you anything, Mrs. Brandt. You've probably done more investigating than I have on this case."

"What do you mean?" Sarah asked, trying to sound innocent.

"You know what I mean. By the time I found some of these people, they'd already talked to you."

"I was only trying to help. I was afraid you wouldn't be able to find all the girls' friends."

"You could've just told me who they were."

"I was also trying to save you some time."

He gave her one of his looks. "Then you should've told me to stop investigating. I wasted a lot of time following in your footsteps."

He didn't seem too annoyed, though. He was only pretending. How and when she had become an expert on Malloy's moods, she had no idea. "Stop complaining, Malloy. I know you talked to a lot of people I didn't. Just as I talked to people you didn't. Let's see your list."

Malloy opened his notebook and handed it to her, then slid her papers over so he could look at them in turn.

Malloy's handwriting was surprisingly small and neat. "You wrote descriptions of the men," Sarah observed.

"A lot of them don't tell the girls their last names. Do you know how many men there are in the city named Frank? I didn't want you thinking I was the killer just because my name turned up on the list."

Sarah looked at him in amazement. His expression was bland, and he was pretending to study her list. Since when had he developed a sense of humor?

"That's a good idea," she admitted. "The descriptions, I mean. That way we'd know immediately if any of these fellows with the same names are the same men."

"Except there aren't a lot of men with the same names."

Sarah had noticed this also. "I made a chart, you see?" she said, pointing to a piece of paper on which she had made four columns, one for each of the dead girls. In each column, she had listed the names of all the men their friends had mentioned. She hadn't done as thorough an investigation as Malloy, of course. She hadn't questioned any friends of Eva Bower, for instance, because the girls hadn't known her. Luisa Isenberg had been fairly easy since she worked at Faircloths and the girls knew her friends. She'd found only a few people who knew Fredrika Lutz. Sarah picked up a pencil and began filling in her chart with the names Malloy had gleaned from his interviews. When she was finished, she made a startling discovery.

"There isn't one single name that appears on all four lists!"

"That would make this job easy, Mrs. Brandt. If it was that easy, they wouldn't need someone with my abilities to solve cases," he told her smugly.

Sarah had to admit he was probably right, even though she could see it gave him great satisfaction that she knew it. "All right, Mr. Detective Sergeant, what do we do now?"

He gloated for a moment, but only for a moment. "We pick out the names that occur most often. Then I find the men—or as many of them as I can—and ask them where they were when these girls were murdered."

"They're hardly likely to remember," Sarah pointed out. "Except for Gerda, the killings happened weeks and even months ago."

"You're right. The average person won't remember where he was on a particular evening even just a week ago, at least not without giving the manner some serious thought. But the killer will know exactly where he was on those evenings. Unless he's very clever, he'll make up alibis for those evenings. He'll pretend to remember exactly where he was those nights and give me an elaborate story to explain it."

Sarah was amazed. "So being clever can be a trap in itself."

"If the police are even more clever."

He was enjoying this too much. "But what if the killer is very smart, too. What if he's smart enough to know he shouldn't be able to remember where he was on a particular night three months ago?"

"Killers aren't that smart, Mrs. Brandt. If they were, they wouldn't be killers."

Sarah certainly hoped he was right, but so far the killer had behaved with unusual intelligence. He'd chosen girls whose deaths would excite no interest in the police and who moved in social circles where they encountered numerous unfamiliar males. He'd killed them far enough apart that no one noticed the connection between the deaths until now, and that was only by accident. He may even have given his victims a false name or made certain the victims' friends didn't see them together. If no one knew they were acquainted, then no one could name him as a suspect. But Malloy had said killers weren't that smart, or they wouldn't be killers in the first place. She clung to that.

Looking over the list, she saw the name George was on three of the lists. "I don't know what he looks like, but remember I told you that Gerda's friends said a man name George was the one who gave her a new hat right before she died. I just found out he also got angry when she danced with another man right before she was killed."

"Jealousy is sometimes a motive for murder, but in this case, I'm not so sure."

"This man must have *some* reason for killing these girls. Maybe he imagines himself in love with them, and when they take up with someone else, he gets insanely jealous and kills them out of revenge."

"Maybe," was all Malloy would give her. "Do you know this George's last name?"

"The girls said they thought it was Smith. They did say they weren't sure it was his real name, though," she added at his skeptical expression.

"George Smith. That narrows it down to about a thousand men in the city."

Sarah ignored his sarcasm. "He sells ladies' notions to the big department stores. He has a sample case, and from what I understand, when a girl allows him, uh, certain liberties, he offers her a gift from its contents."

She'd embarrassed him, although he was trying valiantly not to show it. The flush crawled up his neck, however, betraying him. "Is that all it takes now? A bit of ribbon or a pair of gloves?" He was appalled.

"I'm sure it takes more than that. Gerda got a hat, don't forget."

"And a pair of red shoes. Did this George buy them for her?"

"The girls didn't think so. Seems Gerda took up with another man right before she died, but they never saw him. He spent money on her rather freely, so she gave George the gate. That's when George got angry. I think you'd do well to question him, at least."

Malloy just grunted and continued to look over the list. Sarah wished she'd gotten descriptions for the men on her list. She hadn't even thought to ask for a description of George. It seemed so obvious now that she'd need to know what he looked like. Or rather that Malloy would.

He was making a new list of the names that occurred on three of the lists. A good place to start, she reasoned, when she heard the gate open.

"Oh, Mrs. Brandt, I'm so sorry. I didn't know you had company." Mrs. Elsworth didn't look a bit sorry. In fact, she looked as satisfied as a cat with its head in the cream pitcher. "Good evening, Detective Sergeant."

Malloy rose reluctantly to his feet as Mrs. Elsworth made her way through the flowers to the back-porch steps. "Good evening," he replied without the slightest trace of warmth.

"Oh, Mrs. Brandt, you'll think me such a ninny, but this message came for you this morning, and I completely forgot about it." She had a piece of paper in her hand that Sarah longed to snatch, but there was no point in being rude. Mrs. Elsworth would give it to her in due time. "I should've known," she was saying. "I dropped a fork this morning. You know that saying, 'knife falls, gentleman calls; fork falls, lady calls.' "

Sarah didn't know the saying, but she nodded anyway. "Are you saying a lady called for me?"

"Oh, gracious, yes. I thought I'd said that. And she left this message."

"I hope it isn't a message about a baby being born." That would be a disaster.

"Oh, no, of course not. I told her right away that you were out on a delivery, and heaven only knew when you'd return. Babies keep their own schedule, don't you know. But she said it wasn't about a baby, and she just wanted to leave a message. She didn't look like the sort of person who usually calls on you, if you don't mind my saying so, but she was such a little thing, I didn't believe her to be dangerous. I let her come in and write you a note, and then I forgot all about it until just this moment."

At last she handed over the missive to Sarah, who unfolded it quickly. The spelling was poor, but she had no trouble deciphering the message. It was from Lisle. "One of Gerda's friends saw George at a dance hall last night," she told Malloy.

When she looked up, Mrs. Elsworth was waiting expectantly. "Thank you so much, Mrs. Elsworth. This is a very important message. I wouldn't have wanted to miss receiving it."

"I hope its being late didn't do any damage," she said with a worried frown.

"None at all," Sarah assured her. "Thank you so much for delivering it. You've been a big help."

Sarah was trying to dismiss her, but she didn't want to be dismissed. She wanted to know what they were talking about, and she kept trying see what was on the papers scattered over Sarah's table.

"We don't want to keep you from anything, Mrs. Elsworth," Malloy said. His tone was unmistakable. He wanted her gone.

Her face fell, making Sarah sorry. Mrs. Elsworth was lonely, and her life held little pleasure and absolutely no excitement. Sharing Sarah's life was one of her few enjoyments. But Sarah couldn't share this part of it. "If I don't get a call tomorrow, perhaps you'll come over for lunch," she suggested, softening the rejection.

That seemed to placate her somewhat. "I'll make a pie," she offered. "I'll go to the market first thing tomorrow and see what fruit they have. Good night, Detective Sergeant. Such a pleasure to see you again."

Malloy did not return the compliment. He waited a few minutes after the gate had closed behind her to say, "Let me see the note."

The message was brief. Plainly, Lisle wasn't used to writing formal letters. She had seen George at Harmony Hall the previous night and had come by before going to her job at Faircloths this morning to let Sarah know.

"She says she told him to meet her again tonight," Sarah said. "There's a dance at the same place."

"Do they have dances every night?" Malloy asked, unable to comprehend such a thing.

"It appears they do. And that's just one hall. There are others all over the city."

Malloy looked up from the note. "You think this George is the killer, don't you?"

Sarah hoped he was. She wanted the killer caught quickly, before he could harm anyone else. "I think he may know something," she allowed. "He was angry because Gerda had taken up with another man. Maybe he knows who that man was, at least."

Malloy sighed. "I suppose you want to go out right now and find him."

Sarah smiled sweetly. "Oh, no. The dance won't start for at least another hour."

"YOU CAN'T GO in with me, you know," Sarah said as they approached Harmony Hall. The usual assortment of flashily dressed young men were gathered on the walk at the bottom of the steps, surveying the young women as they arrived.

Malloy cast her an impatient glance. "How am I supposed to question this George fellow if I don't?"

"I'm not sure. I think perhaps we should get Lisle to lure him outside. In any case, he can't see you first. I'm afraid you're just too intimidating, Malloy, and besides, you don't look like you belong in a place like this. You'll frighten away all the patrons."

He looked like he was going to argue with her, but just then the fellows lingering outside the dance hall got a look at Malloy, and they scattered like pigeons, ducking and dodging in every direction.

Malloy frowned, and Sarah said smugly, "You see what I mean? You just look too much like a policeman. You frighten people."

"Only people with something to hide," Malloy argued.

"Maybe this George has something to hide."

Malloy grunted his acceptance.

When they reached the stairs up to the dance hall, Sarah looked around the neighborhood. "We need to decide where we'll meet you."

"*We?*" he asked. "I thought this Lisle girl was going to bring him out. And don't expect to stand around and watch me question this George fellow. You don't have the stomach for it."

Sarah could have argued that point. She'd seen people die in hideous ways during her years of nursing and midwifery, so her stomach was quite strong. But he probably wasn't talking about that sort of thing. She wouldn't approve of his tactics, which she imagined could be quite violent if necessary. If so, then he was right, she didn't have the stomach for it.

"What kind of a place do you need for your interrogation?" she asked. "Is an alley all right?"

"Anyplace out of sight," he replied, also scanning the area for an appropriate spot. "I'll wait in the bar across the street. I'll sit near the front window so I can see them come out."

"You don't know what they look like," Sarah reminded

him. "I'll come out just before or just after them and catch your eye. Then we can follow them until you see a suitable place to . . . to do whatever you need to do."

Malloy didn't like accepting her plan, but it made so much sense, he couldn't argue with it. "All right, but don't think you're going to watch me question him."

Sarah smiled sweetly, then started up the stairs to the dance hall. The music was loud and discordant, and the hall was already crowded and smoky and unbearably hot. The bouncer took her admission fee, but his expression told her he found her presence in a place like this very strange indeed.

Sarah took a moment to allow her eyes to grow accustomed to the darkness of the hall. Then she was able to find Lisle and the other girls sitting at a table on the other side of the room. She made her way over to them, drawing curious glances as she moved through the crowd. Feeling conspicuously out of place, Sarah finally reached the table where Lisle, Hetty, and Bertha sat.

Hetty and Bertha were looking grim, and Lisle was smoking furiously on a cigarette. Sarah noticed her hand was less than steady when she brought it to her lips to take a drag.

"You shouldn't've made her do this," Hetty told Sarah as she took the empty chair at the table. "She's scared silly!"

"Shut up, Hetty," Lisle said, glaring at her friend, even as she took another puff of the cigarette. "I ain't scared. I'm just nervous."

"If you don't want to do it, I can go tell Malloy that—"

"I *do* want to do it!" Lisle insisted, throwing the butt of her cigarette to the floor and grinding it out with the toe of her shoe. "Don't you want to know who killed Gerda?" she demanded of the other girls.

Their gazes dropped. Sarah wasn't sure if it was shame or fear that cowed them. She only hoped whatever it was wouldn't interfere with the investigation.

"I told my friend Detective Sergeant Malloy that when Lisle leaves the hall with George—"

"You mean she's got to go out with him? What if he's the killer?" Bertha wailed.

"Shush!" Hetty said, looking around nervously in case they had been overheard. Fortunately, the music was so loud, they could hardly even hear each other.

"Mr. Malloy is waiting downstairs," Sarah hurried to explain. "He'll follow Lisle and George, then he'll confront George and question him. After I take Lisle away," she hastened to add when Bertha would have protested again, "I'll either follow them outside or go out ahead of them. That way I can point them out to Mr. Malloy. They won't get far, and Lisle will never be alone with him."

The girls didn't seem reassured. Lisle looked around and saw a young man passing their table. "Got a smoke?" she asked with a brittle smile.

He was only too delighted to offer her a cigarette and light it for her. But when he made as if to sit down and join them, she turned away with a faint, "Thanks. See you later."

Stung, he moved away, looking back once with an angry glare. Sarah imagined she saw murder in his eyes. She was becoming much too suspicious lately.

"Have you seen George? Is he here yet?" Sarah asked.

The girls shook their heads. A young man with buckteeth and freckles came over and asked Bertha to dance. She went reluctantly and only after Lisle told her to. A few minutes later another fellow came and asked Hetty to dance. Left alone with Lisle, Sarah watched her smoke the second cigarette down until it was too small to hold any longer. She ground it out with a ferocity that made Sarah wince.

"There's nothing to be afraid of," Sarah tried. "Mr. Malloy won't let you out of his sight."

"I ain't afraid," Lisle snapped, her fragile face rigid with whatever emotions she was feeling. "Not of George, anyways. He won't hurt me. He'd of done it before now if he was going to. I just don't like tricking him like this. And what's that copper friend of yours going to do to him? What if he don't know who killed Gerda?"

Before Sarah could answer, a young man approached them. He was moderately tall and solidly built with the cheerful, open face of a born salesman. If his suit was loud, it was also well made and fit him perfectly. His hair was slicked back with pomade beneath his bowler hat, and his cheeks were clean-shaven. His smile revealed strong, even teeth.

"Lisle, my darling girl, sorry I'm late. The trolley jumped the track, and I had to walk most of the way up from . . . Oh, hello there, miss," he said, noticing Sarah.

"This is my friend Sarah," Lisle said without looking at her.

"George Smith," he said, tipping his hat. "Pleased to meet you." His expression told her he was trying to figure out what a woman like her was doing in a place like this. With Lisle. She simply smiled serenely, trying to picture him beating a young woman to death. The picture simply would not form in her mind.

"Thank you," she said, almost shouting to make herself heard above the music.

George pulled one of the other chairs a little closer to Lisle's and sat down. "You look down in the mouth, kiddo. What's wrong?"

"I'm tired of this place. Can we go somewhere else?" She didn't sound very enthusiastic at the prospect, and George must have been a little suspicious. He glanced at Sarah as if trying to figure something out.

"Don't worry about me," Sarah said. "I was just leaving myself."

"I wouldn't want to run you off," he said with his too friendly smile. "The night's just starting."

"Not for me, I'm afraid." Sarah got up, looking at Lisle to make sure she was going to be all right. The girl's chin rose a notch, and she met Sarah's gaze steadily.

"You go on," she said. "Don't worry none about me. I'll be fine now George is here."

"Very nice meeting you, Mr. Smith," Sarah said to George, who stood politely and nodded. He was still puzzled, trying to figure out who Sarah was and why she was here, but he would get no satisfaction from her.

By the time Sarah reached the relative quiet of the street outside, she felt her own tension quivering along every nerve ending. No wonder Lisle was so nervous.

She walked straight across the street, dodging the late-evening traffic, to the bar where Malloy said he would wait, giving him ample time to see her. Then she paused, looking up and down the street as if trying to decide which way to go. A moment later Malloy was at her side.

"Did you see him?"

"Yes, and I think he and Lisle will be coming out in just a moment. Where can we hide so he doesn't see me watching for him?"

"No need to hide," he said, taking her arm and guiding her to the next building. He put her back against it and stood in front of her, facing her, as if they were enjoying a very private conversation. He put his arm up, bracing his hand against the wall beside her head so her face would be shielded from anyone coming from the direction of the dance hall.

She looked up at Malloy, his face only inches from hers. She could see the tiny hairs where his beard was starting to grow. How odd she'd never noticed before but his eyes weren't solid brown. They had gold flecks in them.

"Do you see them yet?" he asked. His voice sounded a little hoarse. Or maybe she was just being fanciful.

Obediently, she glanced under his arm. People were going into the hall, a group of young men who had obviously been drinking. They were laughing and shoving each other playfully as they unsteadily climbed the steps. Seconds ticked by with agonizing slowness. Sarah was very aware of Malloy. The evening was warm, but it had grown considerably warmer in the past few minutes.

Sarah tried to draw a breath and found her lungs didn't want to cooperate. Just when she thought she would have to duck under Malloy's arm and flee or lose her sanity, she saw them.

"There they are!" she cried with as much relief as triumph.

7

MALLOY GLANCED OVER HIS SHOULDER AND saw a man and a woman—well, a girl, actually—coming down the steps. The girl was small and slender, her hair blond under the oversized hat she wore. The man was dressed the way he'd seen countless salesmen dressed, in a suit tailored more for flash than for style. Apparently, salesmen thought they had to make an indelible impression on people, even if the impression was one of tawdriness.

The fellow had the girl's hand tucked into the crook of his arm, and they turned in the opposite direction from where he and Mrs. Brandt were standing. He should give them a minute to get a start. If he followed them right off, it would look suspicious.

He could hear Mrs. Brandt breathing. Her breath came quickly. Probably she was frightened. This sort of thing wasn't something a midwife usually did in the course of her work. Maybe she was even worried some harm might come to the girl. It was possible, he supposed, but not very likely, not with Frank on his tail.

Frank could feel her breath on his cheek. He could feel the sweat forming all over his body. The night was warm, but not that warm. He was just standing too close to Mrs. Brandt was all. He'd fix that in a minute. There, they were turning the corner.

"Come on," he said, pushing himself away from the wall with a sense of relief. Action, that's what he needed. Anything to distract him from thoughts he shouldn't be thinking.

He didn't wait to see if she was coming. She'd be with him every step of the way. He knew he'd probably have to force her to leave when they caught up with George, too. She'd want to hear everything he had to say. Well, he'd deal with that, too.

He started down the sidewalk in the direction they had gone, watching the traffic for a break so they could cross and follow the other couple. Unconsciously, he reached for her arm, clasping it tightly so she would be with him when he saw an opportunity to cross. It came unexpectedly, a break between two wagons, and he fairly dragged her across the street, just barely missing a pile of horse manure.

She was sputtering a little, but he ignored that. He let go of her arm, and by then they were at the corner. He could see the couple walking up ahead, heading downtown. The girl was still clinging to his arm. Was she looking back? Damn her, she'd tip him off that they were being followed!

No, wait, she was just talking to him. He was leaning down to hear her better. She was pointing, and he reacted in some surprise, but he followed her lead. They disappeared into an alley.

"Smart girl," Frank said in approval to Mrs. Brandt, who was struggling to keep up with him.

"I think I'm starting to understand why there are no female police officers," she said breathlessly. "It's too hard to keep up the chase in skirts."

He tried not to smile, but he couldn't help it. They were almost to the alley into which the other couple had disappeared. He pulled up short and caught her arm again.

"Stay here," he warned. "When the girl comes out, take

her away. I don't care where you go, just get away from here."

"Will Lisle be in danger after this?" she asked, new fears widening her eyes and flushing her cheeks. Or maybe it was just the chase that had flushed her cheeks.

"Not if he isn't the killer, and if he *is* the killer, then I'll arrest him, so no, don't worry about her. She'll be safe. I just don't want either of you around when I question him. Do you understand?"

She didn't like it, but she nodded. And she stayed put when he went into the alley. Thank God for that.

The evening shadows were long now, and no sunlight entered here even at midday. Frank needed a moment to accustom himself to the darkness. He didn't need his eyes to find them, though. He could hear the sounds of their kissing from here. Either the girl was really enthusiastic or she was making sure Frank found them. Considering she thought this fellow might've killed her friend, Frank thought it was probably the latter.

George muttered something Frank couldn't understand. He carefully picked his way through the piles of trash, trying not to alert George before he was in a position to overpower him. By the time he was close enough, however, he realized George probably wouldn't have noticed a brass band marching by.

"Hello there, George," Frank said amiably, startling the fellow as he grabbed his arm and twisted it behind his back.

"What the he—" he cried, ending on a gasp of pain as Frank nearly wrenched his shoulder from its socket.

The girl cried out, but whether it was from fear or in protest, he didn't particularly care. "Get out of here," he told her. "Go on now, run."

She hesitated a moment, looking at George's grimace of pain, but she apparently decided to obey him. She darted away. Frank figured Mrs. Brandt would catch her up and take care of her. At any rate, she was no longer his concern.

"Are you her father?" George said, his voice high with

terror. "Stepfather, I mean. Look, it's not what you think!"

"How do you know what I think?" Frank inquired genially as he smashed George's face into the brick wall.

"Owww!" he cried, but he didn't struggle. He had more sense than that. "She was willing!" he tried. "I didn't force her. It was even her idea!"

"That's not exactly what a father wants to hear, George," Frank said. "Maybe you should try a different story." He gave George's arm a little pull.

"Owww! I didn't mean no harm!"

"What *did* you mean, then, bringing a girl into an alley like that?" Frank asked, his voice still friendly, even if his actions were not. "Maybe you had something in mind. Like maybe you were going to start hitting her."

"Hitting her?" he gasped in surprise. "Why would I do that?"

"Oh, maybe because you hate her. You hate all women, don't you, George? You think they all deserve to die."

"*Die?* What're you talking about? Who are you?" he was starting to sound frantic now.

"I'm Detective Sergeant Frank Malloy of the New York City police, and I'm investigating the deaths of several young women in the city."

"What do you want with me, then?" he asked, his words distorted because Frank was pressing his face a little harder into the bricks. And because he was terrified.

"Because you knew them. You knew all of them," Frank said, exaggerating a bit for effect. "And we know you bought at least one of them a gift right before she died. Also very interesting, she was killed right after you got angry because she danced with someone else one night."

"Who . . . ? Gerda? Is that who you mean?" He sounded almost relieved. "You think I killed her?"

"The thought did cross my mind, especially after I heard you got into a fight with her over her seeing another man."

"If that's all you want, you can let me go." He sounded

relieved. "You don't have to hurt me anymore. I'll tell you whatever you want to know."

"Why don't you get started, then, and when I've heard something I like, I'll think about letting you go." He gave George's arm a little twist that made him shudder with pain.

"I did give her a hat," he said quickly, his voice high again and much faster. He was in a hurry to get this over. "She and I . . . Well, she earned it, is all I can say. She liked pretty things and was willing to do whatever it took to get them."

"It's not very gentlemanly to talk about a lady like that, George," he chastised him.

"Gerda was no lady," he said. "You can ask anybody."

"Maybe I will. So you bought her this hat, and then she found somebody with more brass and gave you the gate."

"Made me mad!" George admitted. "One day she was my girl, and the next day she wouldn't even dance with me. Said she found somebody could give her even nicer things. Showed me these red shoes he'd give her. They wasn't even good quality! I know quality. That's one thing I know. But she didn't care. They was flashy. That's all she cared about. She never cared a fig for me."

"Did you care a fig for her?" Frank asked.

George didn't want to answer that one until Frank gave him a little encouragement. "I liked her all right," he admitted on a gasp of pain. "She was a lot of fun when she felt like it."

"And when she didn't feel like it anymore, you took her into an alley and beat her to death."

"*No!* I never touched her! I never even saw her after that! She went off with some fellow, and I never saw her again. Nobody did. That's the night she got killed."

"Who was the fellow?"

"I don't know. She never said his name."

"What did he look like?"

"I never saw him!"

"And I suppose you can account for your whereabouts for the rest of that night."

"I . . . I don't . . . I stayed at the dance hall until it closed, I think. Then I went home."

"Alone?"

"I think so. I can't remember! I was mad at Gerda, and I drank too much."

"So much you might not remember beating her to death?"

"No! I never touched her! I swear it!"

Frank released him with a disgusted shove. He fell against the wall, caught himself, and straightened slowly, rubbing his face and hugging his injured arm to him.

"I didn't kill her. I swear it!" he tried.

"What about Eva Bower? I guess you didn't kill her either."

"Who?"

"Eva Bower. Her friends said you'd been paying her particular attention right before she turned up dead."

"I don't . . . Eva, you say?" He honestly didn't remember.

"Her friends said you bought her a hat. I assume she earned it the same way Gerda did."

"Eva?" he repeated, still trying to recall. "Oh, yeah, peacock feathers! She wanted one with peacock feathers! Now I remember. She was . . . Did you say she was *dead*?" He was incredulous.

"Yes, I did. She died the same way Gerda did. Last winter. Not too long after you bought her the hat with the peacock feathers."

"I hadn't seen her around, but I didn't know anything had happened to her. Girls come and go, you see. They come to the dance halls for a while, until they get a steady fellow. Then they don't need to go anymore. I thought she . . . I never heard about her being dead!" He sounded aggrieved.

"Well, she is. Just like Luisa Isenberg and Fredrika Lutz."

"I don't . . . no, wait, I remember Luisa. Big girl with yellow curls?"

Frank thought it a rather unflattering description, but he said, "That's right."

"She didn't get a hat. Just some glass beads. She wouldn't . . . Well, you know."

Frank knew, but he didn't say so. He was too disgusted.

"Did you say Luisa is dead, too?" George asked.

"Yeah, just like Fredrika. And what about Fredrika? What did she earn?"

George was still rubbing his face, and he paused, thinking. "I don't remember her. Are you sure I knew her? What did she look like?"

"Maybe I could find out what kind of hat you bought her. Would that help?" Frank asked sarcastically.

His sarcasm was wasted. "I don't think so. I don't think I knew anybody named Fredrika. I would've remembered. My father's name is Fredrick, you see, and it would've made an impression."

Frank had to resist the urge to punch him just on general principles. He wouldn't be of any use if he was unconscious. "How many girls have gotten hats from you, George?"

"I don't keep a count," he said, a little insulted.

"Maybe you should, since so many of them have turned up dead."

"I never knew that Fredrika, so you can't say I . . . Do you think I killed them *all*?" He was horrified. "Good God, what kind of a man do you think I am?"

"The kind who goes around seducing and abandoning as many young girls as he can find."

"I don't seduce them!" Now he was outraged. "Most of the time, they suggest it first! They know I'll give them something nice. The hats are expensive. I get them at cost, but they don't know that. It's the only way they can get pretty things."

"So they trade their virtue for a present."

"It's not like that! They . . . I never took a girl who was a virgin. They ain't innocent, if that's what you're thinking. They ain't looking for romance. It's a business with them."

"Just like it is with you," Frank pointed out. "I guess you brag to your friends that you never have to pay for it, too."

He was insulted again. "Nobody forces them to do it."

Frank had his own opinions about that, but he kept them to himself. He wasn't getting anywhere discussing the reasons these girls did what they did. He wanted to know why someone had killed them.

"So you don't have an alibi for the night Gerda was killed."

"I told you, I stayed at the dance hall. Lots of people saw me there."

"Lots of people who won't remember one night from the other. And what about the nights the other girls were murdered?"

"I don't even know what nights you mean! I didn't even know they was dead!" He was whining now, like a whipped dog. Frank wanted to stuff him into one of the ash cans and leave him here with the rest of the trash. If he did, no one would even care. No one except Sarah Brandt, who wouldn't want to see an innocent man punished, no matter how despicable he might be.

Frank sighed, defeated. "Maybe you ought to be careful for a while, George," he said. "Seems like the girls you play dip the wick with have a nasty habit of turning up dead."

"Not all of them," he protested. "There's been dozens that're still alive and kicking. Ask that girl I was with tonight, Lisle. She'll tell you!"

That was all Frank could stand. Even Sarah Brandt would forgive him for this. He drove his fist into George's soft stomach, hitting him neatly in the spot just beneath his ribs that would leave him gasping helplessly for breath and certain he was going to die, but do no actual harm.

As he doubled over and slumped to the filthy ground, Frank said, "You should learn a little respect for young ladies, George. It would serve you well."

NIGHT HAD FALLEN completely by the time Frank got to Sarah Brandt's house. He didn't ask himself why he had gone directly there after finishing with George. He didn't really want to know the reason. He just knew he wanted to tell her what he'd learned. She'd be anxious to know.

He wasn't even sure if she'd be there. She might have taken Lisle home first. She might not have gotten back yet. She might even have been summoned to deliver a baby somewhere. But when he turned onto Bank Street, he saw a light in her front window. For a moment he wondered if he should go inside. What would her neighbors think? The old biddy next door would certainly see him, even if no one else did.

On the other hand, strange men probably came to her door at all hours of the day and night to summon her to birthings. His presence could hardly shock anyone.

She looked pleased to see him, but she put her finger to her lips, indicating he should be quiet. "I brought Lisle home with me," she whispered. "She didn't get any sleep last night for worrying about meeting George tonight. She was so exhausted, she almost fell asleep in the chair, so I made her lie down in my bed. I think if we go out in the backyard, we won't bother her, though."

He followed her through the shadowy house, enjoying the odd sense of intimacy their silence created. He was beginning to feel too comfortable in her home. He'd have to make sure this case didn't drag on much longer. He'd have to stop seeing her very soon if he hoped to be able to resume his old life again without regrets.

Her backyard was cooler than the house, if only a little. The flowers masked the stench of the summer city, and only when Frank settled into one of the wicker chairs with a sigh did he realize how weary he was.

"I'll be right back," she said, and disappeared into the house. When she returned, she carried a bottle and a glass. She poured him a shot of whiskey. "You sounded like you needed it," she said by way of explanation.

Although he usually avoided the stuff, tonight he made an exception. He downed it gratefully, in one swallow.

She waited until he had to ask, "Is George the killer?"

"I don't think so. In fact, I don't think he knew one of the girls at all. It's that, or he's a very good liar."

"That's possible, isn't it?"

"Of course. He might have killed all four girls and more besides that we don't know about and be able to lie right in my face about it. There's men can do that. Not many of them, though, thank God, or we'd never catch any criminals at all. They all lie. It's just that most of them aren't very good at it."

"Does he remember where he was the night Gerda was killed?"

"Says he stayed at the dance hall. Nobody's likely to remember whether he did or not, since one night's pretty much like another at those places, so he doesn't have a good alibi."

"Which is just what you said would be the case with an innocent man."

Frank rubbed his chin, surprised at the growth of beard there. He should've gotten a shave before meeting her this evening. "Or a very clever killer."

"What do you think?"

"He doesn't strike me as very clever."

She sighed. "I guess I was foolish to think it would be so easy."

"There's nothing wrong with hoping. Sometimes it *is* that easy."

"But not very often, or else they wouldn't need men like

you to be detectives," she said, teasing him with his own words.

He couldn't argue.

"Lisle is a little worried that George might take some revenge on her," she said.

"She can tell him she didn't know anything about it. He's not clever enough to doubt her."

"I'll be sure she knows. She's very frightened."

"Good. Maybe it will save her life."

She sat back in her chair, swallowed up in the shadows. For a long moment they simply sat there, listening to the night sounds of the city. He was just thinking he should take his leave when she said, "What's the next step?"

"I'll try to find the other men on the list. The ones who were on three of the four lists, that is. I'll question them and see if I suspect any of them are lying."

"And what can I do in the meantime?"

He'd meant to say "nothing." It was the only sensible thing to say. Instead, he heard himself saying, "Can you tell me just exactly where that deaf school you told me about is?"

SARAH KNEW MALLOY would not approve of her questioning the friends of the other dead girls again. The problem was, she couldn't just sit by and wait to hear from Malloy again. Luckily, she had insisted on copying the list of suspects over more neatly for Malloy, and she had kept the original. Which meant she also had a list of the names of the men the dead girls had been seeing just prior to their deaths. The list was shorter now that they had virtually eliminated George. That left only three names. Sarah thought if she could find out some more about these men, perhaps she could figure out the most likely suspect. She was certain that someone who had murdered four women must have some notable characteristic that would distinguish him from normal men.

She only hoped she was right about that.

Sarah had sent Luisa Isenberg's sister, Ella, a note asking if she could call on her the following day. She'd also asked if the sister could gather Luisa's friends to answer a few more questions. She was disappointed to find only Ella and one other girl waiting for her at the beer garden when she arrived the next evening.

"Nobody else wants to talk about it anymore," Ella explained when Sarah had greeted them and sat down at the table. Ella was a plump girl with unruly curls which she tried unsuccessfully to tame into the latest style of smooth pompadour.

"They think it'll be bad luck or something," the other girl said. Her name was Ingrid, and she had been of little help the first time Sarah had questioned Luisa's friends.

"I know it's difficult talking about all of it again," Sarah said, trying to sound sympathetic when she was really feeling impatient. "But I have some new information, and I was hoping you could help me figure out what it means."

"New information?" Ingrid asked, glancing at Ella uncertainly.

"Yes, we made a list of all the men who had been . . . uh . . . seeing the girls right before they died. We were hoping to find one man who had known all of them. We didn't, but we found several who knew most of them. I was wondering if you can tell me anything about these three men. Their names are Donald, Robert, and Will."

"I know three fellows named Robert," Ella said with a frown.

Sarah tried not to let her frustration show. "We're looking for the one you said was interested in Luisa right before she died."

"I never knew she was seeing nobody named Robert," Ella protested.

Someone else must have given Malloy this name. She checked the list. "He's tall with brown hair and a handlebar mustache."

"Oh, that's most likely Bobby," Ingrid said. "At least, I

call him that. He ain't the one you're looking for, though. He got married two months ago, right after Luisa . . ."

"Oh, I remember him now," Ella agreed. "Ain't seen him around the dances since then."

This might well eliminate him from having known Gerda, but Sarah knew Malloy would want to check this out. She went on to the other two. "What about Donald and Will, then? Do you remember either of them?"

Donald's name hadn't appeared on Luisa's list, but Sarah figured it was worth a chance. They considered the question for a moment.

"I heard some girls talking once . . ." Ella began, trailing off when Sarah leaned forward eagerly. She forced herself to relax and smile.

"Yes?" she said encouragingly.

Ella glanced at Ingrid as if gauging her reaction. "I only heard this, mind you. I don't know nothing about this fellow myself."

"Any information will help," Sarah assured her.

Still, she hesitated, then leaned forward so no one would overhear what she said. "I heard some fellow named Will was a little . . . rough."

"What do you mean, rough?" Sarah asked, keeping her voice low as well.

Ingrid's eyes were wide as she listened.

Ella glanced around, making sure no one was near. The noise in the hall would easily cover anything she said. "When he didn't like something, he'd . . . well, he'd slap a girl around a bit. Nothing serious," she hastened to explain, as if slapping a girl around at all wasn't serious. "He didn't really hurt her. Just scare her a little so she'd . . . she'd do whatever he wanted."

Sarah felt the surge of excitement and forced it down. She didn't want to frighten Ella with her enthusiasm. "Do you remember who told you about this Will?"

"No." The answer came too quickly and too certainly.

Ella knew perfectly well, but she wasn't going to say, at least not in front of Ingrid.

"What else do you know about him? Do you know what he looked like?"

"Good-looking, I heard. Nice clothes, but I don't know more than that. Oh, he always had plenty of money to spend, too. But that's all I know."

Sarah fought back a sigh. She didn't want Ella to think she was disappointed. Actually, the information was quite valuable. There just wasn't enough of it.

"I remember!" Ingrid said suddenly and a bit loudly, startling herself. She looked around quickly to see if anyone else had noticed. No one had.

"What do you remember?" Sarah asked.

"Will. I remember now. Luisa met him at Coney Island. She talked about it for weeks. Said he spent more than five dollars on her that day!"

Five dollars would have been almost a week's salary for Luisa, and a lot of money for a working man as well.

Ella's expression was tight and disapproving. "Shut your mouth! You don't know anything about it."

"Yes, I do!" Ingrid insisted indignantly. "He gave her a present, too, I think. What was it, now?" She screwed up her face as she tried to remember.

"Luisa didn't take presents from men," Ella informed her in a tone that allowed for no argument.

Now Sarah understood. If Luisa had taken gifts from men, that would make her a Charity Girl. Ella didn't want her sister's reputation harmed any more than it had been already.

Ingrid glared at Ella, but Ella wouldn't back down. Her sister wasn't going to be labeled a whore.

"Do you think she saw him again after that day at Coney Island?" Sarah asked carefully.

Ingrid glanced at Ella before replying. "I wouldn't know," was all she would say.

Sarah turned to Ella. "If you remember anything else

about him, please let me know. It could help catch Luisa's killer," she reminded them. She only hoped that was incentive enough.

FRANK KNEW HE was probably going to make a fool of himself. He didn't know the first thing about schools or education, particularly education for children who were deaf. And his son was deaf. He'd confirmed that with a trip to a doctor—a doctor Sarah Brandt had said was competent enough to make a judgment—who'd said nothing could be done for Brian's hearing. Born deaf. That was the final verdict.

He'd been interested in Brian's foot, too, but Frank wasn't going to let just any doctor take care of that. When he felt he had built up enough credit with Mrs. Brandt that she owed him a favor, he'd ask her to make him an appointment to see her surgeon friend. Until then, he was going to see what he could find out about educating a deaf child.

Not that he believed a deaf child could be educated. If you couldn't hear, how could you learn to do anything else? And of course Brian also couldn't speak, which made it impossible for him to make himself understood, either. The whole thing seemed pretty hopeless to Frank, but he was willing to find out more. Maybe there was something he didn't know. One or two things, anyway, he thought with some self-directed amusement. He hadn't known there were schools for the deaf, for instance. Mrs. Brandt had him on that one.

The sign over the door on Lexington Avenue said NEW YORK INSTITUTE FOR THE IMPROVED INSTRUCTION OF DEAF MUTES. Deaf Mutes. That was Brian, all right. Frank liked the way it said "improved," though. That must mean they used the best methods here.

Inside, the place was eerily quiet. The halls were empty and still, which he supposed was the way any school was when classes were in session. Here, of course, there would be no need for noise at all, since the students couldn't hear it anyway. He entered the first room he came to, which was obviously an administrative office of some kind. A young man sat behind a desk, carefully transcribing a letter when Frank walked in. He looked up and smiled politely. He looked to be less than twenty, his face still spotted and his body thin with immaturity.

"I'd like to talk to someone about my son," Frank said, conscious he was speaking louder than normal. Or maybe it just sounded that way because the place was so quiet.

"Sit down, please," the young man said, although the "please" sounded more like "peas." He indicated some chairs beside the door, and Frank took a seat while the boy disappeared into an inner office.

In a few moments a round man with a shiny bald head and a fringe of black hair beneath it came bustling out of the inner office, followed by the young man.

"Hello, hello," he said, extending his hand as he approached Frank. "I'm Edward Higginbotham. May I help you?"

"Frank Malloy," Frank said, rising and taking the man's hand. It was warm and sweaty, but then the day was warm and sweaty. "I'd like to talk to someone about my son."

"Your son is deaf?" Mr. Higginbotham said.

"Yes," Frank said, amazed at how much it cost him to admit it aloud. He'd already admitted it silently, but confessing to a complete stranger was more difficult than he could have imagined.

"Well, then, come right in. I'll be happy to answer all your questions, and I'm sure you have a few, don't you?"

He didn't wait for Frank's reply. Indeed, he didn't seem to expect one. He was too busy bustling right back into his office. Frank followed obediently.

The inner office was more elaborately furnished than the outer one. There was a rug on the floor and a nicely made wooden desk. The window looked out on an alley, but at least there was a window.

"Please sit down and make yourself comfortable, Mr. Malloy," Mr. Higginbotham said, taking his own seat behind the desk.

Frank settled himself, and Mr. Higginbotham waited until he was comfortable to ask, "How old is your son, Mr. Malloy?"

"He's three. We just . . . I didn't realize he was deaf until . . . just recently."

Mr. Higginbotham nodded sagely. "His mother didn't notice anything peculiar?"

"His mother died when he was born." Another costly admission.

Mr. Higginbotham looked suitably grave. "I'm sorry to hear that. Who cares for the boy, then?"

"My mother."

"An elderly lady?"

"She's not so old."

"And did she not notice anything unusual about the boy?"

"We thought he was feebleminded." Yet another costly admission. Frank was starting to feel a bit sick to his stomach. "He didn't understand what you said to him, and he didn't speak."

"A common mistake," Mr. Higginbotham agreed. "I could tell you stories about so many deaf children who were institutionalized as idiots when they were of perfectly normal intelligence. But you, Mr. Malloy, have avoided that fate for your son by recognizing his true condition. May I ask how you came to identify it?"

"A . . . a friend noticed. She brought it to my attention. I don't spend much time with the boy because of my work. I'm a detective with the police department."

Mr. Higginbotham straightened a bit at this, although not enough to give offense. "I see," was all he said. "And you've had him examined by a doctor?"

"Yes. The doctor said he was probably born deaf. There's nothing to be done for him."

"On the contrary, Mr. Malloy, much can be done for him. We cannot make him hear in the usual sense, of course, but we can certainly educate him and teach him to communicate with others. We can even teach him a trade."

Mrs. Brandt had mentioned that, but Frank still found it hard to believe. "But if he can't hear . . ."

"May I do a little demonstration, Mr. Malloy?"

Frank nodded.

Mr. Higginbotham rose from his chair and went out of his office. When he returned a moment later, the young man from the front office was with him. "This is Alexander, Mr. Malloy."

"Pleased to meet you," Malloy said, wondering what the boy had to do with anything.

"Pleased to meet you," the boy replied. Malloy noticed that the "please" still sounded like "peas."

"Ask Alexander a question, Mr. Malloy," Mr. Higginbotham suggested.

"What kind of question?" Frank asked.

"Any kind," Alexander said.

"How's the weather?" Frank tried.

"It looks like rain, doesn't it?"

Frank noticed the boy's speech was a bit slurred. He'd never heard anyone speak quite that way before. "What did you have for breakfast this morning?" Frank tried.

"Eggs and bacon and bread with jam," he said with a smile. "I live at home with my mother. She feeds me well."

Something was wrong with the boy's voice, but Frank couldn't quite figure out what it was. "What kind of work do you do here?" he tried.

"I'm Mr. Higginbotham's clerk."

The word was so garbled, Frank could only guess that he'd said "Higginbotham." He had to listen carefully to the boy, but he could understand what he was saying, even if he had to guess at some of the words.

"Why is Mr. Higginbotham making you talk to me?" Frank asked, looking at the gentleman in question.

"Because I'm deaf," Alexander said rather proudly.

Now Frank knew they were playing a trick on him. "Then how could you understand my questions?" he challenged.

"I read your lips." The boy grinned proudly.

"Read my what?" Frank was very confused.

"Alexander has been trained in speech reading, Mr. Malloy," Higginbotham explained. "By watching the way your lips move, he can divine what you are saying. Even though he can't hear your words, he can understand them."

"But he can talk, too." Not perfectly clearly, of course, but well enough to make himself understood. Frank had thought deaf people were also mute.

"Yes, we trained him in speech as well. That is what we do here at the Lexington Avenue School. You may have been to other schools where they use different techniques—"

"No, I haven't," Frank said, still looking at the boy as if he were a wonder. Because, of course, he was. A deaf person who could speak and understand, if not exactly hear, words was a wonder of wonders to Frank.

"Well, ahem, we use the oralist methods here," Higginbotham went on to explain. "We force the students to rely on speech reading and speaking to communicate. Then they are able to make their own way in the world."

Frank was still looking at the boy. "Are you sure he's really deaf?"

"Quite sure," Higginbotham assured him with a smile.

"Oh, yes," Alexander said, still grinning at Frank's confusion. "I had scarlet fever when I was five. That made me deaf."

"So you weren't born deaf," Frank said.

"No, but I am deaf now." He seemed almost proud of the fact.

Frank was still mystified. He looked at Higginbotham. "How can he just look at my lips and know what I'm saying?"

"It takes years of training," Higginbotham said, "but you

are fortunate to live here in the city. Your son is a bit young for our school just yet, but when he's older, he can come here as a day student, just the way he would attend an ordinary school. The students who live in the country have to board with us, but we feel they do better if they can live at home with their families."

"And you think you could teach my son to talk and to read people's lips?"

"We'd have to test him, of course, but assuming he is of normal intelligence, then yes, I think we could."

8

WHEN SARAH GOT BACK FROM THE GANSEVOORT Market, carrying her bags of produce, the next morning, Mrs. Elsworth was waiting for her. She was pretending to sweep her front stoop, as usual, of course, but she was really just keeping herself outside where she could observe the activity of the street.

"Is the corn in yet?" she asked when Sarah greeted her.

"I saw some, but it didn't look very good. It's too early, I'm afraid."

"I do so enjoy fresh corn," Mrs. Elsworth said wistfully. "And of course, I always make the corn dollies out of the sheaves." She donated these dolls to the various orphanages in the city. "The dollies bring good luck if you make them out of the sheaves of the last corn of the harvest, but living in the city, how on earth can you find such a thing? Sometimes I think we've become too civilized, Mrs. Brandt."

Sarah thought of the four dead girls and knew she could have argued the point, but she didn't. She didn't have the heart for it at the moment.

"You don't look quite yourself this morning," Mrs. Elsworth observed. "I hope nothing is wrong."

"I'm just tired, I think."

"You have been out quite a lot lately. It's not baby business either, is it? Are you helping that nice detective with another case?"

Sarah knew she shouldn't burden Mrs. Elsworth with such things. "Something like that," was all she said. She wished her neighbor good morning and went on into her own house. She'd just finished putting her purchases away when someone knocked on her back door. Somehow she wasn't surprised to find Mrs. Elsworth there. She held a plate covered with a napkin.

"I baked a cake yesterday, and it's more than Nelson and I can eat, so I thought you might help me by taking some." Nelson was Mrs. Elsworth's son. He was a banker and was seldom at home to eat much of anything.

"Thank you so much," Sarah said sincerely. "Why don't you come in, and we'll share it. I can make some tea."

A few minutes later the two women were sitting on Sarah's back porch, enjoying the coolness of the morning shade and Mrs. Elsworth's fluffy white cake.

"This is delicious," Sarah said.

Mrs. Elsworth waved the compliment away. "Now, tell me what's bothering you. And don't try to pretend it's nothing. I saw that young woman you brought home the other night. She's the same one who left you the message, isn't she? I hope she's not with child. She's so young . . ."

"It's not that. She's . . . well, a friend of hers was murdered and—"

"Murdered!"

"I didn't want to involve you in this," Sarah said. "It's not a very pretty story."

"Do you think I haven't been shocked in my life?" Mrs. Elsworth asked, a little offended. "I could probably tell you stories that would curl your hair. Now, you look like you need someone to confide in, and I'm right here."

Sarah knew she would probably regret doing this, but she told Mrs. Elsworth the story of how the four girls had been beaten to death, probably by the same man. And she told her what Luisa's sister and friend had said about the man named Will.

"It seems as if Coney Island is the place where he met at least two of the girls, then," Mrs. Elsworth observed.

"Yes, it does. And from what the girls told me last night, he may have bought Luisa a gift there, just as he bought Gerda the red shoes."

"Red shoes," she said, her disapproval obvious. "It shouldn't be too difficult to find where those shoes were purchased, now should it? I wouldn't imagine too many places sell such a thing."

She was right, of course. Why hadn't Sarah thought of it? More to the point, why hadn't *Malloy* thought of it? He was the professional detective. They should go back to Coney Island and find the shop that had sold the red shoes and . . . But when Sarah tried to imagine Malloy returning to Coney Island, she realized she was probably wasting her time. Malloy wouldn't go back to that place unless he was chained to a team of wild horses and dragged.

And when she thought about it some more, she realized she didn't need Malloy anyway. It's not like she was going to be looking for the killer himself, just a simple clue. She wouldn't be in any danger. But it would be nice to have an escort all the same. Someone who knew his way around Coney Island. Someone who could tell her things about the place that Malloy wouldn't know. Someone like Dirk Schyler.

"What are you thinking?" Mrs. Elsworth asked.

"I'm thinking I should visit some old friends. I haven't seen them in much too long."

THE OLD FRIENDS would have to be approached delicately, of course. Sarah had given the matter a lot of thought, and there was only one way she could insinuate herself back into the social life she'd left behind all those years ago, which she would have to do if she hoped to encounter Dirk

Schyler again. She'd have to ask her mother for help.

Sarah's parents lived on Fifty-seventh Street, just off Fifth Avenue, in a row of Italianate brownstones occupied by the upper crust of New York society. The Deckers had been born to wealth and privilege as the descendants of the original Dutch settlers of the area, called Knickerbockers, after the style of britches they had worn in the old days, by those who wished to disparage them.

Sarah had dressed carefully for the occasion, knowing her mother would be worried if she saw her daughter in her regular work clothes. She probably thought Sarah lived in abject poverty, when in fact, her profession earned her a comfortable living. Of course, her mother's idea of "comfortable" would not be the same as Sarah's.

It would have made more sense to wait another day, since it was raining when Sarah got up that morning, but she knew if she allowed herself time to think, she might not go at all. In any case, the rain was warm, hardly likely to give her a chill. And it might well keep other visitors away. Sarah was hoping for a private meeting with her mother.

The maid who opened the front door recognized Sarah, even though it had been a while since her last visit. "Good morning, Mrs. Brandt," she said with a curtsy. "Please come in while I see if your mother is at home."

Since this was Elizabeth Decker's usual morning "at home," when she was free to receive visitors, Sarah was fairly certain of being received. The maid showed Sarah into the parlor, which had already been prepared in expectation of callers. Sarah was happy to see her plan had worked and she was the first arrival.

Her mother came in a few moments later, her face flushed with pleasure. "Sarah, my dear, what a happy surprise!"

Sarah could see the questions in her mother's blue eyes, and the silent reproach. She'd promised at their last meeting that she would come for tea one day when her father was home. She had not seen him in over three years, and her mother was anxious for a reconciliation. Sarah wasn't quite as anxious, so she had dodged the issue by simply not having the time to call.

"You don't have to try to make me feel guilty," she told her mother as she kissed her cheek. "I know I broke my promise, but I've been so busy . . ."

"Too busy to give a few hours to your family?" her mother asked.

"No, too cowardly," Sarah confessed.

Her mother frowned. "Your father isn't an ogre, Sarah. He loves you very much."

Of course he did. But he'd loved her sister Maggie just as much, and Maggie was dead because of his stubbornness and pride. Sarah wasn't sure if she was ready to cope with her father's kind of love again.

"I'll see him soon. The first afternoon I have free," she promised.

"Perhaps we should set a date so you won't forget again," her mother suggested, leading her over to one of the sofas so they could sit down.

"Yes, perhaps we should," Sarah agreed vaguely. Then, before her mother could do so, she said, "Mother, I need your help."

This had the desired effect of distracting her completely. "My help? Whatever for?"

"I know this will sound strange, but I'd like to see Dirk Schyler."

"Dirk?" Her mother's surprise instantly gave way to pleasure. "Of course! Oh, Sarah, this is wonderful!" As she had expected, her mother completely misinterpreted her interest in Dirk. "What made you think of him after all these years? Well, no matter. He's perfectly suitable, exactly the kind of man your father and I would have chosen for you!"

Exactly the kind of man they would have chosen for her if she'd given them the opportunity, was the unspoken message. Sarah's parents had never approved of Tom Brandt, but she hadn't sought their approval or needed it. "Please don't make any wedding plans just yet," she told her mother with a smile. "That's not the reason I want to see him."

Her mother was a little surprised, but then she thought she'd figured it out. "Oh, of course not! We wouldn't want him to think you were seeking him out or pursuing him, would we? Nothing is more likely to discourage romance than apparent interest from the female. But don't worry, I will be perfectly discreet. I'm sure that seeing you again will be more than enough to spark his interest, though. His parents have been quite disappointed that he hasn't married yet. He's well over thirty, you know. They've put him in the way of every eligible young woman in New York, but he never even seems to notice them."

Sarah was fairly certain she knew why. Dirk Schyler's interests lay elsewhere. He didn't want a respectable wife taking note of his comings and goings.

Although she should have dampened her mother's enthusiasm for a match between her and Dirk Schyler, she knew that would only defeat her purpose. Her mother would be disappointed when nothing romantic developed between her and Dirk, but her mother had survived other, larger disappointments and would survive this one as well. In the meantime, her matchmaking instincts would motivate her to get the two of them together at the earliest possible moment.

"Can you think of any social engagements coming up at which you might encounter him?" Sarah asked.

Her mother considered. "Not really. He doesn't regularly attend the usual functions anymore. I suppose I could organize a small dinner party and invite him, though," she finally decided.

"That would be perfect," Sarah said.

But her mother wasn't finished. "I *could* organize a dinner party, but of course, your father would have to host it. And that would mean that you must see him first."

See him and reconcile with him, was what she meant, and Sarah understood the conditions perfectly. Hadn't she known this would happen? Her mother might look as delicate as a china doll, but inside she had a will of iron. She might use charm and grace to accomplish her purpose, but she was relentless. And Sarah supposed she was ready to be reconciled with her father. Otherwise, she would have found another way to contact Dirk Schyler, wouldn't she?

"All right, Mother. When can I see Father?"

MALLOY CAME BY that evening. He looked tired. Sarah wished she felt more sociable, but she was too worried about meeting with her father the next day. Her mother had been wise enough not to allow her too much time to change her mind. Her only salvation would be if someone summoned her to deliver a baby. Malloy certainly hadn't come for that.

"I hope you have some news," she told him as he stepped into her office.

"I was hoping you did," he replied.

The rain had finally stopped, and the air was fresh and cool, so they went out to the back porch. Sarah poured him some lemonade, and then she waited to hear what he had to tell her.

"That fellow Robert, the one on the list, he got married," he said. "He hasn't been going out to dance halls since before Gerda Reinhard died."

Sarah pretended to be hearing this information for the first time. "So that probably means he's not our killer."

Malloy sipped his lemonade. "You might want to call on him, though. His wife will be needing your services soon."

Ah, so that explained the hasty marriage and sudden domesticity. "I should give you some of my cards," she teased him. "You could pass them out in your travels."

Even in the fading sunlight, she saw his quick smile, gone in a moment. "What did *you* find out?" he asked, surprising her.

"Me? How would I find out anything?"

"I don't know," he said, settling more comfortably in his chair. "Maybe by questioning some of the other girls' friends again, just like I did."

"Malloy, you're too suspicious."

"And you're a bad liar. What did you find out?"

She sighed in defeat. So much for keeping her activities secret from Malloy. "I found out that Luisa met the man named Will, the one from the list, at Coney Island. He spent a lot of money on her, and he bought her a gift."

"What kind of gift?" She had his interest now.

"I don't know. Her friend told me about it, but her sister denied it. She didn't want me to think Luisa was a Charity Girl."

"Can't blame her for that, but it does make it hard when they won't tell you what they know. Nothing can hurt the dead, but people forget that. You'd think they'd want to find the killer more than they'd want to protect the victims, but they never do."

Sarah remembered the first case they'd worked on together and knew he was right. "They also said this Will could be rough when a girl didn't do what he wanted."

"Rough? You mean he beat them?"

"Luisa's sister said he slapped them around. Not beat. She was clear that he didn't really hurt them."

"Since when doesn't a slap hurt?" Malloy wanted to know.

"Since women want to pretend it doesn't mean anything," Sarah countered.

Malloy grunted. "What do we know about this Will?" he asked.

"He's handsome, dresses well, and has a lot of money to spend. I haven't met anyone who knew him personally yet. Or at least no one who will admit it. Maybe they don't want to be known as Charity Girls, either."

"He sounds a lot like your friend," Malloy observed.

"My friend?"

"The fellow we met at Coney Island."

Sarah hadn't thought of that. Another reason to ask Dirk to go with her. He'd know exactly how a man like that would behave since he himself was a man like that. Except for being a murderer, of course.

"The first three girls all knew a man named Will who fits this same description," Sarah reminded him. "No one remembered Gerda knowing Will, but she'd just met a fellow who sounds like him, the one who bought her the red shoes on Coney Island."

"Could be somebody else," he reminded her.

"And it could be the same man. If all these girls were killed by the same man, there's bound to be some coincidences."

"At least one," Malloy agreed.

"I was thinking," Sarah ventured, figuring Malloy would find out anyway. "I could go out to Coney Island and see if I can locate the store where Gerda got the shoes. Maybe they'll remember something."

Malloy frowned. "That's probably a fool's errand."

Sarah smiled knowingly. "Don't worry, Malloy, I don't expect you to go with me."

"Good, then you won't be disappointed."

"And when I find the clue that solves the case, you'll be awfully sorry you didn't go with me."

"I'll manage to bear it," he assured her wryly.

They fell silent. Sarah thought they had finished, but Malloy didn't get up the way he usually did when he felt they had discussed everything necessary. After a moment she realized he had more to say to her, but for some reason he wasn't saying it.

"Was there something else?" she asked, hoping to encourage him.

He drained his glass of lemonade, set it down carefully on the table, and stared out at the flowers blooming in her yard for a long moment before he finally said, "I went to that deaf school."

"What did you find out?"

He didn't answer right away. Plainly, he wasn't sure himself. "They said they could teach Brian to talk. And to read people's lips so he'd know what they were saying."

"That's wonderful!" Sarah exclaimed.

But Malloy plainly didn't think so. "I can't see it, myself."

"What do you mean?"

"They had a boy there. He could tell what I was saying, even though he can't hear. He could read my lips. And he could talk, too. Not real clear, but I could understand him."

"Then that proves it's possible."

"Yes, but . . . He wasn't born deaf. He had scarlet fever when he was about five, I think. He'd already learned to talk. He knows what people's voices sound like. Brian doesn't."

He'd obviously given this matter considerable thought. She would've been disappointed in him if he hadn't, of course. "I suppose it would be much more difficult to learn to speak if you'd never heard a human voice."

"I also found out there's another way to teach deaf people."

"There is? What is it?"

"I don't know. The fellow I talked to at the Lexington Avenue School told me, though. He didn't mean to. He must've thought I'd talked to the other people first, so he tried to convince me his way of teaching was the best. That's how I know there's another way."

Naturally, Malloy would be suspicious. He was always suspicious. And he wouldn't miss a single clue, even if it wasn't a clue to solving a crime. "You should certainly investigate all the possibilities before you decide what to do," she said.

He scratched his chin and looked out at the flowers again. "I was hoping you'd know what those other possibilities were."

Sarah smiled a little, since he wasn't looking at her. Then

she considered. "I have seen deaf people talking with their hands," she remembered.

"Their hands?"

"Yes, they have some sort of sign language they use."

"Were they talking, too?"

"I don't think so. Did the boy at the school use sign language?"

"No."

"Then maybe that's the other method they use, the one the Lexington Avenue School thinks isn't as good."

"I can see why. A deaf person wouldn't be able to talk to someone who doesn't know the sign language."

"But if the deaf person couldn't learn to talk, how else could he communicate?"

Malloy scratched his chin again. "I guess that's what I'll have to find out."

SARAH DECIDED HER presence at her parents' home was a measure of how desperate she was to solve these murders. She approached their house with a sick feeling in the pit of her stomach. She'd hardly slept the night before, and she'd spent every waking hour reliving all the arguments she'd had with her father through the years. In memory, at least, she hadn't won any of them.

Remembering how they had fought, however, she realized her father must be deranged to want to see her again. He should count himself well rid of such an ungrateful child. But of course he didn't. He either loved her very much or else he couldn't stand the thought that something of his existed outside of his control. Sarah thought it might well be a little of both. She couldn't condemn him, though. Her own motives for renewing their relationship were hardly pure.

The maid opened the door almost before she knocked, and from her wide-eyed expression, she was well aware of how momentous this visit was. "Mr. and Mrs. Decker is waiting for you in the back parlor, Mrs. Brandt," she said. "I'll show you in."

The back parlor was where the family would normally gather, not where they would receive guests. The location was important. It told Sarah they were welcoming her home. She was still an intimate part of their family. She only hoped that was still true when this visit was over.

The maid showed her in, and she found her parents sitting stiffly on the sofa, awaiting her arrival with the same apprehension she herself was feeling. Her mother rose instantly to her feet, but her father was slower getting up. Did he seem reluctant or merely unable to rise more quickly?

Sarah was struck by how much older he looked than she remembered. He was thinner, his face drawn, and although he was still much taller than she, he looked somehow smaller than she remembered, somehow shrunken. She recalled what her mother had said about his stomach problems and wondered if that had caused the change in his appearance.

He didn't smile. He was much too cautious a man to let his feelings show so openly. He would wait for his cue from her. There would be no unseemly display of emotion.

"Father, how wonderful to see you," Sarah said, feeling the nerves fluttering in her stomach. She went forward, offering him both of her hands.

He took them in a grip so hard it was almost painful as his pale blue eyes searched her face, taking in every detail of her appearance. "You're looking well," he determined, his voice strained.

"I'm feeling well," she confirmed. "My work keeps me busy and happy."

She saw the flicker of disapproval he couldn't quite hide, but she had to admire the way he refrained from uttering the slightest word of criticism. By this she judged how anxious he was to repair their relationship.

"Please, sit down," her mother said too brightly. "I'll ring for tea."

Sarah sat in the chair beside her father, amazed at how her hands ached after he released them. He'd been clinging so tightly he'd almost bruised them.

They chatted about the weather and Sarah's trip uptown—her father was probably horrified that she'd taken the elevated train, but he managed not to betray it—until the maid had finished serving and left them alone.

When the door closed behind her, an awkward silence fell. They all knew someone must say something, something momentous, but no one knew quite what that something should be. Perhaps her father thought she should apologize for abandoning them, but she wasn't going to do that. She had been the one offended and felt that she was the one due an apology. She couldn't imagine her father would offer one, however. As far as she knew, he had never apologized for anything in his life. To do so would be to admit he had been wrong, and he probably believed he never had been.

Unable to think of anything appropriate, Sarah sat silent. Sooner or later her father would say what he wanted her to hear. She was prepared for anything. Or at least she thought she was until he said, "We've missed you, Sarah."

"I've missed you, too," she said quite honestly. Although she had friends and a profession that fulfilled her, nothing and no one could take the place of family. Not even a family who had hurt each other as much as hers had.

"Your father regrets . . . we both regret," her mother quickly amended when he gave her a sharp glance, "the harsh words that were spoken after poor Tom . . ."

"I'm sure we all regret that," Sarah said quickly, coming to her mother's rescue. Had her father asked her mother to apologize for him? No, she realized, judging his expression. His impatience was evident.

"I still believe no respectable woman should live alone and earn her own living," he said, confirming her theory.

Oddly, she found his statement reassuring. He hadn't changed. And if he was still the same, as infuriating as he might be, she knew exactly how to deal with him.

"I know you don't understand the choices I've made," she allowed him. "But the fact is, I'm a grown woman. I don't need your blessing to live my life the way I see fit."

His lips tightened a bit. He wasn't used to such resistance, certainly not from a female and his own child. Her mother, she knew, resisted him frequently, but she used feminine wiles and charm to soften the blow. Sarah had no skill and certainly no patience for such wiles.

But to his credit, her father chose not to argue. Instead he said, "You've always had a mind of your own, Sarah. You're very like me in that respect."

"Too much like you, perhaps," she allowed with a small smile.

"Yes, but it's less . . . acceptable in a female."

"To some people," Sarah allowed, proving his point by arguing with it.

"And always to a father," he countered.

She conceded. "I never intended to let so much time pass with matters unsettled between us, but before I knew it, three years had gone by. I don't know how it happened."

"Nor I," he agreed. Did he look relieved at her willingness to take the blame? She hoped so.

"I should have been more understanding," she allowed, taking even more blame. "I realize now that you were only concerned about my well-being."

Her father was prepared to be equally gracious. "And we probably should have given you some time to get over Dr. Brandt's death before discussing the future with you."

"If you had, you might have understood that no discussion was necessary. I'm perfectly capable of taking care of myself."

"Or you might simply be too proud to accept the help we were offering you," he suggested.

She was right. He hadn't changed a bit. "I didn't need

help then, and I don't need it now, Father. I know it's difficult for you to imagine, but I manage my own life quite well. Not every woman needs a man to take care of her."

Instantly, she regretted her hasty words. With them, she had insulted her mother. Fortunately, her mother didn't seem to realize it.

"I'm sure your father was only trying to protect you from any more unpleasantness," she said.

"But I don't want to be protected from it," Sarah explained, hoping she could maintain her reasonable tone in the face of such ignorance. "I want to face it head-on and do something to change it."

Her mother glanced at her father apprehensively, obviously afraid Sarah had incensed him. In times past, she had done so with far less provocation. But her father was no longer so quick to anger. Or at least he was trying harder to be reasonable today than ever before.

"That's foolish idealism, Sarah. You can't change the way things are, no matter how much you might wish to. The world has been a wicked place since Cain killed Abel, and since then people have simply refined the ways in which they harm each other. One woman can't possibly make a difference."

Sarah could have told him how she had made a difference by solving the murder of Alicia VanDamm. She could have told him of the lives she had saved, mothers and babies who would never have survived without her skill. Instead she said, "Are you suggesting I should stop trying?"

She could see the battle he fought with himself. He was used to ordering and demanding and being obeyed instantly. No one challenged him, no one questioned him, not the people who worked for him or the people with whom he did business or anyone in his household. No one except Sarah, that is.

Her mother placed a hand on his sleeve, as if the gesture would restrain him. But he didn't even seem to notice. He was too intent on Sarah, who met his gaze levelly, without flinching.

"I am suggesting," he said when he was in control of his temper again, "that there is no need for a woman of your position in life to waste that life toiling for common people."

She could have said many things. She could have pointed out that women of the upper class wasted their lives every day, squandering their talents and intelligence on visits and gossip and parties and balls. But saying so would not have convinced her father and would have hurt her mother. Her father believed that women should engage only in socially acceptable activities, and he wasn't going to change his mind in one afternoon.

"Father, I know you don't approve of how I spend my life, but you must also know I have no intention of doing anything else. If we are going to make peace between us, we are each going to have to respect the other's opinions, whether we agree or not."

Her father stared at her for a long moment, his eyes sad. "This is what it's come to, is it? You've lost all trace of femininity, Sarah. You reason just like a man now."

He hadn't meant to compliment her, but Sarah felt flattered all the same. "Men have all the advantages in life, Father. If I've adopted masculine ways, it's only because I had no choice."

"You have a choice. You can come home and let us take care of you again."

Now it was Sarah's turn to be sad. "I'm afraid you'd regret your invitation very quickly if I took you up on it, Father. I'm not the biddable young girl you remember."

"You were never biddable, Sarah," he reminded her sharply.

"Well, I'm even worse now. I've lived on my own far too long to be able to be your daughter again."

"But what about your reputation?" His anger was showing again. "How do you ever expect to find a suitable husband if you insist on running around the city like a . . . a . . ."

"A common trollop?" she supplied helpfully, recalling what he had said to her that awful day after Tom's funeral.

His face grew scarlet above his high collar, but he didn't relent. "Respectable women do not walk the city streets at all hours of the night."

"They do if they're midwives," Sarah countered.

"Felix," her mother said, surprising them both. "Sarah's profession is perfectly respectable."

Her father looked as surprised as if the chair had spoken. Indeed, Sarah could never recall her mother disagreeing with her father, not once in all her life. Before either of them could recover from their shock, her mother continued.

"I think it's unreasonable to expect Sarah to come back home to live with us, too. She isn't a child anymore. And if you ever hope to have her come for another visit, you are going to have to accept that."

Sarah's world had just shifted as profoundly as if an earthquake had shaken the Decker home from its foundations. Her father felt the vibrations to his soul, too, if his expression was any indication. Only her mother seemed unmoved. She sat erect and serene, her lovely face smooth and expressionless. It wouldn't do to gloat, of course, but Sarah wished she looked a bit more forceful, or at least determined. She couldn't imagine her father being transformed by such a gentle rebuke, especially when years of her own ranting and raving had accomplished nothing.

But when her father turned back to her, he looked deeply disturbed. "Would you do that? Would you vanish from our lives again?"

"I don't enjoy being insulted and criticized, Father, and browbeating me won't make me abandon my profession. I won't come to see you again if that's what you plan to do."

"I only want what's best for you, Sarah," he insisted indignantly.

"No, you want what you *think* is best for me. I happen

to disagree about what that is. You're going to have to accept me the way I am or not at all."

"But what about your future?" he demanded. "Who will marry you?"

"I don't want anyone to marry me," she said, shocking him thoroughly. "I'm perfectly content as I am."

"But how will you live? Who will support you?"

"I'll support myself!" she said impatiently. "Haven't you noticed? I've been doing so for over three years now, and quite successfully, too. I don't need a man to take care of me, not even you."

She could see his inner struggle. In spite of the facts in front of him, proving that she could be independent, he simply did not want her to be. He could not understand a world in which women made their own way without the help of husband or father. He would never change, and he would never accept that she had.

Sarah saw her hopes of a reconciliation with her father fading. She was just forming the stiffly polite words she would use to take her leave when her mother spoke.

"It appears as if the two of you will never agree on this subject, but must we allow that to keep Sarah away? Perhaps we could simply promise never to discuss this topic again instead."

It was so eminently reasonable a solution that Sarah and her father gaped at her in astonishment. Sarah suddenly realized she had done her mother a great injustice. She had judged her by the wrong standards and found her lacking when she wasn't lacking at all. She was clever and intelligent, and although she abided by a set of social rules Sarah found ridiculous, Elizabeth Decker did have a mind of her own and knew how to use it. Had she been a man, she might have pursued a successful career in diplomacy, if her work here today was any indication of her abilities. Instead, she had managed to negotiate a peaceful settlement to a family matter. Sarah thought such a success almost equal to an international treaty, and to her, of much more importance.

Felix Decker said not a word to acknowledge his wife's suggestion. To do so would have given her more importance than he felt she should have. As if he had thought of it himself, he said, "Sarah, our quarreling upsets your mother. It always has. And your absence from our lives has caused her great pain. I believe we should make every effort to spare her any further pain, even if that means allowing you to continue on the path you have chosen, however much I might disapprove. I am willing to agree not to discuss the subject further, unless, of course, you feel yourself in need of family support once more. In that case, you must not let pride prevent you from seeking help from your family. You must know we would be only too happy to provide you with anything you might need."

Sarah knew that only too well, just as she knew she would never ask for such help, certainly not while she was able-bodied and of sound mind. His offer was condescending, to be sure, but coming from her father, also a near miracle of conciliation. She could not refuse it. "Thank you, Father. Our estrangement has caused me pain as well, and I'm perfectly willing to make concessions to ensure it doesn't happen again. If that means I can't argue with you anymore, then it's a sacrifice I'm willing to make, for Mother's sake."

It took a moment for them to realize she was joking. Her father frowned. He didn't approve of levity, especially at his expense, but her mother visibly relaxed. With a satisfied smile, she reached for the serving plate. "Try one of these tarts, Sarah. Cook made them especially for you because I told her how fond you are of blueberries."

The rest of the afternoon passed pleasantly enough. Her father made an effort not to offend her, and she returned the favor. They spoke of friends and relatives and generally caught up on each other's lives.

Just before Sarah judged it time to take her leave, her

mother said, "I've arranged a small dinner party to welcome Sarah back into our social circle, Felix. I had your secretary put it on your schedule."

"And just who will be attending this dinner party?" her father asked, not certain he could approve of such a thing. Or perhaps he was concerned that it was too soon to draw Sarah back into their social circle or that she might refuse to be drawn. He would have no idea the dinner party was being held at her request, of course.

"I asked the Walkers. Sarah went to school with Amanda Walker. And the younger Vandekamps. She's another classmate of Sarah's. And the Millers. We'll be an odd number, so I asked Hazel Miller's brother, Dirk Schyler, as well, to be Sarah's dinner companion."

Her father didn't approve. "Hardly an appropriate choice. Why not one of the Astors. Surely they have an unattached son about the right age."

"You aren't arranging a marriage for me, Father," Sarah reminded him. "I just need a dinner companion, and I've known Dirk for a long time."

"You haven't known him lately. He hasn't turned out well. His father despairs of ever making a man of him."

This confirmed Sarah's assessment of Dirk as well. She thought she could lower her father's opinion of him even more by telling him about Dirk's excursions to Coney Island, but then she'd have to explain how she knew about them. She'd just made peace with the man, so this wasn't the moment to inform him she was investigating a murder in her spare time. Their truce hadn't covered arguing over something like that.

"Perhaps he just needs to settle down," Elizabeth Decker suggested. "A good woman can work wonders." She glanced meaningfully at Sarah, who pretended not to notice.

"I doubt even Sarah is up to a task like that," her father said.

For once they agreed on something.

9

FRANK HAD LOCATED THE NEW YORK INSTITUTION for the Deaf and Dumb without too much trouble. It was, he had learned, a much older school than the one on Lexington Avenue. This one had been here over sixty years. A long time, if they were doing something wrong, Frank thought cynically.

This school was as silent as the other had been. He entered the main office. The young man working there as a clerk looked up. "May I help you?" he asked, moving his hands quickly in a way Frank had never seen before. Frank realized this must be the sign language Mrs. Brandt had told him about.

"I'm not deaf," Frank told him, unconsciously speaking too loudly.

"Neither am I," the boy replied with a smile, still using his hands. Now Frank was certain it was sign language. "Do you have business with Mr. Peet?"

"Is he the one in charge?"

"Yes, sir. His father founded the school."

"Then I guess I do have business with him."

"I'll see if he's free," the boy said, and disappeared into an inner office.

Frank didn't quite know what to expect when he was ushered in to meet Lewis Peet. He was relieved to discover Mr. Peet wasn't deaf, and he didn't use his hands when he spoke, the way the boy had.

Frank told him about Brian, and he listened intently.

"I went to the Lexington Avenue School first," he told Peet.

"An excellent facility," he said tactfully.

"They said they could teach my son to speak."

Mr. Peet nodded. "I'm sure they did. Did they introduce you to a student who could speech-read and talk?"

"Yes," Frank said. "His voice was a little odd, but I could understand him. He could understand me, too. If my son could learn to do that, he would be able to make his way in the world."

"But the boy you heard speaking wasn't born deaf, was he?"

Frank frowned. How could he have known that? "No."

Mr. Peet nodded again. "When someone is born deaf and has never heard human speech or sound of any kind, it's very difficult for them to ever learn to speak clearly. It's also difficult for them to understand the concept of language, because they have no language of their own."

Frank wasn't sure he understood all of this completely, but some of it sounded reasonable. "You do something different here at your school than they do at Lexington Avenue," Frank said. "You teach them to talk with their hands."

"Yes, we teach them sign language. You may have seen deaf people using it in the street."

"The boy outside used it."

"He always does, if he suspects he might be talking to a deaf person. Sign language is a unique method of communication. Many people assume the signs are letters of the alphabet, spelling out words, but if you think about it, you'll realize that would be a cumbersome method, and very slow and boring to use for actual communication. Actually, the signs are words, motions representing what we in the hearing world hear as sounds. A skilled signer can speak as quickly as you and I can speak with our voices, and one who understands the signs can comprehend as easily as you understand what I'm saying right now."

"But how do they talk to people who don't know the signs?"

"Ah, that's the problem, isn't it?" Peet said, sitting back in his chair and steepling his hands in front of him. "If we could get everyone in the hearing world to learn sign language, then deaf people could get along just like hearing people. Since that doesn't seem likely to happen, what does happen is that the deaf develop their own society. They work at trades which don't require hearing or speech, they marry other deaf people to whom they can speak easily with signs, and they socialize with other deaf people."

"Which means that the Lexington School has a better solution," Frank said. "Their students can speak and read lips. They can communicate easily with hearing people and live in their world."

"Except they don't."

"What do you mean?"

Peet smiled. "The theory behind the oralist method—that's the method of teaching speech reading and speaking that the Lexington School uses—is to give the deaf students the skills to allow them to live and work and socialize with hearing people. In practice, however, they don't do that. In fact, the graduates of the Lexington school have actually organized their own social club, the Deaf-Mutes Union League, which has only deaf members. They have lectures and meetings and dinners and balls for the deaf. They still associate primarily with each other, and work together and marry each other.

"Please understand, Mr. Malloy. I'm not criticizing what they do at the Lexington School. I'm simply pointing out that their results have not been any more successful than ours for most deaf people, especially if your goal is to give your son the skills he will need in life. And for someone like your son, who most probably would never learn to speak clearly enough to be understood or to read lips well enough to truly comprehend, it would be a frustrating and ultimately a fruitless experience."

"Of course you think I should send Brian here," Frank said, still trying to judge the validity of the arguments.

Peet smiled. "Your son is too young to send anywhere at the moment. When he's older, I think he would do very well here, probably better than he would at Lexington Avenue. But you have some time to find out more about both theories of educating the deaf. In the meantime, I would suggest you meet some deaf people and find out their experiences. I'd be happy to introduce you to a family I know who has a boy about Brian's age."

"He's deaf?"

"Oh, no. He can hear perfectly well, but his parents are deaf. However, he uses sign language quite well. He learned it before he learned to talk, to communicate with his parents. Perhaps he could help Brian begin to understand how to communicate."

"A boy that young?" Frank thought of the intricate motions the clerk outside had used. He himself would have a difficult time learning such a thing, much less a boy of three.

"If Brian could hear, he'd be talking by now," Mr. Peet pointed out. "I'm sure he'll have no trouble at all learning to sign once he's exposed to it. It will be his language. You could learn right along with him. You'd be able to talk to your son, Mr. Malloy."

To be able to talk to Brian. To have Brain know who he was. The thought was stunning. Frank had long since given up hope of reaching his son. Until recently, he'd believed there was nothing inside of him to reach. But now . . .

He'd have to tell his mother, of course. He tried to imagine her learning to sign, but the idea was too ridiculous even to consider. She'd continued to pretend Brian was a normal child, totally ignoring all evidence to the contrary.

Being deaf was almost as shameful as being feebleminded, at least by her standards, so she simply denied it.

"Maybe you'd tell me more about these people with the boy Brian's age," he said.

SARAH HAD FORGOTTEN how interminably dull society dinner parties could be. No one talked about politics or philosophy or literature or anything even remotely interesting. Sarah did learn more than she ever wanted to know about her old friend Amanda's trip to Europe and Hazel's twin daughters. She also learned what had happened to most of the friends she had had as young woman, before she'd decided not to follow the course her father had set for her and gone into nurses' training. Unfortunately, none of them was doing anything Sarah found interesting.

After dinner, as custom dictated, the women withdrew while the men smoked their cigars and took their brandy. Sarah could have used some brandy herself. She needed fortification to get through the rest of the evening.

To make matters worse, Sarah had begun to realize that having a private word with Dirk Schyler, which had been the entire purpose of organizing the evening in the first place, was going to be practically impossible. They would certainly never be alone at all, and the chances of them having a moment when no one could overhear them was unlikely, particularly when everyone seemed intent on watching the two of them closely for any signs that they were interested in one another.

Her mother could have done a better job of disguising the fact that Sarah had merely wanted the dinner party as an excuse for seeing Dirk. As it was, everyone present was aware of it, since they were the only two unattached people in the party. To make matters worse, they had also come to the conclusion that Sarah had set her cap for him. If it hadn't been so frustrating, Sarah might have been amused.

Amanda Walker had just asked where she had gotten her gown—a purely idle question since Amanda could have no interest whatever in such an unstylish creation—when the door opened and the men came into the parlor, saving her from admitting it had come from Lord & Taylor. Sarah's mother had insisted she buy a new frock for the occasion, but Sarah had seen no need to pay a dressmaker for an ensemble she might never wear again.

Instantly, Amanda and all the other women lost interest in her, to her great relief. The men filled the room with their energy, loud voices, and booming laughter. Sarah watched in growing frustration as Dirk Schyler spoke to his sister and then wandered away, off to a far corner of the room. She was just hatching a plan to get herself near enough to him to ask for his help when he called out to her.

"Sarah, would you be so kind as to identify the people in this photograph for me?" he asked.

Sarah gaped at him in surprise. Could he possibly know she wanted a private word with him? Or did he want one with her? Perhaps he was simply afraid she would reveal that she had seen him at Coney Island in the company of a working-class girl and wanted to beg her discretion. Or perhaps he understood that he'd been invited for a reason, and that reason involved Sarah. Whatever it was, Sarah was simply glad for the excuse to confer with him.

"Certainly," Sarah said, trying not to appear too eager to answer his summons.

As she crossed the room, she heard a stifled giggle and realized that everyone was watching her. Well, what had she expected? They were all waiting for the two of them to show some signs of interest in each other. They would imagine such interest no matter what really happened. Sarah Decker Brandt's desperate ploy to land herself a rich husband would probably be the talk of visiting rooms for the next month.

Dirk had picked up a photograph of her father's college rowing team and pointed at one of the men. Sarah, of course, had no idea who any of them were. In fact, she would have been hard-pressed to identify her own father, and she was certain Dirk had no true interest in their identities, either. He proved it instantly.

"Now tell me, Sarah, why on earth have you gone to all this trouble to encounter me again?" he asked in a whisper, his eyes twinkling with mischief. He held the photograph up for her to see, as if it were the true subject of their conversation.

"Why, Dirk," she replied, unable to resist, "isn't it obvious? I developed an instant passion for you, and I couldn't wait to see you again."

He gave her a look of feigned shock. "Does Mr. Malloy know about this?"

"He wouldn't be likely to care if he did," she replied. It was the first word of truth she'd spoken in this conversation.

"Don't be too sure about that. I'm quite certain Mr. Malloy wouldn't approve of your consorting with me."

"Fortunately, I don't need his approval."

"What *do* you need, then?" Dirk asked. His face was still handsome, Sarah noticed, although the signs of dissipation were starting to show. The flesh beneath his attractive blue eyes was pouched from too many late-night drinking parties, and his skin was sallow and unhealthy. He was even developing a slight thickening around the waist that would turn to fat in a few years if he wasn't careful.

"I need to go back to Coney Island with someone who is familiar with the place."

He seemed surprised. Fortunately, he was also intrigued. "What on earth for?"

"Because I'm looking for a murderer."

Dirk looked even more shocked than she would have expected. His face actually paled, and he stared at her for a long moment, as if looking for the answer to some question he dared not ask aloud. Most likely, he had never heard a well-bred woman even utter the word "murderer," which would more than account for his reaction.

Thus far, their whispered conversation had the attention of everyone in the room, and clearly, they would need more privacy to continue. Dirk visibly collected himself. "It's awfully warm in here," he said so everyone could hear, setting the photograph back on the sideboard. "Perhaps you'll stroll with me in the garden for a bit, Sarah."

"That sounds lovely," Sarah agreed. "If you'll excuse us," she added to her mother, who nodded her consent. She looked so pleased that Dirk was performing to her expectations that Sarah actually felt guilty for deceiving her.

Dirk offered his arm, and they stepped out through the French doors leading to the fenced enclosure that passed for a "garden" in the city. It was much larger than Sarah's small backyard, and the flowers had been professionally tended. The shade was cool, and the scents fragrant, but most important, no one could overhear them.

They'd walked a ways from the house before Dirk spoke. "Surely, I misunderstood you, Sarah. You could not possibly have said you were looking for a murderer."

"But I did. I know it's hard for you to understand how I could be involved in such a thing, but a young girl I know was murdered recently. Her family has asked me to help in the investigation," she explained, stretching the truth a bit.

"Why would they ask *you* to do such a thing?" He looked horrified, or at least that's how Sarah read his expression. He certainly seemed upset, although he was using all his formal training to conceal any unseemly emotions.

"As you know, I have a friend who is a police detective."

"Ah, yes, the charming Mr. Malloy. Surely, he doesn't need your help finding criminals, though. Why, the police hardly bother doing that themselves!"

Sarah ignored the insulting remark. It was, unfortunately, too true. "I have been of some use to him in that respect in the past," she admitted with a trace of pride.

Plainly, Dirk didn't believe that for a moment. "Sarah, I'm afraid you haven't learned much of the world, for all your independence from your family, if you believe for one moment this Malloy fellow has any interest in you aside from seduction."

Sarah was hard-pressed not to laugh out loud at such a ridiculous notion. If Malloy wanted to seduce her, he was certainly adept at concealing his intentions. He was also the world's most patient—and inept!—seducer. "Is it so difficult to believe a woman could help solve a crime?"

"Quite frankly, yes," Dirk said, his smile condescending.

Sarah wanted to wipe that smile off his face. She wanted to tell him she had helped solve a murder only a few short months ago. She had been of so much help that Malloy had told her she would have made a good detective, if the police hired women, which they didn't. But she really wasn't at liberty to reveal the details of the case, and besides, she doubted Dirk would believe her anyway.

"Well, then," she tried, "perhaps you will indulge me in my delusions. I would dearly love to return to Coney Island and learn more about it, but Mr. Malloy refuses to accompany me."

"More fool he," Dirk said, his grin flirtatious. Sarah wondered who might be watching them from the house. She hoped it looked as if they were having a romantic *tête-à-tête*. Her mother would be pleased.

"Since you obviously know a lot about the area, I was hoping I could convince you to escort me and show me some things I might have missed on my first visit there."

His smile was mocking. "Do you think I can point out potential killers to you?"

Sarah gritted her teeth at his tone, but she managed to maintain her facade of congeniality. "I am hoping you can help me understand the place. The dead girl met her killer there, you see."

This instantly wiped the smirk off his face. "How do you know that?"

"He bought her a gift there right before she died. At least we suspect the man who bought the gift was her killer."

"And what, exactly, was the gift in question?"

Sarah felt silly saying it aloud. "A pair of red shoes."

Something flickered deep in his eyes, something Sarah couldn't decipher, but then he was smiling. It was a dazzling smile, a delighted smile. "Oh, Sarah, what could be more pleasant than helping you discover who killed a young lady of such abominable taste?"

He didn't have to respect her, she reminded herself. He didn't have to take her seriously or even believe her. He only had to go with her and show her around. "Are you free this Sunday?" she asked, and they set the date for the day after tomorrow.

NOBODY KNEW ANYTHING more about the mysterious man named Will than the ones Sarah Brandt had spoken with. Frank had questioned all the girls who knew the four victims well enough to tell him anything. After days of tracking the girls down and interrogating them again, he knew no more than he'd known the first day.

The fellow had been careful not to reveal his last name or to give any indication of where he lived. Uptown was Frank's guess. By all accounts, he always had a lot of money to spend. Even those who had never seen him knew that much. His reputation was excellent among those who judged a man's worthiness by how many times he treated a young lady to a beer or an amusement-park ride. He couldn't have been an average workingman, not if the girls Frank had spoken with were accurate in their estimates of the amount of money he spent on the girls he found attractive. His clothes and his manners, by all accounts, had also indicated he was upper class.

A few of the girls had been more than treated by him, too, if Frank was any judge. They didn't admit it, of course. Why should they? Even if this Will had murdered their friends, they were still alive and had to live here. Destroying their reputations wouldn't bring their friends back, would it? And if he hadn't killed them when he had the chance, he wasn't likely to do it now, was he?

Frank was beginning to wonder why Sarah Brandt was so desperate to avenge the deaths of these girls. He was so annoyed with them, he was beginning to sympathize with the killer.

Frank was bone weary when he climbed the steps to his flat that evening. He hadn't been home in two days, and when he opened the door, he found his mother knitting in her rocker by the front window. Brian was playing on the floor, carefully building a tower of wooden blocks so he could knock it over and build it again.

When he caught sight of Frank, however, he scrambled to his knees, smashing the tower in his haste as he crawled over to greet his father. His mother said something by way of greeting, but Frank hardly heard and didn't even acknowledge her. He was, he realized, really seeing the boy for the first time.

For three years Frank had been torn by the existence of his son. The boy's birth had killed Kathleen, the only good thing that had ever come into Frank's life. If Kathleen had lived, Frank could have borne any disappointment in the child because she would have made it right. She would have loved the boy no matter what was wrong with him, and she would have made Frank love him, too.

But Kathleen had died, taking with her Frank's one source of happiness in the world. That alone would have been enough to embitter him, but the boy had also remained, a painful and broken reminder of what he had lost. Not only had he taken his mother's life, he had left Frank with a burden so enormous, at times he felt it might crush him.

For a time he had hated the child, blaming him for killing Kathleen. But that had passed, leaving only a profound sadness and pity and a bitterness so deep, Frank doubted he would ever find the bottom of it. And, of course, the guilt. Because if the boy had killed Kathleen, Frank had been the one who put the child inside of her in the first place. If he hated the boy, he would have to hate himself as well.

So the guilt drove him to do right by the child, no matter what his true feelings might be. It drove him to take the bribes that had enabled him to move up in the police force so he could ensure the boy would always be provided for. It compelled him to tolerate his mother because she was willing to take care of the boy.

Now he looked at his son, this imperfect remembrance, all he had left of the woman he had loved more than life itself. She would have expected Frank to love the boy simply because he was their flesh and blood. She would have done anything, made any sacrifice for him. Frank had been willing to make every sacrifice except one. He hadn't been able to love him.

He gazed into the face that was so much like Kathleen's, it caused him physical pain to behold it. The boy was looking up at him through Kathleen's lovely eyes, pleading with him for something he couldn't say but understood instinctively.

The small, spindly arms were reaching up even as he held himself back, braced for the rejection he almost always received. For so long, Frank had believed the boy an idiot, too damaged even to feel normal human emotions. He'd shielded himself with that belief, telling himself his indifference didn't matter to the child because he couldn't understand such things. Now he looked down into the boy's face and knew it had all been a lie.

If Frank was guilty of causing Kathleen's death, then there was only one thing in the world he could do to earn absolution. He reached down and caught the boy up into his arms. Small arms and legs wrapped around him, as if the boy felt he had to hold on with every ounce of his strength for fear of being thrust aside. From the comer of his eye, he saw his mother had risen to her feet, her eyes wide with surprise. She crossed herself and pressed a fist to her lips.

He wrapped his arms around the boy's small body, amazed at how slight he was, hardly there at all. He buried his face into the cloud of silken red-gold curls and inhaled the clean, fresh scent of him.

Frank felt a stabbing pain in his chest as years of bitterness cracked and fell away. He'd wronged the boy terribly, but it wasn't too late. He still had a chance to really do right by him.

"Ma," he said, "there's some people I want Brian to meet. They're deaf."

SARAH HAD BEGUN to regret her decision to ask Dirk to accompany her to Coney Island before their trolley had even left the city. He seemed highly amused by the entire escapade, and he felt compelled to share his mirth with everyone they encountered. Sarah found it exhausting, and by the time they reached Coney Island, she was wishing she had come alone.

"Have you seen the Elephant yet, Sarah?" he asked cheerfully as they strolled from the trolley station toward the park.

She looked to where he was pointing and saw the Elephant Hotel, a enormous hotel actually built in the shape of an elephant. It was one of the landmarks of Coney Island. "Seeing the Elephant" had come to mean making a trek out of town to see something extraordinary.

"I saw the elephant the last time I was here," she reminded him.

"I don't think you did," Dirk said meaningfully. "I doubt Mr. Malloy is adventurous enough to allow such a thing. Fortunately, I am."

Yes, fortunately, Sarah thought cynically.

"I'm surprised Mr. Malloy didn't take you bathing, Sarah. I imagine the sight of you in a bathing costume would be quite pleasant. Have you ever bathed in the ocean?"

"Have you?" Sarah countered, trying unsuccessfully to imagine herself wearing one of those skimpy bathing costumes with the skirts that only reached to the knees.

"Certainly! I find the sand a bit annoying. It does tend to creep in where one least desires it to, but the water is quite refreshing. Healthful, too, I'm told."

"I thought warm springs were good for the health, not the frigid ocean."

"It's not frigid this time of year," he chided her.

"No, only very cold."

He conceded defeat graciously. "Where would you like to go first? The Flip-Flap Railroad?" he suggested with a glint in his eye. Malloy had been afraid to go on it.

Unfortunately, Sarah was, too. "I think I'd rather just look around and talk to people. If the killer frequents Coney Island, and we have reason to believe he does, then someone may know him."

"Are you planning to just walk up to everyone you meet and ask if they know any killers?" he asked incredulously.

"Certainly not."

"Then what will you ask?" Plainly, he thought her either a fool or an idiot.

"I'll ask them if they know a man named Will."

Dirk stopped in his tracks and looked at her in amazement. His eyes were darker than she remembered, and his expression was strained. He was so shocked that for a moment he couldn't even speak. "You know his *name*?" he asked when he got his voice back. "If the police know his name, why on earth do they need a midwife to help them find him?"

Sarah was beginning to enjoy knowing more about something than Dirk for a change. "Do you have any idea how many men are named Will? And we don't know what he looks like or where he lives or really anything much at all. Just the name, and that might not even be his real one."

He studied her face for a long moment, his eyes unreadable. "And you think he killed this girl? The one who wore the red shoes. What was her name?"

"Gerda Reinhard. I guess we don't know for sure that he did, but . . ." She debated mentioning the other victims and decided not to. Dirk was already unbearable enough. If he knew all the facts in the case, he might begin to hinder her investigation. "We do know that she met a young man she liked very much here at Coney Island shortly before her death. He spent a lot of money on her and bought her the red shoes."

"That's not very much to hang a man on, Sarah," Dirk chided. "I daresay, most of the men here would have been executed if that was a punishable offense."

"Including you?" she countered.

He grinned boyishly. When he was younger and not quite so jaded, it might have been an appealing expression, but now it just looked grotesque, at least to Sarah. "A gentleman never tells," he said. He took her elbow and directed her toward the entrance to the park.

Dirk took her to the Flip-Flap Railroad with its unbelievable loop, and they watched people going around, shrieking in terror, for a few minutes. "You see, no one ever falls out," he said wisely. "It's perfectly safe."

Sarah watched the people getting off at the end of the ride. Some of them were rubbing their necks. None of them looked particularly pleased with their experience. "I notice no one is going back for another ride," she pointed out.

Dirk shrugged. "I thought you'd have more courage than that, Sarah. How about the Ferris wheel, then?"

Sarah enjoyed the view of the ocean from the top of the wheel, and she didn't even mind that Dirk put his arm across the back of the seat and sat closer than he needed to. He was only teasing her. Since his tastes ran to fifteen-year-old shop girls, she figured her virtue was safe. Besides, she had a hat pin handy if he got any ideas.

They watched Captain Boyton perform his aquatic feats in the reflecting pool. The captain was the owner of the park. He'd had an interesting career that included trying to market inflatable suits for bathing in the ocean. This had led to founding a water park, in which trained seals performed. The seals hadn't drawn enough customers by themselves, so the captain had added Shoot-the-Chutes and some other amusement-park attractions, and Sea Lion Park was born.

They also watched the sea-lion show again, but the alligator was no longer on display. It had tried to attack a large Newfoundland dog, probably thinking it had found an excellent source of dinner, but the dog had won the battle.

After the shows, they ate some Red Hots and rode Shoot-the-Chutes. Dirk put his arm across the back of Sarah's seat again and moved closer when they went through the dark tunnel, but she managed to restrain herself from throwing her arms around him when the boat made its terrifying lunge into the lagoon. Malloy had been as appalled as she when they found themselves embracing at the end of the ride, but somehow she didn't think Dirk would have quite the same reaction. She certainly didn't want to find out for sure that she was right.

As they came off the ride, Sarah saw the photographer waiting to pose people in the replica of the Shoot-the-Chutes boat to have their pictures made. Remembering that Gerda had had her photograph made that last day she was at Coney Island, Sarah wondered if the photographer would remember. If this Will person made a habit of finding his victims here, he might be a familiar character.

"Excuse me," she said, startling the fellow. He had been fiddling with his camera.

"Just get in the boat, miss," he said. "Soon as it's full, I'll take a picture."

"No, I don't want my picture made. I was wondering if I could ask you a question."

"About what?" He glanced uncertainly at Dirk, who shrugged, telling him he had no explanation for Sarah's strange behavior.

"There's a man who comes to the park a lot. He's quite a ladies' man, and he's probably with a different girl every time. I was wondering if you knew him. His name is Will."

The photographer stared at her as if he'd never seen a creature like her before. He glanced at Dirk again, but got no help there, either.

"I know that's not much help," Sarah admitted, realizing how silly her question must sound. Hadn't she pointed out to Dirk how many men were named Will? "I also know that he's well dressed and well mannered," she added lamely, hoping to jog his memory a bit. "He seems to have a lot of money to spend, too."

The fellow looked at Dirk once more, and the two men seemed to reach some sort of understanding. Over what, Sarah couldn't imagine, and it annoyed her tremendously. Why was the fellow looking at Dirk when she was the one asking the questions?

At any rate, the fellow seemed to relax and even smiled at her. "Sorry, miss. I don't know nobody named Will. The men come through here, they don't tell me their names. Now, maybe if you had a photograph of him . . ."

She did have a photograph, of course, but she wasn't sure the fellow in it was the man named Will, and even if he was, his face was obscured too much to identify him. "Thank you for your time," she said, less than graciously.

Dirk was grinning as they walked away. "Did you really think that fellow would know who you were talking about?"

Sarah didn't know what she'd thought. Every time she believed she'd come up with a plan to find the killer, she realized the depths of her ignorance. Malloy would be laughing in her face for being so naive. Her one comfort was that he would never know how stupid she had been.

"Do you plan to ask every man who works here at the park if they know this Will person?" Dirk asked, his amusement all too evident. "Shall we stop here at the freak show? I'm sure the barker would be more than happy to answer any questions."

Sarah glared at him, but that only amused him more. "I don't think the killer is a freak," she informed him. "Or at least he doesn't look like one. Otherwise, he wouldn't have been able to attract the attentions of young women."

"You're right! Maybe we should try asking if anyone has seen a *normal*-looking man named Will, then. Someone who *doesn't* look like a killer. That should help a lot."

Sarah sighed wearily. "You've made your point. It's hopeless. I can see that."

"Oh, perhaps not hopeless. Simply futile," Dirk allowed graciously.

Sarah wanted to smack him, especially because he was right. Asking if anyone knew this Will was a waste of time. She wasn't even sure Gerda had known the man named Will. Still, she couldn't help thinking that the key was here, in Coney Island. If only she could find it.

"Shall we move on then?" Dirk asked, his charm back in place. "What would you like to do next?"

Sarah allowed him to lead her on through the park.

Malloy had won her a prize with his marksmanship, but Dirk had no such skill. Instead, he tried to impress her on the Hi-Striker machine, the one that tested a man's strength. He removed his jacket—today he had chosen to dress conservatively, probably in deference to her—and handed it to Sarah to hold.

"Dirk, this isn't necessary," she protested.

"Of course it is," he replied with that grotesquely boyish grin. "I'll take three chances," he told the barker, who removed the coins from his hand so quickly, Sarah hardly saw his fingers move.

Dirk turned back his cuffs, as if preparing to do a hard day's work, and he spit on his palms and rubbed them together, probably because he'd seen someone else do it and thought it looked manly. Then he picked up the huge hammer.

Lifting the thing was a challenge in itself. Sarah supposed that kept children from making a pest of themselves, trying to ring the bell. If they couldn't lift the hammer, they couldn't play the game.

Dirk raised the huge thing up over his head with practiced ease and brought it down with a crash. The weight rose up more than halfway, then fell back down with a thud. The crowd murmured its disappointment.

"Look at the gentleman here," the barker shouted. "Out to win his lady a prize. Look how far he got it. Just a little more, sir, just a little more'll do it! Ring the bell and win, you pick any of the prizes! Step right up, folks! Watch the gentleman win his lady a prize! Try your luck! You there, young fellow, you could do this with one hand tied behind your back!"

Sarah watched as Dirk lifted the hammer again, swinging it in an arc over his head and bringing it down onto the strike plate with a crash. The weight rose up and up, and Sarah found herself rising on her tiptoes, as if by stretching herself, she could help it reach the top. But it stopped just short and slid back down to the bottom again. The crowd moaned.

They were breathless with anticipation now. They started to cheer Dirk on, encouraging him to try again. He flashed Sarah a grin, enjoying the attention. She felt a little foolish, but she was calling out encouragement, too.

The obnoxious barker was whipping up the crowd's enthusiasm, urging everyone within shouting distance to come and watch. Sarah found it odd that he would be as interested in seeing someone win as the rest of them were, but then she realized that if Dirk won, a dozen more men would be encouraged to try their skill and prove themselves at least as good as he. Few of them would succeed, and the barker would still have their money.

Dirk waited, rubbing his hands together, shaking his arms to loosen the muscles, playing his part to perfection, until the barker had the crowd whipped into a frenzy of anticipation. The look Dirk cast Sarah was one of pride. He was doing this for her, to impress her in some way, or perhaps simply to prove that he had a sort of power. Probably, he had used this tactic to impress his shop girls. The young girls in the crowd were certainly awed. He did look imposing, standing there in the center of the crowd, ready to master the fearsome machine.

He seemed to sense the perfect moment, the time when all eyes who could be on him were. Then he started swinging the hammer again. Back and forth, building up a rhythm, building up momentum. That was when Sarah realized that he had known how to get the bell to ring all along. He could have done so on the very first try, but no one would have been watching. He had to tease it along for a while, until he had the crowd in his thrall. The barker was nearly hysterical, ranting and chanting, the meaning of his words lost to the delirium of excitement building around them.

Sarah watched in fascination as Dirk finally swung the huge hammer up over his head and brought it down with a resounding smack that sent the small weight sailing up and up and up until it struck the bell with a clang that set the crowd to cheering wildly.

Men were slapping him on the back and shaking his hand. Women were gazing at him in admiration. And Sarah was taking it all in with a combination of amazement and amusement. Anyone would think Dirk had just accomplished something important, like saving someone's life or bringing peace to warring nations, instead of just using brute strength to ring a bell.

No one was interested in Sarah's opinion, however, so she stood back, still holding Dirk's jacket, while he finished receiving his accolades. The barker encouraged him to select his prize while the crowd was still interested. He wanted to remind everyone that there was a higher purpose in ringing the bell. The satisfaction of achievement was only part of it. But Dirk finally remembered Sarah, and he insisted she make the selection.

The prizes were cheap trinkets, glass beads and small toys. Sarah thought of Malloy's son, but she knew he wouldn't appreciate her bringing Brian a prize Dirk Schyler had won for her. Then she remembered Gerda Reinhard's nieces and nephew. She chose a small rag doll. She could purchase toys for the other children, and deliver them next time she was in the neighborhood. Perhaps that would gain her admittance to the Otto home.

Dirk was still teasing her about her selection of a prize when they came to the Old Mill ride. "What does this do?" Sarah asked.

"Let's get on and find out," Dirk suggested.

Sarah could think of no reason to refuse, so they got in line and quickly made their way to the front. They were seated in a boat which began drifting down a man-made stream toward the opening of a tunnel, much like the Shoot-the-Chutes tunnel. A mill wheel turned picturesquely in the water, and over the entrance of the tunnel, Sarah saw a tableau of scantily clad girls performing some kind of spring Maypole dance.

"Oh, my," she said, a little shocked at how suggestive the picture was.

"People come to Coney Island to be shocked," Dirk explained cheerfully as their boat was swallowed up into the darkness of the tunnel.

Before Sarah could think of a suitable reply, she was shocked once more. Dirk took her roughly in his arms and covered her mouth with his.

10

For a moment Sarah was too surprised to move. She hadn't been kissed in a very long time, and she'd *never* been kissed against her will. She only needed a moment, however, before she realized she was furious. The anger took over, and she shoved against Dirk's chest as hard as she could and wrenched her mouth free.

"Stop that this instant!" she cried, moving as far away as the confines of the boat would allow and holding him back with stiff arms so he wouldn't try to follow.

"Sarah—" he tried, but she was having none of it.

"Stop making a fool of yourself, Dirk," she said. "What's the matter with you? Have you lost your senses?"

"You've stolen them, I'm afraid, Sarah," he said, his voice breathless and husky. "How can you expect me to control myself? You're a bewitching woman. You must know that. No man can help but fall under your spell."

He sounded so sincere, Sarah was only sorry it was too dark in the tunnel to see his expression. She imagined he would look lovesick and vulnerable. He probably tried this trick on every girl he met. He must be quite practiced at it by now. The only thing she couldn't understand was why he felt he had to work his wiles on *her*.

"Dirk, you're being ridiculous!" she insisted.

"And you're being a tease!" He sounded annoyed now, but she figured it was all part of his game. "What do you expect me to think when you practically throw yourself in my way and then ask me to take you to Coney Island?"

"I told you I wanted to come here to catch a killer," she reminded him, growing annoyed herself. "That doesn't sound very romantic to me."

"I assumed it was simply a ploy to get my attention."

"Why would I want your attention?"

At last he reared back, giving Sarah some room again. "You're a penniless widow, Sarah." The sincerity was gone, replaced by contempt. "The Schylers are one of the wealthiest families in the city."

"And you thought I was looking for a husband?" Sarah could hardly credit this.

"Your mother made it clear to me that I was invited to her dinner party at your request. You had just encountered me here at Coney Island and learned I wasn't married. What was I supposed to think?"

"You were supposed to think I needed your help finding my way around this place, just as I said."

"Women never say what they mean, Sarah," he told her. His voice had changed again. He was growing angry now. "Yes means no and no means yes. They lie and cheat and all they care about is how much money you have to spend on them."

Sarah was beginning to understand why Dirk was still unmarried. "Not all women are like that, Dirk. Perhaps if you spent more time with women of your own class—"

"Don't be a snob, Sarah. Women of my own class are the worst of all. They can't be bought with a few amusement-park rides and a Red Hot. They want jewels and furs and a country estate, but their virtue is for sale just the same. The price is just higher."

"Well, you can rest assured that my virtue is not for sale at any price, Dirk. I have no interest in your fortune or your person, so you can remember your manners and keep your hands to yourself."

"I thought you were different, Sarah."

"I am different. I'm not going to let you molest me."

He gave a bark of mirthless laughter that sent chills over her. Indeed, he could molest her easily if he so chose. The tunnel was dark and no one was likely to heed her screams of protest. Plainly, this ride was designed to provide a few moments of privacy for couples to indulge at least the minimal pleasures of the flesh. She thought of her hat pin and wondered how long it would hold him at bay if he decided to press the issue.

For the first time in her life Sarah felt an inkling of the kind of terror Gerda and the others must have felt at the hand of their killer. As a woman, she had worried about her personal safety many times while making her way through the city after dark, but that had been a nebulous fear, vague and general, a fear of what *could* happen. This was a fear of what very well might happen, with a familiar face to put on the person who could harm her.

His breathing was ragged, as if he were battling some inner demons, and she imagined he probably was. Sarah glanced up ahead, hoping to see some sign that the ride would shortly be coming to an end. She imagined she saw a glimmer of light, but perhaps that was only wishful thinking. How long could a ride like this last?

But to her great relief, Dirk finally drew a deep breath and let it out on a long sigh. "I'm afraid I must beg your pardon, Sarah. It's been a long time since I was in the presence of a true lady."

She considered pointing out that his mother was most likely a lady and decided not to. Perhaps he had a different opinion. Knowing his mother, he probably did. "I could chastise you for keeping bad company, Dirk."

"You'd be right, too. But you're too much of a lady to point out a man's faults right to his face, aren't you?"

"I will be, in this case, at least," she allowed.

"Thank you. Can you ever forgive my abominable behavior? I'm afraid I forgot myself completely."

"Or perhaps you simply misjudged your companion."

"More likely I have forgotten how to conduct myself in polite company. Can you pretend this never happened?"

"Since you were so gracious as to bring me here today and to patiently endure my feeble attempts at playing detective, I can do nothing less." Anything to get through this awkward moment.

"I will be eternally in your debt," he said. He sounded sincere again. Perhaps he had practice at that, too. "I promise you I will behave myself for the remainder of the day. You need not fear a repeat of my boorishness ever again."

"And you need not fear that I will stick you with a hat pin," she replied archly.

"Oh, dear, I hadn't expected such spirit from you, Sarah." She heard amusement in his tone. "I must count myself lucky that I didn't press my suit."

"You must indeed." There, at last the darkness was lifting. The opening of the tunnel had appeared and was drawing ever closer. Or rather they were drawing closer to it.

Sarah looked at Dirk in the growing light, judging his mood. He seemed perfectly composed, his features calm, his eyes expressionless. Whatever passion had possessed him in the tunnel had passed now. She only wished the words he'd said could pass as easily from her mind. He'd displayed a disturbing contempt for women, and she wondered how he had developed it. True, most men of his class believed women to be helpless creatures who weren't very bright and had to be looked after by men. That was far different from the genuine disdain he had shown, though. He apparently believed women were liars and cheats, saying one thing and meaning another. That was sometimes true, of course. Occasionally, one had to conceal one's genuine feelings or risk giving offense. But that wasn't what he'd meant, she was sure.

She remembered how Malloy had taken an instant dislike

to Dirk. She supposed he had much more practice than she at judging a man's character. He'd seen what she hadn't known to look for. She'd have to remember to take his assessments more seriously in the future.

As they emerged into the summer sunshine, Dirk smiled at her. She studied his face, noticing again the signs of dissipation. The puffiness around the eyes, the sagging along his jawline in spite of his relative youth. His eyes were carefully expressionless, or perhaps he had no expression to reveal.

"Can we still be friends, Sarah?" he asked, trying the boyish charm she found so unappealing.

"Of course. We've known each other since the nursery, after all." A slight exaggeration, but what did that matter? She had no intention of ever purposely seeing him again once this day was finished. In the meantime, she would make what use of him she could.

As the boat reached the docking point, a young man caught it with a long, hooked pole and pulled it in. Dirk helped her disembark, taking her hand with just the right amount of pressure but assuming no other liberties.

Sarah felt relief. Perhaps they could get through the rest of the day without any more unpleasantness.

She began to believe it when he said, "I must confess, Sarah. I always was rather fond of you. You were the prettiest girl in our dancing class, but you never looked at me twice. I must have been remembering that and thinking that I could get you to notice me now."

"I noticed you then, Dirk. It's just that I didn't like boys yet. And now . . . well, I think we're much too different to suit, don't you?"

His smile was strange. "Sometimes I think I'm too different to suit anyone."

Sarah had no intention of exploring that subject with him. "Tell me, Dirk, are there shops around here where someone could buy articles of ladies' clothing?"

"What types of articles?" he asked, his good humor returning instantly as he realized she was going to forgive him.

"Shoes."

"Ah, let me guess. Red shoes in particular."

"Exactly."

"Do you really expect to have more success with that than you did with the photographer?"

"Hundreds of people get their photographs taken at the park, but I can't believe that many women would buy red shoes. Surely, the sale would be a memorable one."

Dirk sighed, but it was a patient sigh. "I'll take you over to Surf Avenue. That's where you're most likely to find what you're looking for."

Surf Avenue was the main street in Coney Island, flanked on either side by the impressive hotels built for those with the time and money to spend more than one day at the shore. The crowds here were more sedate that the ones in the amusement park, although Sarah saw a few suspicious-looking couples in which the man was old enough to be the girl's father but was showing her more than paternal affection.

"Do, uh, some men," Sarah began, trying to phrase her question delicately, "take the girls they meet at the park to hotels here?"

"Why, Sarah," he said. "How shocking of you to ask!"

"I'm sure it would take far more than that to shock you, Dirk," she said. "Of course if your sensibilities are too offended, don't feel obligated to reply."

He conceded. "Although I would have no personal knowledge of such things," he began, both of them knowing he was lying, "I have heard that some men, those whose tastes extend to the lower classes of women, will meet those women at the park and then take them to the hotels here for assignations. Of course," he added with a sly grin, "many of the girls in question can't be away from home overnight. Their families would never allow such inappropriate behavior."

"So those are the virtuous ones," she guessed.

"Heavens, no!" he said, taking perverse pleasure in telling her. "Those are the ones who do it standing up in a hallway or an alley."

"Do what?" she asked, certain she must have misunderstood.

"Allow a gentleman to enjoy their favors," he said brutally, leaving her with no room to misinterpret.

Sarah was appalled. "What kind of a man would do such a thing?"

"Any kind of man, if the girl is willing. I'm sure your Sergeant Malloy would confirm it."

Sarah couldn't imagine Malloy doing any such thing, any more than she could imagine discussing it with him in the first place. She was learning far more than she had wanted to know about the society of Coney Island, and more about Dirk Schyler than she wanted to know, too.

Fortunately, they were passing a shop window in which some ladies' shoes were displayed. "Let's try this place," she suggested. She didn't wait for Dirk's reply.

A long time and several shops later Sarah was exhausted and discouraged. More shopkeepers than she cared to count had looked at her with contempt when she had asked to see a pair of red shoes. She couldn't imagine that they believed she wanted to purchase anything like that, but apparently, they did. Unfortunately, none of them could oblige her.

They were coming abreast of the Elephant Hotel, and Sarah was just about to surrender her quest when Dirk said, "I think there are some shops in here."

"Inside the Elephant? I thought it was a hotel."

"They have a few rooms, but it's mostly for people to come in and look around. There's a vista room in the head and a diorama in one of the front legs. The other front leg is a cigar store, I think, and there are several shops inside the body."

Sarah studied the curious edifice. Surely, it was the only

one of its kind in the world, an enormous wooden elephant standing over a hundred feet high.

"What do you think, Sarah? Are you ready to see the elephant?" Dirk teased.

She supposed she was. She could use a vista right now, anyway.

They entered the Elephant through a spiral staircase in one of the creature's hind legs. Their shoes clanked on the metal stairs, echoing hollowly in the building. The place was dim and stuffy. Inside the body was a little better, however. Windows opened to catch the sea breeze, which hardly ever ceased to blow, and people on holiday strolled through the various shops, looking for souvenirs of their visit.

Most of the shops featured useless trinkets. All manner of elephant figures were available in every imaginable size and material, as were picture postcards one could send to one's friends. Sarah considered sending Malloy one of the postcards, perhaps one with a picture of some girls in bathing costumes. Then she reconsidered and purchased a wooden carving of an elephant for his son. Now she had a doll for Agnes Otto's child and an elephant for Brian. Another elephant and another doll, and she was finished with her shopping.

Dirk watched her with amused interest, and she didn't bother to explain for whom she was making her purchases. Let him wonder.

In the end, she almost missed the shop. It was at the end of the row, and the display case was filled with gaudy hats and shawls and cheap jewelry. Only when Dirk stopped to admire something—probably to annoy her—did she see the red shoes. She'd been looking so hard for them, she somehow hadn't expected them to be displayed so prominently. But there they were, in the front of the case, in plain view of anyone passing by. Sarah felt a surge of excitement. When she looked up, Dirk was smirking.

"You knew these were here all along, didn't you?" she accused.

"Don't be ridiculous," he said. "I knew this shop was here, though. I figured if anyone would have such a thing as red shoes, this fellow would."

She wasn't sure she believed him. It would be just like Dirk to make her trudge all over town before taking her right to what she was looking for. She didn't bother to accuse him of it again, though. No use wasting any more time on this. Inside the shop, the proprietor was helping a young girl in a cheap suit and a tasteless hat decide which brooch the older man with her was going to purchase for her. Payment for services rendered, no doubt, Sarah thought sadly. She waited patiently, glancing outside once to see Dirk pretending to be interested in a display of picture postcards in the shop across the way. At least he hadn't come inside with her to roll his eyes at the man while she questioned him.

She pretended an interest in the shoddy merchandise which had been selected more for ostentation than for quality. Along one wall were displayed an assortment of shoes, none of which could be worn for everyday use. They were all too fancy, too fragile, and too vulgar. Just the sort of thing to appeal to a poor shop girl's idea of style and glamour. After what seemed an eternity, the man paid for the brooch, and the couple left. The girl seemed pleased, and the man just looked satisfied. Sarah tried not to picture him taking his pleasure standing up in an alley. Would she ever be able to get that vision out of her mind?

"Can I help you, miss?" the man behind the counter asked. He was an older man, slightly stooped and balding. What hair he had left was pure white and combed carefully in a futile attempt to conceal his bald patches.

"Yes, I'm interested in the red shoes you have on display."

His expression betrayed surprise. "For yourself?" Plainly, he didn't believe it.

Sarah smiled. "No, actually, I'm not interested in buying the shoes. I'm interested in someone who did buy a pair like them a few weeks ago."

The man was worried now. "If she wasn't happy with them, I can't—"

"Oh, no, I'm sure she was very pleased with them. It's just . . . something happened to her. She was . . . murdered."

The old man's eyes widened, and he took a step back, as if trying to get away from Sarah. Or at least from what she was saying. "I don't know nothing about it," he insisted.

"Of course you don't," Sarah assured him, wishing she knew more about interrogating people. Malloy would know what to do. But maybe not. This poor man was terrified. Malloy would have had him reduced to hysterics by now, and they'd never find out anything. She tried another smile, making it as kindly as she could manage. "I was just wondering if you might be able to remember who bought the shoes for the young lady in question. We think he might be the one who killed her, you see, but we don't know anything about him."

"Who's this 'we' you keep talking about?" he asked suspiciously.

Sarah thought fast. If she mentioned the police, she'd get no help at all. "Her family. I'm a family friend, you see, and they've asked me to help them find her killer."

"They would've done better with one of them detectives," he told her. "You can hire men to look into things like this. Females got no business with such things."

Sarah gritted her teeth to keep from telling him she most certainly did have business with such things. "I have some experience in these matters. And I did manage to locate the place where the poor girl got the shoes, didn't I?"

He frowned, not quite certain he should admit to it. "And what good did it do you?"

"None yet, but it might if you can remember who the man was who bought the shoes for her. Her name was

Gerda. She was a pretty, blond girl. German. She hadn't been here very long, and she spoke with an accent. We think the man who bought her the shoes would have been well dressed. Expensively dressed, that is."

"A lot of them is, you know," the man told her. "They come down here where nobody knows them and takes up with these girls. It's a scandal. In my time, girls didn't go off alone with men. They stayed home where they was safe. You say this girl got herself killed?"

"Yes, that's right."

"It's no wonder, then. She was asking for trouble. What kind of family don't know to keep their girls home where they'll be safe?"

Sarah wanted to point out that Gerda had been forced to work to support herself, so she couldn't possibly have stayed home. Arguing would be a waste of time, though, and she might annoy him enough that he wouldn't tell her anything.

"You're right," she said, trying to be patient. "But we still need to find out who murdered Gerda. He's killed other girls, and he'll most likely kill again if we don't catch him."

"Others, you say? That's terrible! But it wouldn't happen if they'd stay home—"

"I know, I know." Sarah had reached the end of her patience. "But can you give us any help at all? Do you remember the German girl who bought red shoes? It wasn't very long ago."

He frowned with the effort at remembering. "I only sold a couple pairs this summer, but I've seen hundreds of people coming through my store. She was German, you say?"

"Yes, and she would have been very excited about the shoes."

He nodded slowly, concentrating as he remembered. "Thick ankles."

"What?"

"She had thick ankles. I see a lot of ankles in my business. A woman tries on a pair of shoes, you see her ankles. Can't help it."

Now Sarah wanted to throttle him, but she restrained herself. He surely wouldn't tell her anything if she did. "So you do remember her?"

"I only sold two pairs of the red shoes, and the other girl was an American."

He really did remember. He was just being difficult. "Do you remember the man who was with her, the one who bought her the shoes?"

He frowned again. "I ain't too sure. Is there some kind of reward or something?"

"If the information leads us to the killer, there's a reward of one hundred dollars," Sarah lied without batting an eye. Quite frankly, if someone could tell her who the killer was, she'd gladly pay the hundred dollars herself.

The man suddenly seemed much friendlier than he had been. "Can't blame me for being careful, can you? Don't know just who might be coming in here, asking questions. Don't want to get mixed up in no murder, now do I? Can't have the police in here. Bad for business, you know."

Sarah could just imagine. "The man who bought the shoes," she prodded.

"Well, they don't usually introduce themselves, if you know what I mean, and I don't notice the men much anyways. But I remember the girl well enough. She was babbling in German, and he kept telling her to talk English, and she kept saying, 'Oh, Will, they're so pretty,' or something like that."

Sarah felt the blood rushing from her head. "Will? She called him Will?"

"I think so." He was hedging, seeing Sarah's excitement but not knowing what it meant. "I wouldn't want to get nobody in trouble, but I'm pretty sure that's what I remember. Now who did you say was going to pay this reward?"

"Her family," Sarah said, "and I'll certainly tell them how helpful you've been."

Now she had it, proof that all the murdered girls had known the man named Will. He must be the one they were looking for. She couldn't wait to get back to the city and tell Malloy. She was mentally answering all of the questions she imagined Malloy would ask when she almost bumped into Dirk in the corridor outside the shop.

"You look particularly satisfied," he remarked with a grin. "Did you find your killer?"

If only it were so easy. "I learned that a man named Will bought the red shoes for Gerda. That means she really did know him, and all the other girls knew him, too!"

His smile vanished. "What other girls?"

Sarah was so excited, she had forgotten her resolve not to tell Dirk about the other murders. Now, of course, there was no reason not to.

"There have been other murders in which girls like Gerda were killed in the same way. That's how we knew about this man named Will. They had all been seeing him right before they were killed. We knew Gerda had been seeing someone new, too, but we didn't know his name, at least not until today."

He was horrified. "So you think this Will character must be the killer? That he's killed . . . how many girls did you say?"

"I'm not sure," she said, hedging. "Three more that we know about, but there may be others. We only found out about these by accident, because some of Gerda's friends knew the other victims."

Dirk was pale. For all his worldliness, he had probably never been exposed to something so ugly before. He tried his usual grin, but it was crooked and strained. "So now that you know this fellow Will is connected to all the murdered girls, how do you propose finding him?"

"We don't have to talk about this anymore, Dirk," Sarah said kindly. "I can see you're upset and—"

"Oh, please, I'll be more upset if I don't know everything. I must believe that you have a plan for catching this . . . this monster, or I won't be able to sleep at night."

"Actually, I'm not sure we do have a plan. Mr. Malloy might be able to come up with some ideas, but . . . I'm afraid that photographer was right. Unless I can find a picture of this fellow, or someone who knows what he looks like, we might never find him."

He was still upset, but he asked no other questions. He just started walking, and Sarah went with him.

By unspoken consent, they strolled over to the entrance to the Vista Room, which was actually the head of the elephant. Long windows on either side, that were actually the slits that formed the elephant's eyes, allowed a panoramic view of the ocean, the beaches, and the Island itself. Other visitors were clustered in front of them, so Sarah and Dirk stood back, waiting for an opening.

"Perhaps one of the dead girl's friends would know this Will," he suggested. "Have you asked them?"

She almost said that of course she had asked them, but then she caught herself. She'd asked them to give her the names of the men Gerda had been seeing. They hadn't mentioned a Will, so naturally, she hadn't asked if they knew a man named Will. "No! No, I didn't!" she exclaimed.

Dirk smiled. It was a funny, crooked thing, but a smile nonetheless. He was trying so hard to pretend he was as unaffected as she by the subject of murder and murderers. "Then you must speak to them again. Why, for all you know, one of them might be able to lead you straight to this man. Who do you think would be the most likely to help you?"

Now he was even trying to help solve the case. She could hardly fault him for that, though, not when she was trying to do the same thing. "Gerda had three friends she worked with. They knew everything about her, so it seems strange she didn't tell them this fellow's name."

"Maybe not so strange. Maybe she wanted to keep him to herself," he suggested. "Girls like that are very jealous, especially when they find a generous companion."

He should know. She considered his theory. "Or maybe it was just the opposite. Maybe the other girls knew him, and she didn't want them to know she was seeing him."

"Because she'd stolen him from one of them."

"Exactly!"

"Now all you need to do is decide which of them was most likely to have been his first choice," Dirk said.

"Oh, that's easy enough. Lisle would be any man's first choice," Sarah said, thinking aloud.

"Lisle?" he echoed, arching his eyebrow at her. "Another German girl, obviously. From the same neighborhood?"

"Yes."

"This fellow doesn't go far afield, does he? He should be easy to find."

Sarah only hoped he was right.

THE NEXT MORNING, Mrs. Elsworth was on Sarah's doorstep bright and early, her wrinkled face pale and drawn and her graying hair done up so hastily, the knot sat crooked on her head. "Oh, Mrs. Brandt, I had to see that you were all right. I had the most terrible dream last night, and then this morning . . ." She clutched at her chest, gasping for breath, and Sarah quickly took her arm and led her inside.

"Sit down right here and let me listen to your heart," she said, putting her in the chair beside her desk in the examining room. "Are you having any pain?"

"Goodness, no," she exclaimed breathlessly. "I'm just . . . I can't seem to get my breath. I was so frightened when I saw it."

"The dream, you mean?" Sarah asked, reaching into her medical bag and pulling out the stethoscope.

"No, the cricket!"

Sarah was just about to put the stethoscope in her ears, but she stopped at this. "You were frightened by a cricket?"

"Not just any cricket! Everyone knows that a cricket in the house is good luck. Unless it's a white cricket, of course. And this one was. Pure white, and you know what that means!"

"No, I don't," Sarah admitted.

Mrs. Elsworth closed her eyes and laid her hand over her heart again. Sarah reached out, fully expecting her to keel over and ready to break the fall, but she didn't move. She only said, "Death."

"Death?" Sarah echoed stupidly.

Mrs. Elsworth opened her eyes and looked straight at her. "The white cricket means a death is coming to someone close."

"Oh, I'm sure that—"

"And then there was my dream. You were in it, Mrs. Brandt. You were running and running, trying to catch someone, but you couldn't, and then I saw her. I couldn't see her face, but she was dead, and I was so afraid . . . Well, I had to make sure you were all right, didn't I?"

"And as you can see, I'm perfectly fine. I'd be better if you'd allow me to listen to your heart, though. Just to make sure you're fine, too," she added with a small smile.

"It's really not necessary, but if it will make you happy," she conceded.

Sarah was relieved to hear the older woman's heart beating rapidly but strongly.

"Didn't I tell you?" Mrs. Elsworth said as Sarah put the stethoscope away.

"I'd be a poor neighbor if I were less concerned about you than you are about me," Sarah pointed out.

Mrs. Elsworth sighed. "At least I'm not going out at all hours of the day and night looking for a killer."

"Neither am I," Sarah said.

"You were out yesterday, weren't you? All day. I think that's what brought on my dream, worrying about you. I knew it wasn't a delivery. I saw the man who called for you yesterday morning."

Of course she had. No one came onto the street that Mrs. Elsworth didn't see.

"If you saw the man who called for me, you should have known there was nothing to worry about."

Mrs. Elsworth sniffed. "I hope you won't think I'm meddling, but I don't believe that fellow is a proper companion for you, Mrs. Brandt."

"Dirk?" Sarah asked in surprise. He had called for her in a hansom cab, which had seemed excessive to Sarah, since they were taking the trolley to Coney Island. She would have thought that would have impressed Mrs. Elsworth, however. "Why do you think he's not proper?"

"I know that look," she said. "He's a man who's seen too much of the world. He'll always be restless and angry. No woman will ever satisfy him for long."

Sarah was awed that her neighbor could make such an accurate assessment of Dirk Schyler just by catching a quick glimpse of him. "You don't need to worry about me, Mrs. Elsworth. I won't be seeing him again."

"That is a relief," she admitted, managing a strained smile. She still looked shaken, though. Sarah might consider her superstitions ridiculous, but Mrs. Elsworth took them very seriously indeed, and this one had truly frightened her. Not badly enough that she forgot important things, however. "And how is that nice Mr. Malloy?" she asked. "I haven't seen him around for a while."

Sarah managed not to choke at the description of Malloy as "nice." "I haven't seen him around in a while either," she said, "so I have no idea how he is."

"Now, you should know Mr. Malloy would be a much better match for you than that fellow from yesterday, Mrs. Brandt," Mrs. Elsworth said.

This time Sarah did choke. "Are you serious?" she asked when she could talk again.

"Perfectly. Oh, I know he's Irish and a Catholic, but I don't imagine that would stop either of you if you decided you wanted to be together."

"I must say, you have an odd idea of what's proper and what isn't," Sarah said, thinking her mother's—and Malloy's mother's and everyone else's—was exactly the opposite.

"Not odd," Mrs. Elsworth said. "Just practical. You'll understand when you're older, or at least I hope you will. Well, now that I've satisfied myself that you're all right, I'll let you be about your business. Just promise that you'll be careful, won't you? Dreams are sometimes omens, and the cricket definitely was. You mark my words."

"I'm always careful," Sarah assured her, not quite accurately. She would be until Gerda's killer was caught, though. And with any luck, that wouldn't be long.

SARAH WAS JUST putting on her hat that afternoon to go out when someone knocked on her door. She was surprised to see Malloy standing on her doorstep. She hadn't sent for him yet, because she'd wanted to talk to Gerda's friends first. If one of them knew this Will fellow, that would save a lot of time. She'd been planning to catch them as they left Faircloth's this evening, but this was even better. Malloy could go with her to question the girls, and she could fill him in on the way.

But then she got a look at his face. "What's happened?" she asked in alarm, thinking of his son.

"That girl Lisle has been murdered."

11

SARAH COULDN'T GET HER BREATH, AND SHE didn't resist at all when Malloy took her arm and guided her to a chair, just as she had done for Mrs. Elsworth that morning.

"Are you sure?" she asked, knowing she was grasping at a straw but praying it would hold nonetheless.

"As sure as we can be. Her face is pretty bad."

She felt the gorge rising in her throat and covered her mouth with both hands.

"You're not going to faint on me, are you? Put your head down," he said.

"No, I'm fine," she said, alarmed at how her voice sounded. She didn't want to be a detective anymore. She didn't want to know about any other young lives being snuffed out.

"You don't look fine," Malloy said, his own voice alarming as well. He sounded frightened. "You got any smelling salts around here?"

She did, of course, but she wasn't going to need them. Her head was clearing now. She swallowed down hard on the sickness in her throat and clung fiercely to her pride.

"Just tell me what happened. Tell me everything."

"You aren't in any condition to hear about it," he said. "I just wanted you to know so you didn't have to find out from some stranger."

She drew in a deep breath. "Thank you for that. I was on my way to Faircloths. I wanted to talk to Lisle"—she had to stop and swallow after saying the girl's name—"about something I discovered at Coney Island yesterday."

"You found out something?" he asked, sounding insulted. "Were you planning to tell me about it?"

"Yes, of course, just as soon as I'd talked to Lisle and the others."

He pulled up her desk chair and sat down facing her. "Tell me now."

Sarah drew another breath. She was feeling more like herself, but the pain was beginning. She could see Lisle, the fragile-looking girl with the will of iron. Sarah remembered how frightened she had been about meeting George and taking him out of the dance hall so Malloy could question him. She'd been too frightened to go home that night, so she'd stayed at Sarah's instead. Sleeping in Sarah's bed, she'd looked like an innocent child, with her hand curled against her cheek and her corn-yellow hair spread out on the pillow.

Sarah thought of her death, how terrified she must have been. The pain and the fear and the knowledge that she knew who the killer was but would never be able to tell anyone. How many others would have to die before they could stop him?

She swiped impatiently at the tears that sprang to her eyes. She didn't have time for that now. "Do you have any idea who did it?"

"Well, I did question our friend George, even though I was pretty sure he didn't do it. He didn't. He was with a group of fellows playing cards all night. They were pretty drunk, but they all said George never left the room for more than a few minutes. He was pretty broken up about the girl, too. I guess he cared for her a little."

Sarah wasn't surprised George was innocent. "I found the place where Gerda got the red shoes. In Coney Island, at a shop in the Elephant Hotel. The shopkeeper remembered that the man who bought them for her was named Will."

"And?"

"And what?"

"Is that all?" he asked impatiently.

"Yes, that's all! It proves that Gerda knew this Will fellow, too. We know it wasn't George, so this Will must be the killer."

"Well, unless this shopkeeper gave you Will's address, I don't think we're any closer to finding him now than we were before," Malloy pointed out.

Oh, dear, she just wasn't thinking clearly. "There's more. I also realized I'd never asked Gerda's friends if they knew anyone named Will. I just asked the names of the men they did know. I was going to ask them today—" Her voice broke, and she had to cover her mouth to hold back a sob.

"There wasn't much chance that they did know him," Malloy pointed out.

Sarah drew a shaky breath. "That's what I thought, too, at first. But then Dirk said—"

"Dirk?" he asked incredulously.

Oh, dear, she hadn't meant to tell him that part. "Yes, I asked Dirk Schyler to go with me when I went back to Coney Island. He knows the area," she added defensively when he made a face. "At any rate, I realized that there was really no reason for Gerda not to have told her friends the name of the man who'd been so generous to her and bought her the shoes unless one of them already knew him and considered him her beau or something. Dirk pointed out that the girls are very possessive of the men who are generous, so if she'd stolen him away from one of her friends, she might not want her to know."

"It's possible," he said sourly. "Or maybe she didn't want anybody stealing him from her, and that's why she didn't tell them who he was."

"There's one way to find out, although I don't suppose this would be a good time to question Hetty and Bertha. They'll be pretty upset."

"I don't know. They didn't seem very upset when Gerda died. Maybe they'll think it's one less woman to compete for the men."

"What a horrid thing to say! Don't you have any feelings at all?" she demanded, suddenly furious.

"Ah, that's more like it," he said, leaning back in his chair. "For a minute there, I was afraid you were going to go vaporish on me."

Now she really was mad. He'd made her angry on purpose so she wouldn't cry. Just like a man, afraid of a few tears. Well, she'd make him pay for getting her ire up.

"All right, now tell me what happened. How did Lisle . . . ?" Angry as she was, she still couldn't say the words.

He winced a bit, but he said, "She was beaten, like the others. In an alley not too far from where she lived. Near where they found the Reinhard girl, too. Why do these girls go into alleys with strange men in the first place?"

"Because they can't go to hotel rooms," Sarah informed him without thinking.

"What?"

Oh, dear, now she would have to explain. How on earth could she do that without embarrassing them both? She drew a deep breath and plunged ahead. "Prostitutes usually have a room or else men take them to a hotel, but these girls can't do that. They have families who expect them to come home at some point for the night. If they want to be alone with a man, their choices are few. Alleys are dark and private and perfectly suitable for a quick . . . uh . . . rendezvous."

Malloy was horrified. "Are you talking about . . . ?"

Sarah nodded reluctantly. "Whatever favors the girls

grant are granted in alleys. Standing up. Which only makes sense, considering how filthy the alleys are."

Malloy took a minute to digest what she was telling him. She hadn't been able to imagine discussing this with him, but for some reason she didn't feel the embarrassment she'd expected to feel. Malloy's attitude probably had something to do with it. Most men would have snickered or made fun, but he was as appalled as she.

"Mother of God," he murmured, and rubbed his face with both hands.

"Had Lisle been . . . interfered with?" An awkward euphemism for rape.

"Not violently. She probably consented to that part, the same way the others did. It's after that the killer gets angry and starts beating them. That's the part that doesn't make any sense. I can understand him getting angry if the girl refuses him, but these girls didn't. It's like he's angry with them *because* they allowed him to use them."

"Maybe he is," Sarah said. "His mind has got to be twisted to kill the girls the way he does."

He gave her no argument.

"So what do we do now?" she asked after a moment.

"*You* don't do anything," he said. "I'm going to see this girl's family and find out what I can about where she was last night."

"Her family won't know anything."

"And I'll question Hetty and Bertha, too."

"They won't *tell* you anything," Sarah warned him. "Why don't you let me talk to them?"

"Because you're not a police officer," he reminded her.

"What difference does that make? They'll tell me things they'd never tell you. If you expect to find out anything at all, you'll have to let me talk to them sooner or later."

She was right, and it killed him to admit it. After a painful inner struggle, he surrendered. "Do you even know where they live?"

"No, but I can find them." She knew just whom to ask. It would give her the perfect excuse to go there, too.

MALLOY HATED THIS part of his job. Questioning the grieving family of a murder victim was never easy. When the victim was a young woman, it was horrible. He could hear the weeping from down on the street. Of course, with the windows open because of the heat, you could hear everything going on in the flats above.

The girl's family lived on the third floor. Frank was sweating by the time he reached it. The door to their flat stood open, and neighbors had gathered in the kitchen to comfort the girl's mother, who was inconsolable.

When they noticed him, the room went silent. Even the mother stopped crying. Her bloodshot eyes looked to him pathetically. Some part of her probably hoped he'd come to tell her it was all a mistake. "Could I talk to you alone, Mrs. Lasher?" he asked.

"It's Frankle," one of the neighbors said helpfully. "She's remarried."

"Mrs. Frankle," he corrected himself.

"My husband, he'll be back soon," she tried, moving her hands helplessly, desperate to be spared the ordeal of speaking of her dead child.

"Then I'll talk to him when he gets here." He looked at the other women in the room meaningfully. Without a word, they filed out. One of them patted Mrs. Frankle's hand and whispered something to her before following the others out.

When they were gone, he closed the door in spite of the heat.

"There's no mistake, then? It's really Lisle?" she asked, her eyes still holding on to the hope.

"No mistake. I thought somebody had identified her."

"My husband, but he said . . . He could've made a mistake. I wanted to go myself, but when they told me . . . I couldn't."

"You made the right choice," he assured her. "Remember her the way she was."

He pulled out a chair and sat down across the kitchen table from her while she dabbed at her eyes with a damp handkerchief.

"Do you know where Lisle went last night?"

She shook her head. "She goes out almost every night, but I do not know the places. She does not tell us where she goes. Dancing, I think. Her friends would know."

"Did she have any special men friends?"

"None that come here," her mother said bitterly. "She does not tell us anything about what she does or who she knows. I tell her this is not good, that she will end up like the Reinhard girl, but does she listen? No, she never listens."

She was working herself up to anger now. Malloy always learned more when they were angry. "Maybe she mentioned someone she was afraid of," he suggested.

"No, never," her mother insisted. "She does not tell us anything. Except . . ."

"Except what?" he asked when she hesitated.

She was thinking, remembering. "There was a photograph . . ."

Frank couldn't believe he would be this lucky. "A photograph of what?"

"Of Lisle. And some other people. In a boat, I think. I do not know when she would have been in a boat. She tried to hide it, but nothing is private here. That is what she always says. The other children, they get into her things, so she cannot keep anything a secret. She cries to me about it, but what can I do?"

"It's hard in a place so small," Frank agreed. "And the other children found this photograph?"

"Yes. Her brothers teased her about it, but she said she did not care because she did not like the man anymore. She told them to burn the picture. I think she said it because she knew they would not hurt it if they thought she didn't care. They kept it to tease her, though."

"Do you know where it is now?" The chances that it would help him were very slim, but he was willing to take even the smallest clue.

"No, I—"

"It could be very important."

"Do you think it could help find who did this?"

"It might."

"I will try to find it."

SARAH HEARD A baby squalling as she climbed the stairs. The cry was loud and strong, a good sign if it was coming from the Ottos' flat. The door was open, and Agnes was moving around, preparing dinner while she bounced the wailing baby on her hip.

"She's really growing," Sarah said from the doorway.

Agnes turned around, obviously startled. Her eyes widened with what looked like alarm. "The baby, she is fine," she said, offering her for Sarah's inspection. "You do not need to worry about her anymore. There is no reason for you to come here."

Indeed, the child was plump and much healthier looking than she'd been the last time Sarah was allowed to see her.

"Sounds like she's hungry," Sarah suggested.

"I will feed her as soon as I am done here. Lars wants his supper on the table when he comes home."

Oh, yes, she had forgotten about the charming Mr. Otto. "I won't keep you. I was just wondering . . . Perhaps you heard that another girl was murdered last night."

Agnes's eyes grew large, and she murmured something that sounded like a prayer in German. Then she noticed her other two children, who had come from the other room to see who their visitor was. She spoke to them sharply in German, and they retreated. Then she turned back to Sarah. "I did not know. Who was it?"

"Gerda's friend Lisle."

Agnes paled, and she sank down into one of the chairs. She was murmuring in German again. The baby was wailing louder now, and Agnes automatically unbuttoned her shirtwaist and offered her breast.

"It was the same? The same as Gerda?" she asked, not quite meeting Sarah's eye.

Sarah hardly heard the question. She was too busy looking at the nasty bruise on Agnes's chest, right above her breast.

Seeing Sarah staring, she quickly pulled her shirtwaist to cover it. "My skin makes the black spots so easy," she said self-consciously. "Is that the reason why you come here? Just to tell me about Lisle?"

It made her sound so cold. "No, not exactly. I wanted to pay my condolences to Bertha and Hetty, but I don't know where they live. I thought maybe you could help me."

She seemed relieved and gave Sarah an address on Seventh Street. "That is where Hetty lives. I do not know about Bertha. Please, you must go now. Lars will be home soon, and he does not want you here."

How well Sarah remembered. "I brought some gifts for the children," she said. "Just some toys," she added when Agnes would have objected.

"I cannot take them," she said, her eyes frightened again. "Lars would want to know where they came from. He would be angry. Please, you must go now." She sounded almost desperate.

Sarah was beginning to understand. How she could have been so dense, she had no idea. Agnes was afraid of her husband, and probably for good reason, if the bruise had come from his hand, as Sarah strongly suspected. Well, she certainly didn't want to be the cause of another beating.

"I understand," she said. "Thank you for the information. I'm glad to see the baby is doing so well."

Agnes's eyes begged her to be gone, so she turned to go, but just as she reached the door, Agnes called, "Do they know . . . ? Do they know who the killer is yet?" She could hardly get the words out.

Sarah was only too happy to be able to ease her mind, if only a little bit. "We have a good idea. I think it won't be long until he's arrested."

She'd expected Agnes to be relieved. Instead, she looked alarmed, almost frightened. "You know who it is?"

"Yes, or at least we're fairly sure it's a man named Will. Gerda and the other girls all met a man named Will just before they died."

"Will?" She repeated the name carefully. "You are sure?"

"As sure as we can be without catching him in the act," Sarah said, exaggerating slightly.

Agnes closed her eyes for a moment, as if offering a silent prayer. Perhaps she was giving thanks that Gerda's killer would soon be caught. "Thank you," she said when she opened her eyes again.

Sarah marveled at Agnes's gratitude, but she also remembered that Lars would be home soon and wouldn't be happy to find her there. "Send for me if you need me," she said, and left. Moving more quickly than she ordinarily would have, she felt a strong sense of relief when she reached the street without encountering Lars Otto.

Good thing for him, too. She wasn't certain she could have been civil to him just then. She could be wrong, of course, but if he was responsible for the bruise she'd seen on Agnes, he was despicable. And now she also remembered how Agnes had clutched at her side the last time Sarah was here. Could that have been another injury inflicted by her husband? She'd seen too many abused wives to be shocked, but she would never be complacent about that kind of violence. She always had an urge to go after men like that with a bullwhip, although she was well aware of the irony of her desire to punish violence with violence. Not that she would ever have the opportunity to punish anyone, but she could enjoy her fantasies all the same.

In the meantime, she had a grim job to do.

SARAH EASILY FOUND the address that Agnes had given her, but Hetty wasn't at home. The woman who answered the door, whom Sarah guessed was Hetty's mother, looked Sarah up and down suspiciously before giving her that information.

"I'm Sarah Brandt," she said, as if that would impress the woman somehow. "I just heard about Hetty's friend being killed, and I wanted to express my condolences. Do you know where—?"

"She'll be with Bertha. The two of them was carrying on so loud, I made them leave. Don't know where they went."

"Could they have gone to Bertha's?"

The woman shrugged a shoulder, indicating she had no idea and cared less. Sarah was able to convince her to give her the address, however. A few minutes later she was walking down Avenue A and found Hetty and Bertha sitting on the front stoop of one of the tenement buildings. They were no longer "carrying on," but they were slumped against each other, their young faces ravaged by tears. They were the very picture of despair.

"Hello," she greeted them gently.

Bertha looked up and her red-rimmed eyes widened in surprise. "It's Mrs. Brandt," she said, poking Hetty in the ribs.

The other girl looked up without much interest, then slowly her expression hardened into anger. "You did this to her. You killed Lisle!"

"What?" Sarah asked in surprise.

"You made her lead that policeman to George, and now he's done for her just like he did for Gerda!"

"George didn't do this," Sarah told them. "Mr. Malloy questioned him first thing. He was with a group of his friends all night. He's not the killer."

Hetty snorted derisively. "So you say. How do we know his friends ain't in on it, too! Maybe there's a bunch of them that goes around killing girls!"

"If there was, we'd have found them out by now. They'd be bragging and fighting among themselves. It's impossible to keep a secret like that when more than one person knows it."

Hetty didn't want to be wrong. She wanted this to be Sarah's fault so she could put the blame somewhere. She couldn't think of a valid argument, so she simply glared at Sarah.

"Could I buy you girls something to drink?" Sarah suggested. "You look like you could use something."

"You just want to ask us more questions," Hetty said bitterly.

"I want to find out who killed your friends," Sarah agreed. "Maybe you know something that will help."

Bertha was crying again. "I want to find out who it is," she told Hetty, scrubbing at her cheeks with her sleeve. "I'm going to help her." She pushed herself unsteadily to her feet.

"I don't know nothing, and neither do you!" Hetty insisted, her chin jutting rebelliously even though her lower lip quivered suspiciously.

"Then you won't be able to help. But my offer is still good. There's a beer garden just around the corner, isn't there?"

Grudgingly, Hetty rose from the stoop and followed as Sarah and Bertha started down the street. In a few minutes the girls each had a stein of beer—which Sarah felt they needed for medicinal purposes—and Sarah had a lemonade.

They sat in silence for a few minutes. Sarah was loath to intrude upon their grief, but finally she said, "Can you tell me what happened last night?"

"Nothing happened," Hetty said, her anger still fierce.

"She means nothing bad," Bertha explained. "We went to Harmony Hall, just like we usually do. There was a dance, but we none of us met anybody we liked, so we left together. We walked home, and Lisle went off by herself, just like she always does, when we got to her street. That's the last we know."

"Then she wasn't with any particular fellow? Nobody she would have willingly gone with?"

"We ain't done that since Gerda died," Hetty informed her haughtily. "We ain't stupid!"

"Then someone must have followed her or seen her alone and accosted her."

"She would've screamed," Bertha insisted. "There's lots of people out on the streets and sleeping on the roofs and porches. Somebody would've heard if she screamed."

"Maybe she couldn't scream," Sarah suggested, thinking out loud. "Maybe he grabbed her too quickly."

"Or maybe it was somebody she knew," Hetty said with surprising insight. "Maybe she wasn't even afraid at first."

Sarah hadn't thought of that. "Somebody she wasn't afraid of, so she went with him willingly."

"Maybe," Hetty said, not quite convinced. The idea didn't appeal to Sarah, either. Since the girls didn't know who the killer was, how could any man have been considered safe?

Sarah tried a different tack. "Did either of you ever hear Lisle speak of a man named Will?"

The girls exchanged a glance. "Was he the one who . . . ?" Bertha began.

Hetty nodded. "Lisle met him a while back. In the spring, I think. He took her to Coney Island and bought her a pair of ear bobs. He seemed like the perfect beau, and then . . ."

"He hit her," Bertha said baldly.

"What do you mean?"

"They was . . ." Bertha caught herself, glancing at Hetty, whose frown held a warning.

"I know you don't want to speak badly of your friend, but we can't let that stand in the way of finding out who killed her," Sarah reminded them.

"Lisle didn't never want anybody to know, especially you," Bertha told her.

Sarah was touched. Lisle had wanted her good opinion. "I thought Lisle was a fine, brave girl," she said, her voice unsteady as she tried to hold back her tears. "Nothing you tell me now will change my mind. And no one else will ever know."

Hetty still wasn't convinced, but Bertha needed to unburden herself. "A lot of the girls do it, Mrs. Brandt. It's the only way we can get pretty things."

"I understand," she assured them. "I like pretty things, too."

"Lisle liked this fellow, and he treated her real good," Hetty said, her tone daring Sarah to contradict her. "She never would've done it otherwise."

"Of course not," Sarah agreed.

"She went with him one night," Bertha said. "Not to a room or anything. Just someplace private. She let him, you know, and after he was done, he slapped her. Called her a whore."

"He had no call to do that! He knew she weren't no whore," Hetty said.

"She was scared, but she's been beat by her stepfather, so she wasn't going to take it from him," Bertha said.

"He must've been surprised. Maybe he thought 'cause she's so little, she wouldn't put up a fight," Hetty said.

"But she did," Bertha reported. "Kicked him and bit him, and she got away before he could hit her again."

"She was mad," Hetty remembered. "Couldn't hardly tell us about it without spitting and hissing. Wanted to scratch his eyes out, only he never came around again."

Sarah was trying to put it all together, but the puzzle pieces didn't quite fit yet. "Did Gerda know about this?"

"Sure she did," Bertha confirmed. "Lisle told all of us right after it happened."

"Do you think Gerda might've gone with him, even knowing he'd hit Lisle?"

The two girls exchanged another glance. Plainly, they weren't sure about this.

"It's not that Gerda was so brave," Hetty began, feeling her way.

"She just didn't worry about things," Bertha clarified. "Maybe he hit Lisle, but she'd figure he'd never hit *her*. She always thought she was smarter than the rest of us and could get men to do things we couldn't."

"Sometimes she was right, too," Hetty said, "and that only made her worse. She went with anybody who'd treat her. We tried to tell her that was stupid and maybe even dangerous, but she wouldn't listen."

Now it was beginning to make a sort of sense. "So if Gerda had met this Will and realized he was the same one Lisle had warned her about, then you think it's possible she'd have gone with him anyway if he wanted to treat her?"

"Sure. She didn't care." Hetty still sounded angry.

"But she probably wouldn't want the rest of you to know that she was seeing him," Sarah guessed.

"Not unless she wanted us to give her what for," Hetty said.

That explained how the killer had been able to get to Gerda, but not how he'd gotten to Lisle, who would have been more wary.

"I suspect Lisle wouldn't have been likely to go with this Will willingly if he came up on her in the dark," Sarah guessed.

"Not even in the daylight," Hetty confirmed. "Not after the other girls got themselves killed."

Sarah was thinking, trying to picture how it must have been. He'd been looking for Lisle. Maybe he'd been following her, waiting to catch her alone. Or maybe he saw her by chance and remembered that she'd escaped him once. He'd somehow dragged her into an alley without her managing to scream and attract attention. Then he'd beaten the life out of her, taking revenge for her earlier escape.

One strategically placed blow to her stomach would have robbed her of breath and effectively silenced her. By the time she recovered from that, he could have beaten her senseless. Sarah only hoped oblivion had come quickly. She couldn't stand the thought that Lisle had suffered for long.

"Did either of you ever see this man?" Sarah asked. "Do you know what he looks like?"

They considered, trying to remember.

"I saw him that first night," Bertha said, "when he came to ask Lisle to dance. But I wasn't paying much attention. He was just another fellow in the crowd. I didn't know . . ." She shrugged helplessly.

"And you don't remember much about him?" Sarah asked, her hopes dying.

"I doubt I'd know him again," she confirmed.

Sarah thought of the storekeeper who had sold Gerda the red shoes. He'd been so busy looking at her ankles, he probably hadn't even noticed the man who'd paid for the shoes. The only people who could have identified him for sure were dead. And nobody even knew his last name.

Sarah was starting to believe they would never find him.

LISLE'S FUNERAL THE next day was better attended than Gerda's had been. Her family had more friends, it seemed. They filled the United German Lutheran Church, and many of them were weeping audibly. Sarah wondered if it was out of genuine grief over Lisle's death or simply to show support for the family.

Lisle's mother was a tired-looking woman who probably wasn't nearly as old as she looked. Three young boys sat in the pew between her and the man who must have been Lisle's stepfather. He looked like the kind of brute who would beat his stepdaughter. Or maybe he'd just wanted to keep her from going bad and used the only method he knew. Sarah couldn't judge others. Her own shortcomings were too real.

Sitting near the back, she was surprised when Malloy

walked in just as the service began. He slipped into the pew beside her, forcing her to move over to make room for him.

"Thought I'd find you here," he said before the organ music drowned any attempt at conversation.

Sarah wasn't sure if she was glad to see him or not, but the expression on his face warned her he did not have good news to share. In fact, he looked haggard, as if he hadn't slept well. He wouldn't meet her eye, either. Another bad sign.

She studied him as the service progressed. He needed a shave. And a haircut, too. His clothes were rumpled, but then, they always were. Probably, he cultivated his slovenliness so he wouldn't stand out in the poorer neighborhoods where crimes usually occurred.

She tried to concentrate on the minister's words of comfort, but Malloy's presence was too disturbing. He'd come looking for her. What did he know?

Whatever it was, he didn't seem to be in any hurry to share it. He could've pulled her out of the church. She would have willingly gone if he'd had something to tell her. Instead, he seemed intent on studying the crowd. What was he looking for?

Then she realized he was probably looking for someone who might have been Lisle's killer. Was it possible? Would the killer be brazen enough to attend his victim's funeral? Then she realized that a man who would beat young women to death within spitting distance of a public street would probably be brazen enough to do just about anything. But brass didn't count in this instance. He'd have to be a fool to show his face where someone might recognize him or notice that he didn't belong. Sarah doubted he was a fool, but Malloy was looking around anyway. Just in case.

The service seemed interminable, probably because Sarah was so aware of Malloy and so anxious to speak with him alone. No words of comfort would bring the dead back to life, nor could they make the pain of loss more bearable, as Sarah well knew. She didn't want comfort, in any case.

She wanted vengeance. While the others prayed for Lisle's soul, Sarah prayed that Malloy had learned something about the killer. While the others sang of a life hereafter, walking the streets of heaven, Sarah's heart thrummed with a desire to send one particular man to the fires of hell.

Finally, the service ended. The family filed out, following the casket, and Sarah and Malloy waited until the last of the guests had gone. In the quiet of the now empty church, Sarah clutched at his sleeve when he would have followed the others.

"You know something. What is it? Tell me!"

He looked down at his boots, as if seeking wisdom. When his gaze met hers again, his eyes were bleak. "I think I've found out who this Will character is."

"Who?"

He didn't reply. Instead he reached into his coat pocket and pulled out a cheap cardboard photograph cover. It looked just like the one she'd found among Gerda's things, the one that held the picture of her on the Shoot-the-Chutes ride. He handed it to her.

She opened the cover, and for a moment she thought it was the same picture. In the dim light of the church, it might well have been. The boat was the same, and it was filled with people, just like the other photograph. But closer inspection revealed that the occupants of the boat were different. She tilted the picture, trying to catch the light. After a moment she found Lisle. She was trying to look frightened but anyone could she was having the time of her life. She was clinging to a man's arm, and unlike the man in Gerda's photograph, this fellow was looking up, his face full to the camera.

He was Dirk Schyler.

12

"IT'S DIRK," SHE SAID STUPIDLY. HER MIND couldn't quite grasp the significance.

"Yeah, it's him all right. And he's with that girl, Lisle."

She still wasn't certain what it meant.

"Turn the picture over," he suggested.

She turned the cover over and found nothing on the back. He took it impatiently from her hands, pulled the photograph from its frame, and handed it back to her. She recognized Lisle's handwriting from the note she had left with Mrs. Elsworth. The words were scrawled in pencil, but they might as well have been written in blood: *Me and Will at Coney Island.*

"Dear heaven," Sarah breathed, and then she couldn't breathe anymore. She felt as if all the air in the church had suddenly evaporated.

She could see Dirk's face, laughing and smirking at her efforts to find the man named Will out at Coney Island. She remembered how he'd stood there winking at the photographer when she'd inquired about him. Had the photographer recognized him and just pretended not to?

Then she remembered how he'd kissed her, pressing his

mouth against hers so insistently, and how angry he'd been when she'd resisted his advances. Someone made a small, moaning sound, and she vaguely realized it was she.

"Sit down," Malloy said gruffly, laying one of his beefy hands on her shoulder and forcing her down onto the pew.

Dirk had touched her. Dirk had *kissed* her. She felt unclean. She scrubbed the back of her hand across her lips in a vain effort to wipe away the memory of him.

Malloy, who missed nothing, said, "Did you *kiss* him?" His voice held equal measures of disbelief and disgust.

"Not willingly," she informed him, equally disgusted.

"He tried to force himself on you?" Was that outrage? Malloy hardly seemed capable of such a thing, so Sarah must be imagining it.

"He tried to steal a kiss when we were in the tunnel on one of the rides," she recalled, feeling sick to her stomach at the memory. "I pushed him away and told him to stop, and he did."

"He didn't get angry?" Malloy was sitting beside her now, leaning close, watching her face as if for clues.

Sarah tried to remember every detail. "I couldn't see his expression because it was dark, but he *sounded* angry, at least at first. Not for long, though. He said something about my being a lady, and how he didn't encounter many real ladies. He'd forgotten himself, he said." She looked into Malloy's dark eyes, searching for some reassurance. "I made him angry, Malloy. If he was the killer, then he would have killed me, too, wouldn't he?"

She wanted so desperately to be right. She *needed* to be right, because if she wasn't, then a man she'd known all her life was a killer.

But Malloy shook his head. "All the other girls let him have his way. He didn't even have to force them. That's when he beat them to death."

"But we still don't know for certain that Dirk is the one who killed them," Sarah reminded him almost desperately, "even if he really is the man they all knew as Will."

"I believe I've mentioned that before," Malloy reminded her, although she could see it gave him no pleasure to be right. He wanted Dirk to be the killer, and not just because he wanted the killer caught. He wanted Dirk especially to be the guilty one, because he didn't like him. "We need some proof."

Sarah remembered what she'd learned yesterday. "I met with Bertha and Hetty yesterday. They said Lisle knew a man named Will, but she'd stopped seeing him because he hit her."

"When was this?"

"It must have been earlier this summer, just after Coney Island opened on Memorial Day," she guessed, glancing at the photograph she still held. "They said she let him . . . let him have his way. Then he got angry and called her a whore, and he hit her. She fought back, though. Apparently, she's stronger than she appears. *Was* stronger," she corrected herself, her voice catching. "Somehow she managed to get away."

"Did Gerda know about this?"

"That's the strange part. They said she did, which should have made her wary of him, but they also said she was the kind of girl who'd think something like that would never happen to her. She may not have told the others the name of her new benefactor because she didn't want a lecture from Lisle."

Malloy considered this for a moment. "It fits what we know about the killer. Maybe he gets mad at women who give in to him because he thinks they're immoral or something and deserve to die. But why would he have gone after Lisle again? He must've known she'd be wary of him."

"Oh, dear heaven!" Sarah exclaimed, covering her mouth as if she could stop the words that may have led to Lisle's death.

"What is it?" he demanded, his voice too loud for a church.

"I . . . I led him to her!"

"What do you mean?"

"I . . . He was asking me about the crimes. I thought he was just interested!" she cried in her own defense.

Malloy nodded. "Go on. What did you tell him?"

"He asked me . . . No, he *told* me! He was the one who came up with the theory that Gerda hadn't told anyone her new beau's name because she wanted to keep the others from knowing who he was. He suggested they might want to steal him or maybe that Gerda had already stolen him from one of the others. He *knew* that's what had happened!"

"Maybe," Malloy reminded her. "What else?"

"He asked me . . . He wanted to know which of Gerda's friends was most likely to have had a beau that Gerda would want to steal. I told him Lisle. Oh, Malloy, I led him right to her!" she wailed.

"We don't know that for sure," Malloy said with a kindness that surprised her. He was trying to assuage her guilt, but it wasn't working.

"Yes, we do! I killed her, Malloy, just as surely as if I beat her myself!" The tears were welling in her eyes, hot as lava, burning and stinging and begging to be shed.

"Don't be a fool! He would've figured it out himself eventually. Or else he would've just killed every girl who might've led us to him. You probably saved some lives by giving him Lisle's name."

She couldn't bear his vindication, and she certainly didn't deserve it. She'd caused Lisle's death, and she would carry the knowledge to her grave. The only hope she had for retaining her sanity was to put a noose around the killer's neck.

"What can we do now?" she asked. "Will you take him in and question him?"

"Not likely, a man in his position," Malloy said. "If I did and couldn't prove he was the killer, he'd have my job. More important, he'd be free to keep on killing, because he'd know the other detectives wouldn't dare detain him again either, for fear of what he'd do to them."

"Then we need some proof," Sarah said, her mind racing as she considered and rejected one idea after another. "Maybe some of the other friends of the dead girls would recognize him."

"And what if they did? We already know he knew the victims. Unless one of the friends saw him committing a murder, which we know they didn't, then he'd still go free."

Sarah felt the old frustrations welling up, the helpless, powerless feeling she'd had when her husband Tom was killed and no one could find his murderer. Behind that came the wave of guilt and shame for her part in all this. "Then *I'll* get him to confess," she said.

Malloy reared back at that. "And exactly how will you do that?" he asked, his voice heavy with sarcasm.

"I don't know yet, but I'll figure it out. I was thinking maybe I'd take him back to Coney Island. He's never killed anyone out there, so I should be safe."

"Are you crazy?" Plainly, he believed she was. She'd never heard that tone in his voice before. It sounded almost like panic.

"I assure you, I'm perfectly sane. You've already said the usual methods won't work with Dirk. He's too rich and powerful for you to take him into the Mulberry Street cellar and beat him into confessing. He isn't likely to come to you voluntarily to clear his conscience, either. That leaves us no other choice but to trick him."

"Mrs. Brandt, you're not a detective," he reminded her with more than a hint of condescension. "You couldn't trick a man like that."

She gave him a disdainful glance. "Women of my social class are trained to trick men like Dirk Schyler from the time we can talk, Mr. Malloy. All I need is some time to decide the best method to use."

He was looking at her as if he'd never seen her before. "And exactly how will you do that?"

He still didn't believe her capable of such a deception. He obviously knew far too little about upper-class society.

"First of all, I have to figure out why he's doing these terrible things." She waited a moment while the ideas formed in her mind. "Unfortunately, it's not all that difficult to imagine. Dirk has been a slave to social conventions all his life. That sort of constraint can drive people to do strange things. It drove me to become a midwife," she confessed with a shrug. "I think it's probably the reason he chose to spend his time with shop girls. With them he didn't have to worry about all the rules that he'd been taught to obey, and he certainly didn't have to observe any sexual restraint," she went on, thinking aloud.

"Why not just go to a prostitute then, if that's all he's interested in?"

Sarah considered. "Possibly he has some compunction about using the services of prostitutes. Perhaps he doesn't like the lack of romance he encountered with them. But the shop girls were different. They actually liked him, or at least pretended to, and they willingly granted their favors in exchange for trinkets instead of money. This would remove some of the taint. That was what he wanted, but when he got what he wanted, for some reason he couldn't accept it. Perhaps he felt he had to punish these girls for not adhering to the stringent rules of morality he'd been taught. He might even believe they deserved to die. If I could get him to admit that . . ."

"And what if you can't? What if he decides you know too much and kills you, too?" He was furious or outraged or perhaps simply exasperated. She was too distracted to figure it out, and besides, it didn't matter.

"He won't kill me, Malloy, because you'll be following us, ready to arrest him the instant he admits what he's done."

THIS WAS CRAZY. The whole idea was crazy. Sarah Brandt was crazy for thinking of it, and Frank was crazy for agreeing.

Not that he'd had any choice. She was going ahead with

her plan whether Frank helped her or not. Guilt was a terrible thing, and he knew she felt guilty for causing Lisle's death. Maybe it was even a little bit her fault, but she didn't deserve a death sentence for it. If Dirk Schyler really was the killer, that was what she might very well get, too.

Frank had gone over and over it in his mind. He didn't like Schyler. He rarely liked men of that class, probably because men of that class usually treated him like Irish scum. Schyler was less discreet about it than most, which made it even easier to hate him.

And then there was the matter of him taking liberties with Mrs. Brandt. She wasn't the kind of woman men took liberties with. He'd known that the first time he'd set eyes on her, and his opinion had been confirmed many times since then. When he thought of Schyler forcing himself on her, he wanted to commit murder himself.

Frank wanted Schyler to be the killer so he could cart him off to prison and watch the bastard sizzle in that fancy electrical chair. What he didn't know was whether he was letting his personal feelings color his professional judgment. Was he overlooking some important clue in his quest to lock Schyler up? Was he damning an innocent man just because he happened to be obnoxious?

Frank had a lot of time to consider all this while he paced at the Coney Island trolley station and waited for Sarah Brandt to appear with Schyler. They'd discussed various methods of surveillance, and they'd quickly discarded the idea of having Frank follow them out from the city. Dirk knew what he looked like, and he'd be hard to miss in the close confines of the trolley. So Frank had assigned Broughan the task of overseeing their trip out. He only hoped Broughan was sober enough not to lose sight of them. Frank didn't think Schyler had any reason to kill Sarah Brandt just yet, but he hadn't really had any understandable reasons to kill anyone else, either. Frank didn't want to take any chances.

He scratched absently at the false beard he wore in an

effort to keep Schyler from recognizing him. He doubted the beard would fool anyone, though. His best bet was simply to stay out of sight, which was what he planned to do most of the time. Now, if Mrs. Brandt could be trusted not to go looking for him in the crowds and tip Schyler off that they were being followed, he would be fine.

He'd been pacing for over an hour, watching trolleys arrive and disgorge their passengers without seeing his quarry. Another one was approaching the station, and Frank stepped back inside the building, where he could watch without being seen.

He saw her at once, even before she got off. He'd seen her wear that hat many times, but he probably would have recognized her no matter what she was wearing. She was the kind of woman who stood out in a crowd. Something about the way she carried herself. He'd never known another like her. Not even Kathleen, with all her sass, would have gone after a killer all alone. At what point did courage become folly? Frank only knew he was not the proper person to judge such a distinction.

Schyler looked the part of gentleman-about-town. He was dressed as if he was going to the races with his society friends. Sarah Brandt looked just as she always did. Was her smile too bright? Perhaps a little strained? Would Schyler notice? If he was the killer, he'd miss nothing. Frank had to resist the urge to rush out there and confront him, which told him more than he wanted to know about his feelings for Mrs. Brandt. Usually, he had all the patience in the world waiting for the trap to spring on his prey. But usually, he didn't particularly care about the fate of the bait. Today he cared very much indeed.

Another reason to hope Schyler was the killer. As soon as they locked up the man who'd been murdering all these young women, Frank would no longer have to encounter Sarah Brandt. He could return to his solitary existence and everything would be as it was before.

He only wished he believed that.

He watched the two of them as they made their way out of the trolley and onto the platform. Schyler offered her his arm, and Frank felt his hackles rise. But she pretended not to notice and pointed at something instead of tucking her arm into his. They started off toward the park. Did Schyler look suspicious? Had she given herself away already? Frank no longer trusted his instincts.

Waiting until they were almost out of sight, Frank finally stepped out of the station. That's when he saw Broughan stumbling down the steps of the trolley. He was drunk and making no effort to hide it. Frank wanted to thrash him. What if Sarah had needed help? What if she'd asked the wrong question and angered Schyler? What use would a drunk have been?

Frank wanted to slam Broughan up against the wall and ask him those questions rather forcefully, but if he did, he'd lose Sarah in the crowd. He settled for giving him a black look before setting out after them.

They had paid their admission and gone into the park. Frank waited until he saw what direction they were headed before doing the same. The laughter and screams of delight from the crowd mocked him as he made his way into the throng. He'd never felt less carefree in his life.

SARAH SMILED AT Dirk, although her face felt stiff. She hadn't expected to be frightened. Not that she was afraid exactly. Dirk wouldn't harm her here, not with hundreds of people around, and certainly not with Malloy nearby. But she was nervous. Anxious. Unable to relax. Her mission was so important, and one false word could spoil everything. She should have let Malloy talk her out of this. He'd certainly tried hard enough. He was probably right, too. Even if Dirk *was* the killer, he was hardly likely to confess it to Sarah, no matter how clever she might be.

"What are we looking for today?" Dirk asked pleasantly as they strolled through the park. "Do you have more information on this fellow you think killed the girl . . . ? What was her name? Gilda?"

"Gerda," Sarah supplied, wondering if he could really have forgotten. "No," she said. "Today I want to forget all about killers and their victims. I just want to have a good time."

"You chose an odd destination for our outing, then," Dirk pointed out. "I could have taken you to a museum or to dinner or a show or—"

"Don't you ever get tired of doing the proper things, Dirk?" she asked, hoping she sounded as rebellious as she should. "I do. Sometimes I think I'll scream if I have to sit through another dinner party." Not that she attended many anymore, but Dirk wouldn't know that.

He arched an eyebrow at her. "Most women I know would faint to hear one of their own talking like that."

"Most women you know?" she repeated skeptically. "Probably not that girl I saw you with that day we first met here."

"Ah, *touché*," he said. "I forget, you know my ugly secrets."

"Do I?" she asked.

"Well, you know about my fondness for shop girls, at least," he replied with a secretive grin.

"Is there more, then? What other ugly secrets could you have?"

"None I would share with a lady," he replied.

"Do you share them with your shop girls?"

He frowned at this. "Is that why we came? So you could berate me for my lapses in judgment?"

"Is that what you consider them?" She didn't wait for an answer, knowing he wouldn't admit to it. "No, I'm just curious. How did you happen to discover that you had a . . . a fondness for shop girls in the first place?"

"Oh, Sarah, you really can't be interested in hearing about my follies," he protested uneasily.

"Nonsense, I'm fascinated. Are you doing it to embarrass

your family? Are you planning to bring one of these girls home one day and present her as the future Mrs. Dirk Schyler?"

"Don't be ridiculous." He seemed shocked at the very idea.

"But you are trying to rebel, aren't you? Why else would you keep company with girls of that sort?"

He was plainly uncomfortable discussing this, which was all the better. "I've never given the matter any thought," he insisted.

"Well, think about it now," she insisted right back. "At first I thought it was just that you . . . Well, I've been married, so I understand that a man has needs. I thought you were simply using these girls to meet those needs. But then I realized that a man of your means could keep a mistress to satisfy him in that way if that was all he was interested in. Such an arrangement would be safer, surely. You wouldn't have to worry about disease or even about possible rejection. Surely, *all* these girls don't succumb to your seductions, Dirk."

"Sarah, you shock me," he said, his voice hoarse with disbelief.

"Do I? I've shocked many people with my attitudes. That's what comes of living alone and earning your own living, I suppose. You lose all sense of what is proper. I thought I'd found a soul mate in you, however. I thought you were a man who understood what it's like to break the bonds of society. At least tell me how you first discovered an interest in pursuing these girls."

"Are you thinking of following in my footsteps?" he asked in an effort to put her on the defensive.

"Perhaps," she allowed with a small smile.

He smiled back, reluctantly. "I was coerced," he said. "In the beginning, at least. My friends were bored one evening, and one of them said he knew a place where we could meet some attractive . . . uh . . . harlots. He took us to one of those places where they have dances. We asked the doorman to introduce us, but he insisted that he was unable to tell the respectable girls from the other kinds, and he left us to our own devices."

"And were you able to tell?"

"Not at all," Dirk assured her, warming to the story. "They all looked alike. And they all seemed quite pleased to have such well-dressed gentlemen paying attention to them. We bought drinks for some of them and engaged them to dance. Their behavior was quite outrageous, but they were insulted when we offered them money for their favors. My friends quickly lost interest when they learned they had been misled about the kind of female who frequents such dances, but I was intrigued."

"You like a challenge," she guessed.

He shrugged. "What man doesn't?"

Indeed, she knew few who didn't. "So you rose to that challenge."

"I went back on another night, alone. This time I met a young woman who wasn't quite so coy." He grinned, a smile that chilled Sarah's blood, but she managed to smile back.

"Your first conquest?" she asked, tempting him to brag.

"Ah, a gentleman never tells," he replied.

"Does a gentleman seduce shop girls?" she countered.

He pretended to be offended. "Sarah, you cut me to the heart."

"That assumes you have one, Dirk."

"How cruel you are. When you lived in your father's house, I'm sure you had better manners."

"No, I didn't," she said. "I just had less opportunity to prove it."

She surprised a bark of laughter from him. The sound wasn't pleasant. "Are we quarreling?" he asked.

"Are you angry?"

"Not yet, but I can't promise not to become so if you continue to insult me."

"I can't resist a challenge either," she confessed. "What

if I told you that all the murdered girls were killed after attending a dance? And they also had one other, very important thing in common."

"What was that?"

"They all knew a man named Will."

Dirk didn't so much as blink. "You told me this before, and I believe I pointed out that it's a fairly common name."

"They all knew the *same* man named Will. A man who gave them all gifts right before they were murdered."

He gave her a pitying look. "I'll admit I don't know as much about murder and murderers as your friend the policeman, but is it common practice for killers to give their victims gifts before murdering them?"

It did sound strange, but everything about this was strange. "We believe this man named Will seduced these girls, and when they succumbed, he became enraged and beat them to death."

"Sarah, my dear, that is preposterous. Who would believe that a man would become enraged and kill a woman *because* she submitted to him? Isn't it usually just the opposite?"

"Yes, it is, which is why this case has been so difficult to solve. But just the other day, we discovered a clue that puts everything into perspective."

"A clue?" She had his interest once again. "What kind of clue?"

"We have a photograph of the man named Will, Dirk. I don't think it will surprise you to learn that it's a picture of you."

She watched the play of emotions across his face. Surprise came first, but the others followed so rapidly, she couldn't even keep track, much less identify each one. The final one was, of all things, amusement.

"You think I killed those girls?" he asked in astonishment.

She didn't want to admit it. She wanted to be wrong.

"You knew them all," she reminded him.

"So you say. I don't know which girls were murdered, so I can't deny it. But I know dozens of girls like that, Sarah, much as it must shame me to admit it. Surely, not all of them have been murdered. Not a *tenth* of them, or the newspapers would have been raising a hue and cry against such a slaughter!"

"We don't know why the victims were singled out," Sarah said.

"And who is this *we* you keep talking about? You and that Irishman? Sarah, don't you know anything at all about the police? They're nothing more than uniformed criminals themselves! That detective—what's his name?"

"Malloy," Sarah supplied.

"Malloy," he repeated, making a face as if the word left a bad taste in his mouth. "I already told you why he's so interested in this case, if you don't. He doesn't care who killed these girls. He's only pretending to in order to impress you. Any fool can see he has designs on you, Sarah. He must consider you quite a prize to spend so much time chasing a killer of women no better than prostitutes. Why should he care how many of them die? The world would be a better place with fewer such creatures in it!"

"Dirk!" she cried, horrified by his attitude, although she knew far too many others shared it. She could also have set him straight about Malloy's interest in her, but she didn't think it was worth the effort.

"Don't bother to be offended, Sarah. You've accused me of murder. I think I've got a right to be offensive in return."

"Can you explain how you happen to know all the dead girls?" she asked.

"I told you, I know dozens of these girls, dead and alive. I've given them gifts and enjoyed their favors. At least give me an opportunity to defend myself. I probably have an alibi for the crimes. When were these girls killed? I'll consult my calendar and give you a full report!" He seemed genuinely offended.

Sarah was starting to feel foolish. Although she wanted

him to be innocent, she hadn't really considered the possibility that he was. "Dirk, really, this isn't necessary."

"Of course it is. I can see I must prove myself to you or live under a cloud of suspicion for the rest of my life. Tell me. You must know when these girls died. What about this Gretel, the one you knew? You must have the date of her death engraved in your memory."

Sarah wanted to deny it, but she did know the date. "Her name was Gerda. She died on the night of July sixth."

He stared at her for a moment, then slowly a smile spread across his face. "I knew it. I thought I'd have to go home and check, but that's a date I'll never forget. Timothy Vandervort. You remember him. He got married a few weeks ago. I was his best man. That was the night we had a bachelor party for him. There were about twenty of us. We had a suite at the Plaza Hotel, and several young ladies came to . . . uh . . . to entertain us. All of the men are from the best families in New York, and every one of them will vouch for the fact that I was there with them all night. So you see, I could not possibly have killed your poor little Gerda."

Malloy would make discreet inquiries, of course, but she knew Dirk wouldn't lie about something that could be so easily disproved. He wasn't the killer.

"What's the matter, Sarah? You look disappointed."

"No, I . . . I'm just so relieved," she said, realizing that she was. So relieved that she was weak from it.

"Here, let's find a bench," Dirk said, taking her arm and leading her over to where two old men were sitting, feeding crumbs to the pigeons. "Excuse me," he said to them. "The lady is feeling faint. Do you mind?"

They jumped up and scurried away, allowing Sarah to sit down just before her knees gave out completely. She felt like a complete fool.

"Do you want something to drink?" he asked solicitously.

Now she felt guilty. The man she'd just accused of murdering half a dozen young women was concerned about her welfare. "Oh, no, I'll be fine. I just . . . Oh, Dirk, I'm so sorry. How could I have ever believed . . . ?"

"I don't know," he replied, looking hurt. "How could you?"

"Everything seemed to suggest . . . And then Lisle was killed, right after I told you about her."

"Lisle?"

"She was the one I said was most likely to have had a beau that Gerda would want to steal. She was murdered just a few days later."

"Good God, how awful."

"And Malloy found a photograph of you and Lisle that had been taken here at the park. She'd written the name Will on the back of it."

"So Malloy's the one who convinced you I'm a killer," he said, thinking he understood everything.

Had he? Sarah couldn't really remember. She'd thought it had been her own conclusion, but now she wasn't sure. And Malloy hated Dirk. That much was certain. He'd wanted Dirk to be the killer. Had his prejudice colored his judgment? Had she let it color her own? She didn't know. All she knew was that Dirk was innocent. Well, perhaps not innocent. His conduct had been too degenerate for that, but at least he wasn't guilty of murder.

"Is that why you brought me here, to get me to confess to you?" he asked. He seemed to be amused again.

"It does sound silly, when you say it out like that, doesn't it? Even if you *were* the killer, that hardly seems likely to happen. I'm terribly sorry, Dirk. Can you ever forgive me?"

"I'm not sure," he said with amazing good nature. "But I will allow you to grovel a bit to get back in my good graces before I decide."

"You're very generous," she allowed.

He shook his head in wonder as he considered the situation. "I can't believe you came here alone with me if you believed I'd murdered those girls."

Sarah had an urge to look around for Malloy, but she resisted. She didn't want to alarm Malloy, and she didn't want Dirk to know the extent of their folly. It was enough that she was embarrassed. No use embarrassing Malloy, too.

"We're hardly alone, Dirk," she pointed out, glancing meaningfully at the throngs of people passing by. "All the murders were committed in the city, in the dark of night."

"And Malloy agreed to this idiotic plan?" he asked incredulously.

"I . . . I didn't tell him," she lied. No use making Malloy look as foolish as she did.

"Oh, Sarah, I thought you were such a sensible woman. When I think of what could have happened if you'd confronted the real killer this way . . ."

"I know." She drew in a deep breath and let it out in a long sigh. "I suppose I'm not cut out to be a detective. I should leave that to the police."

Dirk made a rude noise, reminding her of how infrequently the police did any detecting of their own. She ignored him, choosing instead to begin making up for her ugly suspicions.

"I suppose you'll want to go back to the city now."

"Why?" He seemed genuinely surprised at the suggestion.

"Because I can't imagine you want to spend any more time with me after the way I treated you."

He shook his head again. "Sarah, you may find this hard to believe, but I'm actually sort of flattered."

"*Flattered?*" She couldn't believe it.

"Do you know, I believe this is the most interesting thing that has ever happened to me? I shall have the most fascinating story to tell at my club, about how I was suspected of murder! It's too delicious."

Sarah could hardly believe anyone would be bragging about such a thing to his friends, but Dirk seemed actually delighted.

"And we most certainly will not return to the city, at least not yet," he went on, his face alight with excitement. "First we will enjoy the amusements to be found here, we will eat a delicious dinner, and then we will dance under the stars. I want to remember this day forever."

Sarah didn't want to remember it at all, but she couldn't be rude, certainly not after the way she'd treated Dirk. If he wanted to spend the day here, she'd do her best to help him enjoy himself. She knew a pang of guilt over knowing Malloy would be traipsing around after them all day, but perhaps she could slip away at some point and tell him what had happened so he could go home. She pasted a smile on her face and said, "What would you like to do first?"

"Let's ride on the Ferris wheel."

Sarah found this the most pleasant of all the rides at the park, so she readily agreed. The line was long, but it moved quickly since the wheel was large and held many cars. Dirk was in boisterous good humor, almost unnaturally so. She tried to match his enthusiasm, but her heart wasn't in it. She didn't really like him, after all. Even if he wasn't a killer, he'd taken terrible advantage of many young women to satisfy his own lusts, and she could never overlook such a damning character flaw. When this day was over, she would make a point of never encountering him again.

When they reached the head of the line, Dirk stepped over to the ride operator and spoke quietly to him, slipping something into the fellow's shirt pocket.

"What did you say to him?" she asked when he returned.

"I asked him to give us an extra-long ride. And to make sure we stop on the very top. The view is breathtaking." He smiled, eager for her approval, and she gladly gave it. She couldn't fault him for trying to make sure she had the best time possible, could she?

At last it was their turn. Dirk helped her into the car, then took his place beside her. The attendant fastened the gate across the front and then stepped back as their car swung up a notch to allow the people on the next car to exit and new ones take their place.

Soon they were halfway up, stopped momentarily for another car to load, when Dirk began to rock the car back and forth.

"What are you doing?" she cried in alarm, grabbing onto the gate for support.

"Are you frightened, Sarah?" he asked without a trace of concern. "Don't worry, the car won't tip over." He lurched forward, leaning over the gate, so that the car tipped so far forward, Sarah could imagine them both tumbling out to their deaths.

"Dirk, stop it!" she cried, bracing her feet and clutching the back of the seat with one hand while still clinging to the gate with the other.

The wheel lurched into motion again, carrying them up another notch. When they stopped, the car swayed, and Dirk made it rock dangerously again.

Sarah saw his expression, and then she understood. He was frightening her on purpose, punishing her for her suspicions. "This is childish, Dirk. I told you I was sorry."

"You're going to be even sorrier, Sarah," he assured her. "You know, you weren't far wrong when you suspected me of murder."

"*What?*"

"You heard me. I *am* a murderer, Sarah." He smiled, and the coldness in his eyes chilled her to her bones.

"What do you mean?" She was glad to hear her voice sounded almost normal.

"Just what I said. It happened by accident the first time. I didn't mean to kill the miserable little wench. She was just another one of those whores. You wouldn't believe how cheaply they sell themselves, Sarah. A string of glass beads or a pair of gloves, and they'll lift their skirts practically on a street corner."

The wheel lurched again, and they rose another notch.

At least Dirk had forgotten about rocking the car. He was too engrossed in his story.

"They're disgusting, Sarah. They whimper and moan and pretend they enjoy it while you're pressing them against a wall in a filthy alley. Even while I was using them, I hated them. I despised them. Each time the urge to punish them somehow got stronger and stronger, until I couldn't stand it anymore. I'd just finished with her, and she was simpering, pretending it had been so lovely when it was cheap and dirty and disgusting, so I hit her. I used an open palm the first time. A gentleman would never strike a woman with his fist, you know. You should have seen the look on her face. She was so surprised that I hit her again. She ran away, but I'll never forget that feeling of triumph."

Sarah could only stare. She seemed paralyzed with her horror. It was just as she'd imagined when she and Malloy had been trying to figure out what had happened. She felt no satisfaction, though. How could she take pride in having guessed such an awful truth?

"After that, I hit all of them. Each time I hurt them worse. I was trying to experience that surge of power I'd felt the first time, but it became more difficult each time. I had to hit them harder and more often. I had to beat them until they begged for mercy, and finally I hit one of them until she stopped begging at all. I didn't know she was dead at the time. I just thought she was senseless. Then I saw something about her in one of the newspapers a few days later. They'd found her body."

"Dirk, if you're just trying to frighten me—"

"I think I'm doing more than trying, aren't I?" he asked confidently. "It's nice to see you at a disadvantage for once, Sarah. I knew I could manage that, given the appropriate opportunity."

She'd been trying to convince herself he was making it all up just to terrify her. How could anyone speak of these horrors so matter-of-factly? But now she understood. He'd really committed these murders, and for some reason he wanted her to know all about it. "So after that first time," she guessed, "you killed the next girl on purpose."

"Of course I did. How could I do less? There was no going back after that, Sarah. And nothing else would appease me. I can't describe to you the pleasure of feeling their flesh and bones breaking beneath my fists. There's nothing else like it."

His eyes shone with a light that she might, under other circumstances, have described as divine. Indeed, he looked transported.

She cringed away from him as far as the confines of the car would allow, which wasn't far. She tried to reason, tried to find an escape from the truth.

"But you told me about Tim Vandervort and the party!" she remembered. "You couldn't have killed Gerda."

"Don't you understand?" he asked with a sneer. "That's the irony here. You started out looking for the man who killed this Gerda and then found out about the other girls who'd been killed. I killed the other girls, but I didn't kill this Gerda. I might have. I was considering it. She would probably have been next, but someone else beat me to it."

The car lurched again, and they rose higher into the summer sky.

"And what about Lisle? You couldn't have killed her either." At least her conscience would be spared this agony.

"Oh, but I could. And I did. I had to, you see. She was one of my failures. That happened sometimes. I could usually judge which ones would put up a fight, but Lisle surprised me. She looked so fragile, I never expected—"

"But why go back and kill her later if you didn't kill Gerda?" Sarah cried, horror choking her.

"Because she might have remembered what happened between us and made the connection with the other murders. I had an alibi for Gerda's death, but not for the others. If your detective had suspected me, I would have had to answer some difficult questions. Ordinarily, I'd think a decent-sized bribe would get me out of trouble with the police, but I don't think I can offer the one thing that might appease this Malloy. His lust for you makes him very dangerous indeed."

"Dirk, you shouldn't have told me all this."

"Why not, Sarah?" he asked, as if he really didn't know.

"Because I have no choice but to tell Detective Sergeant Malloy. Surely, you must know that. I can't allow you to kill anyone else."

He waited until the car had moved again, bringing them to a stop at the very top of the wheel. "Don't worry, Sarah. You won't have to tell Mr. Malloy anything, because you're going to have a terrible accident, and you won't be able to tell anyone anything ever again."

13

SARAH LOOKED DOWN FROM HER PERCH AT the top of the Ferris wheel. The view indeed was breathtaking. She couldn't seem to breathe at all. Somewhere below, Malloy would be watching, but even if she could signal him somehow, there was nothing he could do to help her. She must save herself.

"Dirk," she tried, amazed that she could speak at all. "You don't have to hurt me. Surely you know that wealthy people don't go to prison. Your father will hire the best attorneys for you. No jury will ever believe a man like you could be capable of committing murder." The words almost gagged her, but unfortunately, she also knew they could well be true. Justice might be blind, but she wasn't above accepting a bribe.

"But I'd have to stop killing women, Sarah," he pointed out, his voice so calm and reasonable, it turned her blood to ice. "And I'd be a social outcast. No one would see me. What kind of life would I have?"

"What kind of life will you have if you kill me in front of thousands of people?" she argued.

"I'm not going to kill you, Sarah," he said, giving the

gate she still clutched a sharp tug that pulled it loose from the latch that held it closed. "I told you, you're going to have a tragic accident."

"No!" she cried, fighting him for control of the gate. But before she could stop him, he'd flung it out straight, far beyond her reach, and they sat there, a hundred feet above the park, with nothing but air between them and the ground.

"You're terribly distraught, Sarah," he told her, his voice so calm he might have been discussing the weather. "You are desperate to remarry, but I told you that you must stop pursuing me. I have no interest in you, and you're making a fool of yourself. I have no intention of marrying you, and the news caused you to fling yourself off the Ferris wheel to your death."

He grabbed her by the arms. He was strong, much stronger than she, but she held on to the sides of the car fiercely as he tried to pry her loose.

"You'll never get away with it, Dirk! Malloy is down there! He's watching everything! He'll know what happened!"

"You're lying," he reminded her. "He doesn't even know we're here."

"No, it's true! He's been following us since we got here! There was a policeman on the trolley, too! Someone's been watching us the whole time we've been together!"

"There's no one here now, Sarah."

He'd pulled one of her hands loose and was using her arm to drag her off the seat, but she'd braced her feet, and he couldn't budge her.

"Don't do this, Dirk!" she begged as he reached down and slid his arm beneath her knees. He was going to lift her off the seat! If he did that, she'd be helpless. All he'd have to do was toss her over, and she'd be lost.

As he lifted her legs, releasing the hold her feet had on the floor of the car, she kicked up and the toe of her shoe struck him soundly on the side of his head. He cursed her, rearing back and dropping her legs. The look in his eyes was wild, like an animal cornered and ready to fight for its life. Sarah imagined her eyes must look the same as she screamed Malloy's name in some vain hope he might be able to do something.

Dirk sneered at her. "It's over now, Sarah," he said, and drew back his fist.

Everything seemed to move slowly, as if they were underwater. She saw Dirk's fist coming toward her, and she knew that when he struck her, she would be helpless. Stunned, she couldn't resist when he threw her out of the car. Some primal instinct responded, and without thinking, she ducked her head, bending nearly double in the last second before his fist would have slammed into her cheek. In that same instant the whole world jolted, nearly unseating her from the car. If she hadn't been holding on for dear life, she might very well have gone tumbling to the ground.

Dirk's cry was a shriek of terror as his body kept going, following his swinging arm, carrying him out of the car into oblivion. Sarah's instinct was to catch him, but her hands clutched only thin air, and she very nearly fell herself as the car reacted to the loss of Dirk's weight by swinging violently. Only then did she realize the wheel was moving. The lurch of the start, coming just as he was swinging to hit her, was what had unseated Dirk and sent him toppling from the car.

Seconds later she heard the sickening thud as his body struck the ground beneath the wheel, and the crowd's anguished reaction. Sarah clasped the side and back of the car, hanging on for her life as the wheel came to another precipitous halt that set her car rocking madly. But someone was yelling down below, giving orders. She recognized the voice, even from way up here near the top of the wheel, and in another moment it started again, lurching like a drunk before falling into the smooth rhythm of the usual ride. It didn't stop until Sarah's car was on the loading platform.

Malloy was there. She almost didn't recognize him because of the ridiculous beard he was wearing, but she knew his voice and responded when he told her to let go, she was safe now. Even still, he practically had to pry her hands loose to get her out.

Only when her feet were firmly planted on solid ground was she able to comprehend what had happened. And what had almost happened.

"Are you all right?" Malloy asked. His arm was around her waist, supporting her as he led her away from the wheel.

"Where is he?" she demanded. "I want to see him."

"He's dead," Malloy said.

But another voice called, "He's still alive! Somebody get a doctor!"

The words rejuvenated her. All weakness and terror evaporated. She broke from Malloy's grasp and whirled, searching for the voice. "I'm a nurse!" she called.

Picking up her skirts, she ran back the way she'd come, dodging the descending cars that the ride operator was emptying as quickly as he could.

Dirk's body lay in the barren, rocky area beneath the wheel, which was barely high enough for a man to stand upright. Several men had gathered around him, but no one was doing anything. Probably they were afraid to touch him, and she could guess why. She could tell from the angle at which he lay that his back was broken. He wasn't moving, and his breathing was shallow. He was probably going into shock, which would be a mercy. The pain from his injuries must be excruciating. If he could feel anything at all, that is.

"Are you Sarah?" one of the men asked as she approached.

"Yes," she said.

"He's asking for you."

The men stood aside for her. Dirk's face was twisted and gray, his scalp bloody from a gash. His lips were moving, but she couldn't hear his words. She knelt beside him, anxious to hear what his last words would be. Would he confess and clear his conscience? She wanted to hear him admit he'd killed Gerda, too, and then this nightmare would be over.

But when she leaned close, he said, "You are another of my mistakes. I can usually tell when they're going to fight back. I thought I was ready for you."

"The wheel started moving," she said. "It unbalanced you."

"I told them to get you down." It was Malloy, standing over them. She'd known he wouldn't be far away. "I saw he was trying to throw you off."

She cast him a grateful glance. There would be time for proper thanks later. She turned back to Dirk. "Tell me the truth about Gerda, Dirk. At least you'll die with a clear conscience."

His lips curved into a grotesque parody of a smile. "I didn't kill her, Sarah. You'll have to keep looking."

She heard Malloy's reaction, but she didn't want to waste time filling him in on the whole truth. She had only a few more minutes with Dirk. "Why did you do it, Dirk? Why did you kill the others?"

His smile became a grimace. "Because I could," he said simply.

"Get back, step back." The command came from an officious-looking fellow in a bowler hat and a plaid shirt with sleeve garters. He was followed by two men carrying a stretcher. "Out of the way, miss. We've got to take him to a doctor."

"If you move him, he'll die," Sarah protested.

"If we don't move him, he'll die, too," the fellow said reasonably. "Better he shouldn't die in front of all these people."

"Don't touch me!" Dirk protested in alarm when the two men laid the stretcher down beside him.

"It's all right, mister. We're going to get you some help," one of them said.

The expression on Dirk's face was naked terror, the kind Sarah had felt moments before when she had been certain Dirk was going to throw her to her death.

"This is how those women felt, Schyler," Malloy said to him. "Think about that. The pain and the fear. It isn't pleasant, is it?"

Dirk didn't reply because the men were lifting him on the stretcher, and he was screaming in agony. Sarah instinctively moved to help him—although she had no idea how she might have accomplished that—but Malloy held her back as the men carried Dirk away.

"Are you all right, miss?" the short man in the sleeve garters asked. "Did you get hurt at all?"

Sarah hadn't even considered whether she had or not. "I don't think so. I was just frightened."

"How did it happen?" he asked. "I'm the park manager," he added, in case she thought he was just being nosy.

Sarah thought quickly. She'd have to explain this to many people, Dirk's family included. She glanced at Malloy. His expression was grave, but he offered no suggestions. "It was a terrible accident," she said, sickeningly aware that she was quoting Dirk. She didn't look at Malloy again. If he disapproved, she would never be able to lie convincingly. "Mr. Schyler was acting silly, trying to frighten me, I think. He had an odd sense of humor. The gate came loose and flew open, and just as he tried to reach for it to pull it back, the wheel started to move, and he lost his balance."

"You sure he didn't jump on purpose? A lot of them does, you know," the man said by way of apology for asking.

"If he'd wanted to commit suicide, he hardly would've taken a lady up to accompany him, now would he?" Malloy pointed out.

"I suppose not," the man allowed. "I just don't want nobody telling the newspapers he jumped. It gives all the crazy ones ideas. Gives the park a bad name, too."

"No one will say he jumped," Sarah assured him.

The man sighed. "Is he your husband or something?"

"Just a family friend," Sarah said. "I should go with him, though. Where are they taking him?"

"To a doctor down on Surf Avenue."

"I'll take her," Malloy said. "How do we get there?"

The park manager had one of his men drive them in a park wagon. As they made their way through the crowded streets, Sarah thought of Dirk's broken body being subjected to the jostling of a wagon ride, and winced. Malloy would say it was no more than he deserved, and Sarah knew he was probably right. Still, the thought of anyone suffering so horribly sickened her.

"What were you thinking to go up on the Ferris wheel with him?" Malloy demanded as the wagon jounced along. He sounded angry.

"I was thinking we would have a lovely ride," she replied defensively. "He'd managed to convince me he was innocent, you see."

"You confronted him?" Malloy was incredulous.

"I'm not sure you'd call it that, exactly. We were talking, and I let him know that all the murdered girls knew a man named Will and that we knew he was that man."

"Did you think he'd just break down bawling and beg you to absolve him?" He was angry again.

"No," she said, becoming annoyed. "I thought he'd get angry and betray himself."

"But he didn't."

Sarah sighed over her own naïveté. "He was much too clever for me. He asked me the date of Gerda's murder, and he had an alibi for it, one we could easily check."

"You couldn't have checked it if you were dead," he pointed out. "Which is exactly what he had planned. Didn't it ever occur to you that he was lying through his teeth just to get you to let down your guard?"

"Of course it didn't, or I wouldn't have gone on the Ferris wheel with him!" she snapped. It occurred to Sarah that they were probably giving the driver enough gossip for the rest of the season, but she couldn't help that.

Malloy frowned inside the awful-looking beard. "But you did get him to confess, finally?"

"Yes, I think . . . I think he wanted to brag. He must have wanted someone to know about his successes, even if I'd only know for a few moments before he killed me. He said he'd killed the other girls. And Lisle. I'll have to live with that for the rest of my life. But he swears he didn't kill Gerda. That was the one he had the alibi for."

"Probably he was lying. He knew that was the one you cared most about. He was just trying to torment you."

"I cared about Lisle, too, but he readily confessed to killing her. No, I'm afraid he might be telling the truth. He said he was at a party with a group of men. They'll be able to tell us if he was or not. Then we'll know for sure."

Malloy sighed his disgust. They rode in silence for another block before he said, "Are you going to be all right? He didn't hurt you, did he?"

Malloy's concern was gruff but sincere. It almost undid her. "He was going to throw me off the Ferris wheel, Malloy! In front of all those people."

"He might've managed to convince everyone it was an accident, too. Nobody would believe he'd do something so brazen. Would your family have wanted an investigation?"

"Certainly not," she said, knowing it was true. They would have mourned her for the rest of their lives, but they never would have been able to accept that her death had been anything but mischance. They wouldn't be able to believe someone like Dirk, a gentleman of their own class, capable of a heinous crime. "And the worst part is, he would've been free to keep on killing."

"Didn't you tell him I was watching?" Malloy wasn't going to let this alone.

"He . . . he thought I was lying."

Mercifully, Malloy didn't question her further on that

point. She didn't want to have to admit she'd let Dirk believe she was unprotected.

The wagon stopped in front of an unassuming house set back a little from the avenue. "This is where they took him," the driver said. Was he looking at them strangely? Sarah wished she could say something to reassure him, but that wasn't possible.

Malloy helped her down from the seat and slipped some coins to the driver, asking him to wait for them.

Inside they found the doctor looking grim. "You his family?"

"No, just . . . just a friend," Sarah said, almost choking on the word.

"I'm sorry. Wasn't anything I could do. He was near dead when he got here. I gave him something for the pain so he didn't suffer too much at the end."

Malloy made a rude noise, which the doctor obviously mistook for grief. He murmured some condolences, which Malloy ignored.

"What arrangements do you want to make for the body? It won't keep long in this heat," he added apologetically.

"I'll inform his family when I get back to the city," Sarah said. "I'm sure they'll send for the body immediately. Can you keep it until then?"

A few moments later Sarah and Malloy were back in the waiting wagon. Malloy told the driver to take them to the trolley station. At Sarah's questioning look, he said, "There's nothing else we can do here, is there?"

She had to agree.

MALLOY HADN'T WANTED Sarah to visit Dirk's family alone. He thought this was a police matter and that he should be the one to notify them. Sarah had argued that it wasn't a police matter unless he was going to charge someone with murder, and since the suspect was dead, he wasn't likely to do that. Sarah saw no need to blacken the name of the entire Schyler family by accusing their son of murder when he wasn't able to defend himself. In fact, doing so would only bring down the very considerable wrath of that family and all their friends and relations. Malloy didn't need that any more than Sarah did. Justice had been served with Dirk's death, and they would have to be satisfied that they were the only ones who knew it.

Sarah still had one last duty to perform before she could be completely satisfied, however. Somehow she had to test Dirk's alibi for Gerda's murder. If Dirk hadn't been guilty of that crime, then a killer was still on the loose.

The Schylers lived in one of the unpretentious brownstone town houses a few blocks from her parents' home. Outside, the homes were quietly elegant. The Dutch weren't much for ostentatiously flaunting their wealth. Inside, however, the dwellings were as plain or elaborate as the occupants' tastes—and fortunes—allowed. The Schylers, Sarah discovered when she was admitted to their home, were apparently still doing very well, indeed.

The marble floor shone brightly in the summer evening sunlight, and fresh flowers filled the Oriental vase that sat on the imported English table standing in the center of the entrance hall. The butler had looked at her queerly when he'd seen her standing on the front stoop. He'd have no idea who she was, of course, and her clothes marked her as distinctly middle class. Only her message—that she had some news about Dirk—had gained her admittance. She just hoped his parents recognized her name so she wouldn't have to explain too much. She didn't think she was up to any more fabrications today. She'd already composed enough lies to last her a lifetime.

After a few minutes the butler escorted her into the back parlor, where she found Dirk's mother alone, ensconced on a sofa in a room far less grandly furnished than the formal rooms reserved for company. She was wearing a simple, at-home dress, and her hair hadn't been arranged. Plainly, she hadn't been receiving visitors today, and she looked annoyed at having one now.

"Sarah Decker, is that you?" she demanded when Sarah walked in. "James said another name, but that's who you are, isn't it?"

"Yes, ma'am," Sarah said. "Brandt is my married name."

"But you're widowed, I think," she said, looking Sarah over with no apparent approval. The years had scoured away any excess flesh from her face, leaving her gaunt and sharp looking. From the way the lines on her face ran, she also seldom smiled.

"Yes, I am. Mrs. Schyler, is your husband at home? I'm afraid I have some unpleasant news, and I think it would be better if—"

"Nonsense," she said, waving away Sarah's suggestion. "Just say what you've come to say. It's not the first time some female has come in here mewling that Dirk has ruined her and demanding this or that in compensation. He won't marry you, I promise you that! You may be a Decker by birth, but anyone can see that you're as common as dirt now. You can't expect Dirk would waste himself on the likes of you. You should have thought about that before you took up with him."

"I didn't 'take up with him,' Mrs. Schyler," Sarah said, reminding herself that she was about to shatter this woman's life. Only the thought of her grief allowed Sarah to hold her temper.

"You certainly wanted to," she said. "Everyone knows how you pursued him. You've made yourself a laughing-stock, young lady."

Sarah felt a twinge of annoyance at the thought of her ruined reputation among society matrons, a sad remnant of her previous life. Well, if they were gossiping about her before, just wait until they found out where her pursuit of Dirk had led.

"Mrs. Schyler, the news I have isn't about me. It's about Dirk," she said. Although she hadn't been offered a seat, she sat down anyway, taking the fragile damask-covered chair opposite her companion. "I'm afraid there's been a terrible accident."

There it was again, the phrase Dirk had used. Sarah shuddered slightly at the realization that if things had gone as he planned, Dirk might well be delivering this same news to her own parents instead.

"What kind of accident?" Mrs. Schyler didn't believe it could be very important.

Oh, dear, where to start? "You see, Dirk and I went to Coney Island today and—"

"*Where?*" she asked, horrified.

"Coney Island," Sarah repeated, hoping she wouldn't question everything Sarah said. This could take all night! "There is a park there with rides and—"

"What on earth were you doing in a place like that? I can't believe my son would consent to such a thing. Although I suppose your tastes have grown common. They certainly have if that gown is any indication."

Sarah was rapidly losing patience, but she reminded herself of her mission and bit back the sharp retort that sprang so readily to her lips. "Dirk enjoyed going to the park there," Sarah said, not really caring whether the other woman believed her or not. "We were on the Ferris wheel this afternoon and . . . and that's when the accident happened."

When Sarah hesitated, Mrs. Schyler grew impatient. "Go on, spit it out," she said. "I don't have all day."

Sarah drew a deep breath and began to recite the story that was almost starting to sound true to her own ears. "We were on the Ferris wheel, at the very top, and the gate across the car came loose. It flew open, and just as Dirk reached to pull it back again, the wheel started to move. He lost his balance and . . . and he fell."

"That was very careless of him," his mother said with disapproval. "I suppose he was injured or else you wouldn't be here." She sighed with long-suffering. "All right, where is he? We'll see that our doctor attends him immediately."

Sarah would have liked to see a bit more concern from Dirk's mother, even if she truly believed he'd only been injured. She had no reason to believe the injuries were minor, after all. "He . . . he was taken to a doctor there, but . . . there was nothing he could do. I'm sorry to tell you, Mrs. Schyler, but Dirk died of his injuries."

Mrs. Schyler stared at her through faded blue eyes as the truth slowly penetrated. *"Died?"* she echoed, as if she'd never heard the word before.

"Yes," she said, and manufactured another lie to add to her long list for the day. "You'll be relieved to know he didn't suffer, though. The end came quickly."

Mrs. Schyler's face had gone white. Sarah was wondering if she should summon a servant to fetch some smelling salts, but before she could, Mrs. Schyler disabused her of the notion that she was about to faint.

"Are you telling me my son died from a fall from a . . . what did you call it?"

"A Ferris wheel," Sarah explained patiently. "It's an amusement-park ride. It's a large wheel, about a hundred feet high, that goes around. It has cars that people sit in—"

"And you made Dirk ride on this . . . this *thing*?"

"Actually, it was his idea to ride on it," Sarah said. She wanted to add that he'd intended to push her off of it, too, but that would accomplish nothing.

"Nonsense," his mother insisted for the second time that evening. "My son would never choose to do anything so common. I'm sure he never visited this Coney Island place before he met you, either. How will we ever explain this to our friends?"

She seemed outraged. Sarah had seen unusual reactions to grief in her time, and anger was fairly common. Blaming the messenger was also fairly common. She tried not to be insulted. She had, however, expected at least a rudimentary form of grief. "It does seem a rather unpleasant way to die, but I assure you, there's nothing to be ashamed of—"

"Ashamed! How dare you even suggest such a thing!

You, who are nothing more than a fortune hunter who tried to trap my Dirk into marriage and ended up killing him instead!"

The truth burned inside of Sarah, but she knew Mrs. Schyler would never believe her now. On the contrary, she'd accuse Sarah of making up lies about Dirk to cover her own guilt. She reached into her purse and pulled out a slip of paper. "I've written the name and address of the doctor in Coney Island. You may send someone there for Dirk . . . Dirk's remains. I'm very sorry, Mrs. Schyler." She laid the slip of paper on the table between them.

"Sorry! You haven't begun to know the meaning of the word! I'll ruin you! No other respectable man will ever speak to you again!"

Sarah didn't bother to point out that hardly any respectable men spoke to her now, in the course of an average day. "I'll see myself out," she said, rising from her chair and only too happy to put an end to this conversation.

Mrs. Schyler wasn't finished, but Sarah didn't listen to the rest of what she was saying. Or rather, shrieking. She'd already heard enough. At least she had a better understanding now of what might have inspired Dirk to kill women. It was small comfort.

"OH, MY DEAR, what on earth is wrong?" Mrs. Elsworth exclaimed when she saw Sarah coming down the street that evening. "I dropped a pair of scissors today, and the point stuck in the floor. That always means bad news. It's not another lost little one, I hope!"

"Oh, no, nothing like that," Sarah assured her.

"Is it something to do with that fellow I saw you with this morning? I knew he was trouble the moment I set eyes on him! I warned you, didn't I?"

Sarah only wished she could tell Mrs. Elsworth just how right she'd been. "Dirk won't be any trouble to anyone ever again," she said, knowing at least a small measure of relief at the thought of how many young women would be safe now that he was dead.

"Oh, my, that sounds serious," she said, coming down the steps she'd been sweeping to meet Sarah in the street. "From the looks of you, it is, too!"

Sarah toyed with the idea of telling her the fable she'd invented to protect Dirk's family, but she no longer had the stomach for it. "You were right, Mrs. Elsworth, he was an evil man. Today he was trying to frighten me on one of the rides at Coney Island, and he accidentally fell to his death."

"Good heavens! You poor dear! You must be devastated!"

"Not exactly," Sarah admitted, "but I am exhausted. If you'll excuse me, I'd—"

"Let me take you inside and make you a cup of tea. I've got some lamb stew left from supper. I don't suppose you've eaten, either. No matter, I'll take care of you."

"I'd really rather just go home and—"

"Of course, dear, go on. I'll be over in a minute with something to eat."

Sarah was too tired to argue. She let Mrs. Elsworth feed her and put her to bed, where she dreamed of the faceless man who had killed Gerda Reinhard.

THE NEXT DAY Sarah visited her mother, knowing she would soon hear of Dirk's death and demand to know the details. Their visit was a trial for Sarah. Her mother assumed she had been romantically interested in him, and nothing she could say would convince her that she wasn't grief-stricken at his loss. At least she had no trouble explaining why she wouldn't be attending Dirk's funeral. Sarah knew it was because she wouldn't be welcome by his family, but she allowed her mother to believe it would be too difficult for her.

That evening, Sarah took advantage of the coolness of the evening to weed her garden. That's where Malloy found her.

"Your neighbor told me where you were," he explained when he came through the back gate.

Sarah rose from where she'd been kneeling and pulled off her work gloves. She felt a little self-conscious to be dressed in the shabby gown she used for cleaning, but she reminded herself she had no need to impress Malloy. "Have you found out anything?"

He didn't look very pleased. "I found out that Schyler really was entertaining his friends the night Gerda Reinhard was killed. There's no chance that he killed her."

"Damn," Sarah said, throwing her gloves down in disgust.

"Mrs. Brandt, I'm shocked," he said, pretending to be.

"Shut up, Malloy. You're as annoyed as I am about this!"

"You're right, I am. I wanted him to be the killer, and it looks like he was, but not in this case."

Sarah sighed. "Come and sit down. Mrs. Elsworth brought over a bottle of homemade elderberry wine last night. I think we deserve a glass, don't you?"

"Homemade, did you say?" Malloy asked, following her to the back porch. "My opinion of the old bat just went up a notch."

Sarah smiled in spite of herself. It was the first time she'd felt like smiling since Dirk had plunged to his death.

When they were seated at the table on her back porch with glasses of wine in front of them, Sarah said, "What do we do now?"

Malloy stared out at the garden for a long moment. "I'm not sure we can do anything at all. We're right back to where we started—too many suspects to even hope to find the right one. And now so much time has passed that any chance we might have had of finding the killer are pretty much gone."

He was right, of course. They were back to suspecting every man Gerda had known, and that was a lot of men. Even if Malloy had the time and resources to question all of them, there was no way of proving which one of them—

if any of them!—had actually killed her unless he chose to confess, which seemed highly unlikely. She may have even been the victim of a total stranger, someone she didn't know at all, which meant that all the investigation in the world probably wouldn't find him.

"How do you deal with it?" she asked him. "With knowing that a killer is walking free and there's nothing you can do, I mean?"

His dark gaze met hers. His eyes were unfathomable. Finally, he said, "How do you deal with it when one of your patients dies?"

There was, of course, no answer to his question. She simply went on, learning from past mistakes and doing the best she could in the future. Now she understood that he did, too.

They sat in silence for a while, sipping their wine. It was very good, and after a while Malloy poured himself a second glass without asking, then refilled her glass, too. Perhaps it was the wine that gave her courage.

"How did your wife die, Malloy?"

She felt the instant tension, but she waited, refusing to take back her question.

"I told you," he finally said. "A midwife killed her."

"What happened exactly?"

At first she thought he wouldn't answer, but she waited, giving him time. Her patience was rewarded.

"It was a difficult birth. After three days, the baby still hadn't come."

Sarah couldn't help the sound of protest that escaped her.

He glanced at her. "Would you have taken her to the hospital?"

"Probably," Sarah said. "Although there are some things you can do to help the baby along. I would've tried those first, and then—"

"Kathleen wouldn't go to the hospital. Her mother died in a hospital. She was terrified of them. Didn't want a doctor either. Didn't want a strange man to see her like that.

In the end, I sent for one anyway, but it was too late by then."

"Didn't the midwife do anything?"

"Oh, yes, she did something all right. She used these . . . these instruments to pull the baby out."

"Forceps," Sarah guessed.

"Yes, that's right." The bitterness was thick in his voice.

"Do you know it's illegal for a midwife to use them?" she asked him.

"I do now. And I guess I know why, too, don't I? She got the baby out, but she tore something inside . . . inside Kathleen. She was bleeding and . . . I sent for the doctor, but by the time he came, she was gone."

His efforts to conceal the depths of his anguish only made it more profound. Moved beyond tears, Sarah reached over and laid her hand on his arm. She understood the pain only too well, the agony of losing someone you dearly love in such a senseless way. "I'm sorry," she said.

He looked down at where her hand rested on his arm, then up to meet her gaze. "It's not your fault," he reminded her. Or perhaps he was reminding himself. He'd hated her on sight because of what she was, but now he was saying he no longer held that against her. Or at least she hoped he was saying that.

As for herself, she'd long since forgiven him for being a policeman. Now that she understood his reasons, she could not condemn him for doing the only thing he could to make sure his son was well provided for.

Aware that they had reached a new level of understanding, she self-consciously withdrew her hand and placed it in her lap. The silence between them was no longer comfortable, but heavy with unspoken things. She cast about for some way to break it.

"What do we do now?" she asked again, not even certain this time to what she referred.

"About Gerda's killer, you mean?" he asked.

"Yes," she said, glad to have that settled.

When she met his gaze, she thought she saw her own relief mirrored in his dark eyes.

"I told you, there's not much we can do," he said.

But Sarah wasn't going to give up quite so easily. There was still one more thing she could do, and if that didn't work, well, then maybe, just maybe, she'd give up.

14

SARAH KNEW SHE HAD NO REASON TO FEEL APprehensive. It was the middle of the day. No one would know she was here. At least Lars Otto wouldn't know, unless his wife chose to tell him. Since it seemed unlikely Agnes would do so, no harm would be done. And she did need to see Agnes and the baby, to make sure they were still doing well. It was her duty.

All that rationalization didn't remove the butterflies from her stomach, though. The building was quiet as she made her way up the dark stairway. All the children were outside, playing in the street on this summer afternoon. She could hear the faint echoes of their cries and laughter, but only dimly. She'd been practicing what she would say all the way over here so she could adequately feign surprise at just happening to see Agnes on her way someplace else, but when she reached the landing, the Ottos' door was closed tightly.

Sarah found this strange, since it was so hot today, but perhaps Agnes was out. As she'd planned, she went up the stairs to the third floor, where another of her patients lived. Mrs. Gertz was genuinely happy to see her. Her time was drawing near, and since this was her first baby, she had a lot of questions. Sarah answered them patiently, then allowed Mrs. Gertz to serve her some cookies. As she nibbled politely, she managed to turn the subject to where she wanted it to be.

"How are Agnes Otto and her baby doing?"

Mrs. Gertz frowned. She was a plump woman made bigger still by her pregnancy. Her yellow braids had been wound around her head so tightly, Sarah wondered that her features weren't distorted. Everything about her was spotlessly clean and relentlessly tidy. "*Ach,* you should look in on her, Mrs. Brandt. She hardly comes out of her flat anymore. I hear the baby cry sometimes, but mostly I hear yelling."

"Yelling? From whom?"

"From Mr. Otto. He is not happy with anything she does. The baby cries too much, the food is not to his liking, he thinks the floors are dirty. Things like that. I know she still misses her sister, too, but he will not even let her say the girl's name. That part she told me. I would like to help her, but I do not know how."

Sarah wasn't sure she did either, but she was certainly going to try. "I was going to say hello to her just now, but her door was closed. Is she out, do you know?"

"Oh, she keeps her door closed all the time, even in the heat. We never see her anymore. She does not even let her children come down and play with the others."

"They must be stifling in there," Sarah said, horrified.

"*Ja,* I am sure they are. But she will not listen to reason. We have tried to talk to her, but it does not help. She is afraid."

"Of her husband?"

Mrs. Gertz looked away, perhaps worried she had gone too far, but after a moment she said, "*Ja.* And she is right to be."

That was all Sarah needed to hear. If Lars Otto was mistreating his wife, as Sarah had suspected, she would do whatever she could to put a stop to it. Mrs. Gertz didn't even make a token protest when Sarah said she had to leave. She merely nodded.

Sarah hurried down the steps and stopped outside the Ottos' door, listening for any sounds from within. She thought perhaps she heard weeping, but she couldn't be sure. She knocked. The sound she thought was weeping ceased abruptly. Someone was inside, but no one answered her knock.

She knocked again, more loudly this time. Still no response.

This time she pounded, so there could be no mistake. "Mrs. Otto, it's Mrs. Brandt. I know you're in there, and if you don't open the door, I'll have to get a policeman."

There, knowing how frightened Agnes was of the police, that should do the trick, although she had no idea what she would do if it didn't. Malloy seemed hardly likely to come over here and force his way into this poor woman's home, and she certainly didn't know any other policemen who would do such a thing, either.

After a long silence, she heard a slight scuffling sound that might have been footsteps. Then the sound of a bolt being drawn, and the door opened a crack. "Go away, Mrs. Brandt," a disembodied and very frightened voice said. "Lars will be angry if he knows you come here."

"He won't know unless you tell him. I just want to make sure you're all right," Sarah said. "Your neighbors are worried about you."

"I am fine," she insisted, although she had yet to show herself.

"What about the baby?" Sarah asked. "How is she? This heat can't be good for her."

"She is . . ." The voice broke, and Sarah felt the hairs on her arms rise as every nerve in her body sparked to attention. "She will be all right," Agnes insisted after a moment.

"If she's sick, you should let me see her. I can help." In the city, bringing children safely into the world was only the first of many battles that must be won in order to raise a child to maturity.

Sarah let her think this over, but when Agnes didn't respond, she tried another tactic. "If you won't let me in, I'll have to got to the settlement house for the visiting nurse. She might take your baby away if she thinks you aren't taking good care of her." It was a stretch of the truth, but Sarah was desperate enough to try anything.

Just as she'd hoped, the door flew open, and Agnes cried, "You cannot take my baby away!"

Sarah would have reassured her, but what she saw shocked the breath from her body. Agnes's fragile face was swollen and discolored. Both eyes were black, and her jaw was puffed out on the left side and mottled black-and-blue. The instant she saw Sarah's horror, she tried to close the door again, frantic to hide herself, but Sarah threw up her arm and pushed her way inside.

"Agnes, what happened?" Sarah demanded, closing the door behind her now that she was safely inside. No use airing Agnes's problems for the entire building to hear.

"Nothing, nothing," Agnes insisted frantically, holding up her hands to shield her face backing away from Sarah as if afraid she might strike her, too. "I am very clumsy. I fall down the stairs and—"

"You didn't get those bruises from falling down the stairs," Sarah said. "Someone hit you. Was it your husband?"

"No, no one hits me!" she insisted even more frantically, then clutched at her side and nearly doubled over from the pain.

Sarah rushed over and helped her to one of the kitchen chairs. "Is it your ribs? Show me where it hurts," she asked as she seated Agnes.

Agnes might have denied the pain if she'd been able to get her breath, but Sarah had no more patience with such denials. Gently moving Agnes's hand away, she felt along her midriff until she located the source of the pain.

"I think you may have a cracked rib. I don't think it's broken, because if it was, you wouldn't be able to move around the way you were. I can bind it for you so it won't hurt so much, though."

"No!" Agnes gasped. "He will know you came here."

"You can tell him you bound it yourself, because it was hurting so much," Sarah suggested.

But Agnes shook her head. "He will know!"

Sarah signed in frustration. "Where else are you hurt?"

But Agnes only shook her head again. She didn't want Sarah's help. She was too afraid of what it would cost her.

"Agnes, let me at least make sure you aren't more seriously hurt. If you die, who will take care of your children?" Sarah tried.

Sarah would have thought the other woman couldn't be more terrified, but she would have been mistaken. Every last vestige of color drained from Agnes's face, leaving the bruises standing out in stark relief. "My children," she whispered.

"You must think of them. Where are they now?" Sarah asked, almost afraid to find out.

Agnes pointed an unsteady finger at the bedroom door. Sarah hurried over and opened it. She found the two older children huddled on the bed, staring at her with wide, terrified eyes. The baby was lying in a cradle in the corner. Her eyes were open, but she wasn't making a sound. She wore only a diaper, and her little body was covered with a rash. Sarah hoped it was only prickly heat. The room was like an oven, without a breath of air, but the children didn't seem to be sweating. Most likely they were dehydrated, even the baby. How long had they been cooped up like this? Sarah didn't even want to think about that.

The next hour passed in a blur as Sarah got the children to drink large amounts of water and bathed them to help them cool off and dusted them with cornstarch and examined Agnes to make sure she had no more serious injuries than the ones she already knew about.

When she was satisfied that everyone was physically as comfortable as possible, she turned her attention to the rest of it.

"Agnes, you can't go on like this. You're going to have to do something to protect yourself and your children."

"I do," Agnes insisted. "I work very hard. I try to have Lars's supper on the table when he comes home, and I keep the children as quiet as I can, and I clean until my hands are raw. But I am not a good enough wife. Lars is so nervous. He must have peace and quiet in his home. I try, but I cannot do things the way he likes them. But I will try harder. I promise!"

"No, Agnes, I'm sure you already try as hard as you can. I've seen men like Lars before. No matter how hard you try to please him, you'll never be able to. He'll always find a reason to beat you. There's nothing you can do to stop him."

"Yes, there is!" she insisted. "I will be a better wife. That is what he says he wants. I will work harder and take better care of the children. Then he will be happy, and he will not have to hit me anymore."

Sarah wanted to scream. She knew all the logical arguments, but rarely did they work on women like Agnes. Not only did their husbands injure their bodies, they also injured their minds, twisting them until they actually believed they deserved the beatings they received. This time, however, Sarah had an argument she'd never been able to use before.

"Agnes, do you want to end up like Gerda?"

Her eyes grew wide with renewed terror. "What do you mean?"

"I mean, do you want to end up beaten to death?"

Agnes reached out and grabbed Sarah's arm, squeezing with surprising strength for one so frail. "What do you know? Tell me the truth? Do you know who killed my Gerda?"

Sarah couldn't identify the emotions burning in Agnes's bloodshot eyes, but they frightened her. "No, we haven't found her killer yet," she admitted reluctantly.

"But you told me . . . You promised! You said you would soon know!" Agnes reminded her brokenly.

Sarah swallowed down the lump that rose in her throat. "You know that other girls were killed the same way as Gerda, don't you?" Agnes nodded. "Well, we found out who murdered them, but . . . but he didn't kill Gerda. He couldn't have. He was somewhere else that night. So we still don't know who killed Gerda."

Sarah watched Agnes's eyes fill with tears that spilled over and ran down her battered cheeks, but still she didn't release Sarah's arm or her gaze. She wanted to tell Sarah something. Sarah was sure of it, although she couldn't imagine what it might be. So she waited, willing Agnes to unburden herself as she prayed for the wisdom to know how to reach her.

After what seemed an eternity, Agnes said, "He did not hurt her."

"I know," Sarah assured her. "I told you, that man wasn't the one who hurt Gerda."

Agnes shook her head. "No, not that. Lars. Lars did not hurt Gerda."

Once again every nerve in Sarah's body leaped to attention, but she willed herself to calmness. "What do you mean?"

"Gerda was a wicked girl," Agnes said, almost as if she were trying to convince herself. "She stayed out late and went with strange men. She was always flaunting herself in front of Lars. She made him so angry, but he did not hurt her!"

"No, of course, he didn't," Sarah said, her mind racing with possibilities. "Why would anyone think he did?"

She swallowed, as if trying to get some moisture in her mouth. "He . . . he was so angry because she did not come home that night. He went out to look for her. We know where she goes because she tells us. He came home very late. He was very nervous. He said he did not find her, but . . . but his hands are . . . are . . . like my face."

"Bruised?" Sarah guessed.

"Yes, bruised," Agnes confirmed. "And cut. He is bleeding. I try to take care of him, but he will not let me. He said some men tried to rob him, and he had to fight them. That is how he got hurt."

Sarah remembered noticing Lars's hands when she saw him at Gerda's funeral. She had thought he'd injured himself at work.

"But you didn't believe him?" Sarah asked.

Agnes's eyes widened with renewed terror. "Yes, I believe him! He would not hurt Gerda. He is not that kind of man."

Sarah was looking at living proof that Lars Otto was *exactly* that kind of man, but she didn't say so. "But you said Gerda made him very angry," she reminded her gently.

"He told her she was disgracing us. He told her she would come to no good, but still she goes out every night. She would not listen to anyone. I knew something bad would happen to her, but she would not listen!"

"Agnes, is it possible that Lars did find her that night and—"

"No! He would not hurt her! But if the police know he was out that night, they might think he did! The police, sometimes they punish the wrong man. I know this is true. If a man is poor, they will put him in the jail even if he is not guilty. You must tell them Lars did not do it. Please, Mrs. Brandt, you must tell them! If they take Lars away to the jail, what will become of us? We will starve!"

Sarah's heart was beating so loudly, she wondered Agnes couldn't hear it. Could Lars Otto have been the killer all along? That would explain so much, such as why he had ordered Sarah not to see his wife anymore and why he'd forbidden Agnes to mourn her sister's death. Of course, she could be wrong again. Malloy would most certainly remind her that she had no proof. Perhaps Otto really had gotten his bruised knuckles from a street fight, as he'd said. Perhaps he was simply ashamed of his sister-in-law and didn't want to hear her name mentioned again.

Or perhaps he had been so ashamed that he had sought her out on a dark street corner and beaten the life out of her before she could bring even more disgrace to his family. Fortunately, it wasn't Sarah's job to find out. Malloy could do that. And if he had to use force to get Otto to tell the truth, for once Sarah wouldn't criticize his methods. Looking at Agnes's battered face, she couldn't think of a more fitting punishment for Otto, killer or not.

Meanwhile, however, Sarah had more pressing issues to be worried about. "Agnes, your husband is probably worried about the same things you are. He's probably afraid the police will blame him for Gerda's death. That's probably why he has been so nervous lately."

"Yes," Agnes agreed eagerly. "I am sure that is why. He is very frightened."

Sarah sent up a silent prayer for wisdom. "That is also probably why he's been so . . . so violent with you. He might be afraid you'll tell someone he was out that night."

"I would never do such a thing!" she cried, then covered her mouth in horror, realizing she had just done so.

"Even if he only suspects, he'll be very angry," Sarah suggested reasonably. "Agnes, I think your life is in danger."

She was horrified. "Oh, no, Lars would never hurt me!" she insisted.

Sarah stared at her in astonishment. "Agnes, he's already hurt you terribly!"

"He did not mean it! I just made him so angry. He is very sorry. He will not hit me again. He promised!"

"I'm sure he means that promise, too, but I'm also sure he's made the promise before. Sooner or later you'll make him angry again, and he'll forget it. One night, he might start beating you and not be able to stop himself. You'll be dead, and who will take care of your children? You must get away from him before it's too late."

Once again, terror twisted her face. "I have no place to go! No one will take a woman with three children, and I cannot work. How will I live? My children will starve!"

"I can take you to the settlement house."

"They will take away my children!" she wailed, and Sarah silently cursed herself for using that threat.

"No, they won't. They'll help you there. They'll give you a place to live and food, and your children won't have to hide anymore, and neither will you."

"Lars will find us! He will be so angry!"

"We won't tell him where you are." Sarah didn't add that Lars might well be in jail and unable to find anyone. "You'll be safe, I promise you. Agnes, if you stay here, you might die. If you don't care about yourself, think of your children! They need their mother."

But Sarah could see she was fighting a losing battle. How many times had she made this argument to women like Agnes? Even in the few cases when she'd succeed in getting a woman to seek safe shelter, she had eventually returned to her husband. Life for a woman alone, especially if she had children, was simply too terrifying and uncertain. The settlement house would keep such women only for a short while, and then they would have to make their own way. The choice between destitution and an occasional beating—especially when the woman probably believed her husband had every right to beat her if she didn't please him—was no choice at all.

"Mrs. Brandt, you should go," Agnes said, her fear plain. "Lars does not want you here."

"There's no reason for him to know I was," Sarah reminded her. "I certainly won't tell anyone. Just please, promise me you'll take the children outside for some fresh air every day and make sure they get plenty of water to drink. Otherwise, the heat can make them sick."

Agnes nodded absently, glancing at the door to her flat. She was probably worried that her husband might be coming soon. If he found Sarah there . . . But he wouldn't. She was leaving. She gathered her things. Before she let herself out, however, she said, "If you need anything, please don't hesitate to send for me, Agnes. And if you're ever afraid, you can come to me. I'll make sure you're safe."

Agnes wouldn't even look at her.

As Sarah made her way down the stairs to the front door of the building, she knew her only hope was to find Malloy and send him after Lars Otto. If he really was the one who'd killed Gerda, then Agnes and her children would be safe. Safe from Lars Otto, that is. Sarah would have to figure out how to keep them safe after that as well.

MERCIFULLY, MRS. ELSWORTH was nowhere in sight when Sarah finally made her way home that evening. Unutterably weary after leaving Agnes's flat, she'd had to walk over to Fifth Avenue to find a cab. Then she'd had to go to police headquarters on Mulberry Street to leave word for Malloy, and since no cab would wait for her in that neighborhood, she'd had another long walk ahead of her. Now, at last, she was home.

Too tired to cook, Sarah made herself a sandwich with some cheese and drank what was left of the elderberry wine. She'd earned the indulgence. Only when she felt the warmth of the alcohol seeping into her blood did she begin to question her actions that day.

What right did she have to try to convince Agnes to leave her home? Many would condemn her actions. She had, after all, tried to break up a marriage. Not many people would consider the fact that Lars had beaten his wife savagely as grounds for such a desertion. Many men beat their wives, and they considered it their right. The law, in most cases, supported them, too. A man might go to jail for beating up a total stranger, but if he did the same thing to his wife, the law would turn a blind eye, even if she died from her injuries. Just one more injustice to feel outrage about in an unjust world. Sarah would go mad if she allowed herself to feel outrage for all of them, so she had to focus on righting the ones she could. If she was able to put Lars Otto in jail for murder, she would have won another battle.

She wished Malloy were here. She'd just discovered that this was the answer to his question about how she coped with losing patients: she coped by saving the ones she could.

Unutterably weary, she decided to go to bed, even though it wasn't very late. She'd taken down her hair and begun to brush it when she heard someone pounding on the front door. It was the unmistakable sound of a panicked man whose wife had just gone into labor. Suddenly her weariness vanished. She always had the energy to bring a new life into the world.

She was almost to the front door when she realized that the pounding wasn't quite right. Usually, they stopped after a while to give her a chance to answer the door, but this pounding hadn't stopped. In fact, it seemed to be getting even more frantic. Her instincts had just warned her not to open the door when it burst open on its own, the wood splintering around the lock as Lars Otto stumbled in.

"You!" he cried, pointing at her. "You tried to take my family away!"

"You're crazy!" she tried. "Get out of my house this instant before I call the police!" Sarah only wished she didn't sound quite so frightened. He'd startled her, bursting in that way, and now he glared at her with utter contempt.

"I know what you tried to do! You tried to make Agnes run away with my children! You were going to hide them from me!"

"I was worried about Agnes's safety," she tried. "You hurt her very badly."

"She will not listen!" he roared. "She makes me hit her. I cannot help myself."

"You can help yourself now," Sarah said, fighting to keep her voice steady. "Get out of here before the police come and arrest you."

His face contorted with hatred. "Why would the police arrest me?"

Sarah wanted to accuse him of murder but decided that would be foolish. "For breaking into my house."

"When they find out what you have done, they will praise me! A man must protect his home."

"And you protect yours by beating your wife?" Sarah asked before she could stop herself.

"What happens in my home is none of your business, you meddling bitch!"

Sarah had been mentally plotting her escape, and when he lunged for her, she bolted, heading for the kitchen and the back door. Once outside, he wouldn't dare harm her, and if he tried, neighbors would come running.

She dodged around the kitchen table, but her foot caught on the leg of a chair, throwing her off balance. She grabbed the edge of the sink and righted herself, but before she could take another step, Otto grabbed her by the hair that was hanging loose down her back.

Sarah screamed with both terror and pain as he yanked savagely on the fall of her hair, dragging her backward to the ground. She reached up, instinctively trying to grab his hands, but he wrapped her long hair around his fist and dragged her across the floor. She was screaming in pain now, fighting and clawing and trying to get at him, but the worst damage she could do was a few scratches to his hands. He hardly seemed to feel them.

"You cannot steal a man's family away! I will get the law after you!" he was saying.

"The law is on their way right now!" Sarah cried. "I sent for Detective Sergeant Malloy! He knows what you did!"

Twisting in a vain attempt to free herself, Sarah caught sight of the poker she kept beside her kitchen stove. If she could reach it . . .

But Otto jerked her head back and put his face right against hers so that she could feel the spittle when he shouted, "What did I do, you whore? Tell me what I did!"

"You killed Gerda!" she shouted right back.

She shocked him so much that he reared back, loosening his hold on her just enough that she could lunge for the poker. Her fingers closed around the cool metal just as he dragged her back again, wrenching a scream from her throat.

But she had the poker now and the element of surprise. She swung it, aiming for his knee, the most vulnerable part of the leg. The angle was poor, but she felt the satisfying thump of solid metal hitting solid flesh and heard his answering grunt of pain.

He swore as she lunged for freedom, but she hadn't hurt him badly enough or else his fingers were too tightly woven into her hair, because he pulled her back with a howl of triumph. She swung the poker again, unable to aim, just hoping for a good, solid hit, but this time he grabbed the end of it with his free hand.

Although she clung with both hands, he was stronger than she, in spite of his lanky frame, and he wrenched it from her fingers and flung it away. Lars Otto didn't need a weapon to hurt a mere woman.

When she looked up, she saw his eyes blazing with a hatred she could only imagine. He drew back his fist, and Sarah covered her head with both arms.

"If you hurt me, they'll know who did it! I left word at the police station that you're Gerda's killer!"

"You're lying!" he cried, but at least he didn't hit her.

"Agnes told me you killed Gerda! She said you came back that night with your hands all bruised and bloody. She said you were nervous, and you've been angry ever since Gerda died."

"She was a whore! I saw her that night. She was in an alley with a man. She lifted her skirts for him like it was nothing! She had no shame!"

"And she wouldn't lift her skirts for you, would she?" Sarah guessed. "Is that why you killed her? Because she wouldn't give you what she gave others so freely?"

"You do not know what it was like. You do not know how she tormented me. Showing herself like a harlot, telling me the things she did with other men! She wanted me to lust after her. She was not happy unless every man lusted after her."

"And so you started hitting her, just the way you hit your wife, but you couldn't stop yourself, could you?" Sarah said. "You kept hitting her and hitting her until she was dead."

"She deserved to die!"

"And what about Agnes? Does she deserve to die, too?" Sarah tried, trying to break through his blood lust. "Are you going to kill her next?"

Sarah watched in horror as his expression changed from fury to evil satisfaction. "No," he said, suddenly very calm. "I am going to kill *you* next."

Sarah screamed as loudly as she could as she watched his doubled fist draw back to strike her, and she lashed out herself, aiming a punch at the vulnerable area between his legs.

He howled with pain and released his grip on her hair enough that she was able to scramble to her knees. Still his fingers tangled in her hair too tightly for complete escape, but ignoring the tearing in her scalp, she made a lunge for the poker, now lying in the corner where he had flung it.

This time she caught it with both hands and swung wildly, hoping for any kind of contact that would allow her a precious second to escape. But once again, he caught the other end of the poker, and for what seemed an eternity, they struggled for it, Sarah grasping the pointed end with both hands while he grasped the handle with one and tried to tear out her hair with the other.

Her eyes streaming with tears from the pain, Sarah hung on for dear life, until, from out of nowhere, his boot struck her in the ribs. The pain knocked the breath from her body, and he easily wrested the poker from her now nerveless hands.

The expression on his face was chilling, eyes gleaming with pleasure, teeth bared in a feral grin. Holding her fast by the hair of her head, he raised the poker over his head while she struggled helplessly, fighting for the breath for one last scream. In the second before the poker came slamming down into her head, her last thought was that at least Malloy would know who'd killed her, and she threw up her hands in a futile effort to ward off the blow.

The sound was like nothing she could have imagined, a dull thud and oddly far away. She waited for the searing pain and instead felt nothing at all. Then something very large and very heavy came toppling over on top of her.

"Mrs. Brandt, Mrs. Brandt, are you all right?"

Sarah needed a second to realize that the large, heavy weight lying on top of her was Lars Otto's now unconscious body, and the voice she was hearing was . . . no, it couldn't be!

"Mrs. Brandt, did he hurt you? Can you help me get him off of you? He's awfully heavy!"

"Mrs. Elsworth?" Sarah said, still not quite certain she wasn't mistaken.

Suddenly her strength returned, and she was able to push herself free of Otto's weight. His hand was still tangled in her hair, but Mrs. Elsworth's nimble fingers quickly freed her, leaving an alarming number of broken strands still locked in his motionless fist.

Only when she was free could Sarah finally see that Lars Otto did, indeed, lie unconscious on her kitchen floor.

"How on earth . . . ?" she started to ask, and then she saw that Mrs. Elsworth still clutched her cast-iron skillet in her other hand. "Did you hit him with *that*?"

"He was going to hit you with the poker!" Mrs. Elsworth replied defensively. "What else could I do?"

Sarah looked at the back of Otto's head. His skull didn't seem to be misshapen, so perhaps he was only unconscious and not even very seriously injured. Gingerly, as if touching a live snake, she placed her fingertips on the inside of his wrist and found a pulse.

"We'd better get him tied up before he wakes up," Sarah said. "He won't be in a very good mood when he does, I'm afraid."

"Oh, my," Mrs. Elsworth said. "Perhaps I should hit him again."

Sarah felt an hysterical urge to laugh. "I'd much rather let the police take care of him. I'm sure they'll be more thorough. Now, let me see, I think I have some clothes rope around here somewhere."

"MOTHER, REALLY, I think you should go home. All this excitement can't be good for you," Nelson Elsworth said for what Sarah guessed was the tenth time in as many minutes.

"Nonsense," Mrs. Elsworth said to her son, also for the tenth time. "I've never felt better in my life. Besides, I have to tell Detective Sergeant Malloy what happened, don't I?"

"He can come to our house to speak with you," Nelson insisted. Nelson Elsworth was a tall, slender man approaching forty who wore wire-rimmed glasses and was trying to disguise the way his hair was thinning on top by growing the hair on the sides longer and combing it over the bald spot. He'd arrived home from his job at the bank a short while ago to find his neighbors gathered in the street in front of Sarah's house and his mother inside enjoying the attentions of a red-faced police officer who didn't quite know what to make of the entire situation.

"Officer O'Brien," Nelson said to the policeman, "Can't you tell my mother it's all right if she goes to her own home? We only live next door."

O'Brien shrugged. "I'd stay around if I was her. Malloy can be awful testy if he's irritated, and it irritates him to have to go chasing down witnesses." He'd used a call box to notify police headquarters of the incident, and they were trying to track down Frank Malloy to handle the investigation.

"I'm not a *witness*, young man!" Mrs. Elsworth reminded him indignantly. "I am the one who subdued this miscreant!"

"Yes, ma'am," O'Brien said, coughing to hide a chuckle.

Sarah was coughing, too. She knew she must be in shock. Why else would she be fighting the urge to laugh when a semiconscious killer was lying trussed like a Christmas turkey in her kitchen?

"You know," Mrs. Elsworth was saying, "it's the oddest thing. I didn't see a single omen today, either. You'd think that with something this important, I would've seen *something*, wouldn't you? But not a hint! However was I supposed to be prepared?"

Sarah could think of no reasonable answer to that. Luckily, Malloy chose that moment to arrive, so she didn't have to. He, too, was red-faced, probably from rushing in this heat. Sarah and Mrs. Elsworth were sitting in chairs in Sarah's front office, while O'Brien, the beat cop, and Nelson Elsworth stood around helplessly.

Frank took in the scene with one swift glance. His main concern was making sure that Sarah Brandt was all right, and she appeared to be, although her hair was loose and tangled, something he'd never expected to see. He found the sight more than a little disturbing.

Before he could ask her what had happened, she said, "Lars Otto killed Gerda. He'd gone out looking for her that night, and he saw her go into an alley with a man. That made him furious, so he apparently accosted her afterward and started beating her. He may not have intended to kill her, but he did. His wife saw that his hands were all bruised when he came home that night, but he told her some men had tried to rob him, and he'd fought with them. She wanted to believe him, so she did. Oh!" she added as a new and apparently very disturbing thought occurred to her. "He also beat his wife. We should send someone to make sure she and the children are all right. I went to see Agnes Otto this afternoon, and she told me what happened. He may have beaten her again, too!"

Malloy glanced at O'Brien, who nodded his understanding. "What's the address, ma'am?" he asked Sarah.

Sarah gave it to him, and he went out to use the call box again.

Frank walked over to the kitchen doorway and looked down at where Lars Otto lay, moaning softly. Blood was oozing from the back of his scalp, and he was tied hand and foot with what appeared to be about a mile of clothes rope. "Somebody want to tell me what happened here tonight?"

"I heard Mrs. Brandt screaming," Mrs. Elsworth said rather proudly. Plainly, she couldn't wait to tell him her story. "So I ran over to see what was the matter. Luckily," she added with a twinkle, "I thought to take my cast-iron skillet with me, just in case."

Frank glanced at where the skillet now sat on the kitchen table. "You hit him with *that*?" he asked incredulously.

"My mother isn't a very strong woman," Nelson Elsworth said, rushing to his mother's defense. "I'm sure no permanent damage has been done to this gentleman."

"I can't say I'd mind if there was, if what Mrs. Brandt here says about him is true," Frank allowed. "I'm just amazed that he held still for you to do it, Mrs. Elsworth."

"Oh, he was rather busy trying to kill Mrs. Brandt with that poker at the time," Mrs. Elsworth informed him cheerfully. "I don't think he even knew I was there."

Frank felt the impact of her words like a blow to his gut. He struggled to get his breath, but before he could, Sarah jumped in with her version.

"He broke in," she told him somewhat defensively, pointing toward the smashed door lock. "He was quite angry that I'd tried to convince his wife to leave him for her own safety. I think he also must have realized that she'd told me enough to make me realize he'd killed Gerda. He must have thought if he killed me, no one would ever find out what he'd done."

Somehow Frank managed to find enough breath to speak in a fairly normal voice. "He told you he killed the Reinhard girl?"

She nodded.

Frank looked down at Otto again and noticed something he'd missed the first time. He bent and retrieved a hank of long, golden hair that clung to the man's trousers. It had been pulled out by the roots. Impotent rage twisted in his stomach at the thought of how Sarah's hair had come to be clinging to Otto's trousers.

"Mrs. Brandt put up quite a struggle," Mrs. Elsworth informed him. "He was dragging her around by her hair and trying to hit her with the poker when I came in."

Sarah reached up and rubbed the back of her head. Frank swallowed hard on the gorge that rose in his throat. At the thought of Otto putting his hands on Sarah, he wanted to do murder himself, and it took every ounce of willpower he possessed not to kick the life out of the man lying bound on the floor. At least he would have the satisfaction of watching him pay the ultimate price for his crimes in New York's new electric chair.

"Did he . . ." Frank had to clear his throat and start again. "Did he hurt you in any other way?"

She rubbed her side. "He kicked me, but I don't think it's more than a bad bruise."

Frank was going to take great pleasure in seeing Otto fry. "We'll get a doctor here to look you over."

"Nelson," Mrs. Elsworth said, "go fetch Dr. Pomeroy, will you? We want to make sure Mrs. Brandt is all right."

"I can't leave you alone with that killer!" Nelson protested.

But just then they heard the clatter of wagon wheels, and a Black Maria, one of the police wagons, pulled up outside. A moment later, two uniformed officers came in, and Frank directed them to collect Lars Otto and carry him off to the Tombs.

As he stood on the sidewalk, watching the wagon pull away, Frank suddenly realized he still held the lock of Sarah's hair. He could have dropped it, but he stuffed it discreetly into his pocket before going back inside to send Nelson Elsworth after that damned doctor.

Epilogue

FRANK DIDN'T BOTHER MAKING EXCUSES TO HIMself for going to see Sarah Brandt. He owed her a visit, if for no other reason than to tell her the news about Lars Otto. The city streets were shimmering with heat, and Frank stopped on her doorstep to mop his brow before knocking on her door. He noted with approval the new lock and the repairs to the door in the moment before it opened.

"Malloy," she said the way she always did. She looked pleased to see him, and not at all surprised. He always forgot how her smile seemed to glow.

"Thought I'd come by and see how you were," he said.

"I'm glad you did," she said. "It saved me from having to send you a message or brave your mother's wrath by going to your place. Come in."

As usual, they sat out in the shade of the back porch. The heat seemed almost bearable here amid the fragrant blossoms. She served him lemonade and cookies she said Mrs. Elsworth had baked. "She's been fussing over me quite a bit since that evening," she explained with a smile. "I think she just likes talking about it. She was quite the heroine."

Frank didn't want to think about what might have happened if Sarah didn't have such an intrepid old woman living next door. "Yeah, I guess I'll have to stop saying insulting things about her."

"And I'll have to have more patience with her superstitions. She's been trying to figure out if she saw an omen of what was going to happen and just didn't interpret it correctly. She likes to think she sees things that are going to happen, you know."

"She did all right, even without any warning," Frank allowed.

"She certainly did."

They fell silent. Frank was dying to know why she'd wanted to contact him, but he wasn't going to ask. He cleared his throat. "I wanted to tell you that Otto confessed. They only gave him twenty years, though."

"You thought he'd get a death sentence?" she asked.

Frank didn't want to say he'd been hoping so, mainly because of the way the bastard had tried to kill Sarah. "They went easy on him because the girl wasn't very respectable."

"That's outrageous!"

He'd expected her to be angry. "I guess we're lucky they didn't decide she deserved to be killed and let him off scot-free. How's his wife doing?"

She frowned and looked away. "She won't see me. She blames me for Lars going to prison. She still thinks Gerda's death was an accident and Lars shouldn't be punished for it."

"After the way he treated her?" Frank couldn't believe it.

She shrugged. "I've seen it too many times. You'd think that a woman would hate a husband who beats her, but it's usually just the opposite. Those women tend to be even more loyal than women whose husbands are good to them. They never say an unkind word about them, and they defend them with their dying breath. And of course there's the problem of her being left with no one to support her with her husband in jail. She blames me for that, too."

"What will she do?"

"Take in lodgers, I suppose. And washing, perhaps. I don't know. I've asked my friends at the settlement house to keep an eye on her. That's about all I can do."

She fell silent again, sipping her lemonade. Frank took a long gulp of his, then asked, "Is that what you wanted to tell me?"

"What?" she asked, as if her mind had been wandering. "Oh, no, that was something else entirely. It's about Brian."

Frank felt his defenses rise, but he tried not to sound defensive. "What about him?"

"Have you made a decision about which school you're going to send him to?"

Frank shrugged. "He's still too young. And I've got to convince my mother to send him anyplace first. At least I've gotten her to agree to meet some deaf people who have a boy Brian's age. We can see how the sign language works."

"I'm sure it's a hard decision for you to make. But at least you know he can be educated now. That's important."

Frank nodded, not trusting his voice.

"But that's not what I wanted to talk to you about. Do you remember I told you that I was going to contact a surgeon who might be able to help Brian's foot?"

Frank had forgotten all about that. He nodded again, not liking where this was going.

"Well, I talked to him the other day. He'd be happy to examine Brian and see if there's anything he can do. No promises, of course, not until he's done an examination, but he's very good. There's even a chance Brian might be able to walk almost normally."

POLICE HEADQUARTERS WAS quiet when Frank returned that evening. A few drunks were chained together, sitting on the benches, and the desk sergeant barely spared him a glance when he strode past.

He climbed the stairs, past the commissioner's offices, where Teddy Roosevelt still held court during the day, past the chief of detectives' office, and on to the dusty room where the old files were kept. Even in the feeble light of the gas jet on the wall, Frank didn't have much trouble finding what he was looking for. The file of an unsolved murder, three years old. Dr. Thomas Brandt.

Frank was relieved to discover he hadn't worked on the case. The file was thin. No one had worked very hard on it at all, in fact. The trail would be stone cold, the killer probably long since dead or in jail for some other crime. Solving the case was virtually hopeless. Just as finding the killer of those young girls had been hopeless. Just as finding out who killed Gerda Reinhard had been hopeless.

But Frank wasn't going to let that stop him. When Brian went to visit this surgeon, Frank would owe Sarah Brandt a debt of gratitude. And if Brian was someday able to walk, he'd owe her more than he could ever repay. If he could find her husband's killer, however, he just might make a start of it.

Author's Note

Usually, I pride myself on the historical accuracy of my novels, but this time I took one small liberty with the facts. By 1896, the Elephant Hotel, where Sarah finds the merchant who sold the red shoes, had been abandoned for several years. In fact, it burned shortly afterward, in September of 1896. It did exist, however, and was very much as I described it during its heyday. Since it was such a delightfully absurd part of Coney Island, I just had to use it in the book, and I hope you'll forgive my lapse in accuracy for the sake of whimsy.

If you missed the first book in this series, *Murder on Astor Place,* I hope you'll track it down and find out how Sarah first got interested in solving murder mysteries and how she happened to join forces with Detective Sergeant Frank Malloy. And don't worry, I tried very hard not to give away the ending of that book in this one, so you can still be surprised! By all means, let me know how you liked both books, too. You may write to me at P.O. Box 638, Duncansville, PA 16635, or send me E-mail via my Web page at:

www.victoriathompson.com

Until next time!